THE D.A. TAKES A CHANCE

THE D.A. TAKES A CHANCE

Erle Stanley Gardner

Chivers Press • G.K. Hall & Co.
Bath, Avon, England • Thorndike, Maine USA

LP
Gar
c1

This Large Print edition is published by Chivers Press, England, and by G.K. Hall & Co.

Published in 1996 in the U.K. by arrangement with Thayer Hobson & Co.

Published in 1996 in the U.S. by arrangement with Thayer Hobson & Co.

U.K. Hardcover ISBN 0–7451–3980–9 (Chivers Large Print)
U.K. Softcover   ISBN 0–7451–3992–2 (Camden Large Print)
U.S. Softcover   ISBN 0–7838–1634–0 (Nightingale Collection Edition)

The text of this Large Print edition is unabridged.
Other aspects of the book may vary from the original edition.

Set in 16 pt. New Times Roman.

Printed in Great Britain on acid-free paper.

British Library Cataloguing in Publication Data available

Library of Congress Cataloging-in-Publication Data

Gardner, Erle Stanley, 1889-1970.
   The D.A. takes a chance / Erle Stanley Gardner.
     p. cm.
   ISBN 0–7838–1634–0 (lg. print : lsc)
   1. Public prosecutors—United States—Fiction. 2. Large type books.
I. Title.
[PS3513.A6322D28   1996]
813'.52—dc20
                                           95–49587

CHAPTER ONE

Since it was only seven-fifteen in the morning when Doris Kane arrived in Madison City, and since she had been driving all night, her road-weary eyes at first failed to notice that the town was preparing to renew its early Wild Western youth. Such citizens as appeared on the street were wearing two- to five-gallon hats, and for the most part had grown moustaches or beards. Occasionally someone would sport a cartridge-belt with dangling holsters.

A sign flapping indolently over the main street, suspended from the windows of two office buildings, bore the red-lettered announcement: 'Wild West Celebration, November 1st to 5th.'

Looking at her wrist-watch, Doris Kane decided that it was a positively indecent hour to call upon her daughter. Marriage, of course, might have changed Paula's habit of sleeping late in the morning, but Mrs Kane was afraid to take chances. She wanted her visit to appear to be elaborately casual, a 'just driving through' sort of thing. And Paula's husband, Jim Melvin, might well resent the intrusion of his mother-in-law within two months of his marriage.

Mrs Kane slid the station wagon in close to the kerb in front of the Owl Café, above which

1

an illuminated sign announced: 'WE NEVER CLOSE.'

There was but little trouble finding a parking space at this hour in the morning, and Doris Kane, after carefully locking the car, entered the restaurant, started back towards the section devoted to booths, then changed her mind and decided on the more sociable half-filled lunch counter.

It wasn't until she had seated herself on a stool that she recognised the extent to which Madison City had dressed itself for the pending celebration. So far as appearances were concerned, Mrs Kane might have stepped into a Hollywood set featuring an episode in the life of Billy the Kid.

There were moustaches, beards, cowboy hats, loud-coloured shirts, and there was a general atmosphere of over-all incongruity.

A young man waited on Mrs Kane.

She looked at the moustache, at the cowboy shirt.

The man grinned. 'Stranger here?'

She confessed that she was.

'Celebrating the city's birthday,' the man said. 'Ninety years ago the place was founded. She was wild then, mostly cattle and mining. All the citizens are co-operating. Everyone has to grow a moustache or a beard, and wear a costume until the celebration's over. We're going to have a big *fiesta*, covered wagons, cowboy escorts, all the rest of it. What do you

2

want to eat?'

She smiled, conscious of her weariness, now that she was no longer driving. 'Lots of coffee,' she said, 'and ham and eggs. The coffee beginning immediately.'

Seven-thirty apparently was an important hour to the handful of men who were eating in the Owl Café. One by one they paid their checks, hurried out of the place, and by seven-thirty-one, Doris Kane was the only person at the counter.

It seemed an auspicious time for a guarded, cautious question or two.

'You've been here for some time?' she asked the young man behind the counter.

'Born here,' the man said. 'Served a stretch in the army and then right back to the old town. She looks pretty good. Used to think it was a hick place. Now I like it.'

'It seems a very nice little city,' she said. 'I believe it's the county seat?'

'That's right. The court-house is right up there on the hill. How's the coffee? Want some more?'

'I will have another cup. Thanks.'

As he pushed the newly refilled coffee-cup across the counter, she asked casually: 'Do you happen to know a James L. Melvin?'

'Melvin,' he said, 'Melvin—oh, sure, Jim Melvin.'

'You know him?'

'Sure. I've known him quite a while. He

3

sometimes eats here. Working on a deal with the city trustees on some kind of a parking device. He's got State right to it, he tells me.'

'That's right,' she said, and then realised that the man behind the counter was looking at her, waiting for her to say something else.

She laughed nervously and said: 'He's my son-in-law.'

'Oh. Seems to me he got married just a short time ago, didn't he?'

'Yes.'

'Nice chap. Been mixed up in politics here lately, but I suppose you know all about that.'

'I'm not certain I do.'

'Doug Selby, our district attorney, was mighty popular. He resigned his office to go to war. When he came back, the man who had taken his place wanted to hang on. Public sentiment made him quit. People even started a recall. Doug Selby's back in the D.A.'s office now. It was a nasty fight—while it lasted.'

'I see. Jim was for Mr Selby?'

'No, he was tied up with the other side.'

'He hasn't been in this morning?'

'No. He doesn't eat here regular. He comes in sometimes about nine or ten o'clock. Usually he comes in with someone, talking business, for a cup of coffee or maybe a sandwich. Reckon you came here to see our big *fiesta*, huh?'

She smiled and said: 'No, I'm just passing through. It was a little early to run up and see

4

the young folks.'

'*Young* folks,' the man said, looking her over appraisingly. 'That's a good one. You're as young as he is!'

Doris felt herself flush with pleasure. There was no mistaking the sincerity of the man's compliment. Paula had, of course, just turned nineteen, and Doris, herself, had celebrated her thirty-ninth birthday—just three days ago. But the years had developed a habit of marching rapidly past. The thought of Paula's being married was a shock to her. It had been only four or five years ago that Paula was an awkward youngster, all knees and elbows. Now she was married. It seemed simply incredible.

Mrs Kane paid her check, returned to her station wagon. It was still ten minutes before eight. She had, in her mind, fixed nine o'clock as the earliest hour at which she dared give Paula a ring, but she didn't want to sit there at the kerb, dozing behind the steering-wheel of the station wagon. And, after all, Paula, as the wife of a young business-man, was quite probably up and cooking breakfast.

Mrs Kane entered the restaurant again. 'I want to use your phone,' she said.

'Help yourself.'

She consulted the telephone directory and found: '*Melvin, James L., r., 1641 Hillcrest Drive.*'

She dropped a coin, dialled the number, then

5

waited while she heard the phone give the sound of steady ringing.

There was no answer.

As soon as Doris Kane realised that there was going to be no immediate answer, she had to fight a guilty desire to drop the receiver back on the hook and leave the restaurant, but she stood by her guns until it was quite apparent no one would answer. Then she dropped the receiver back into place. The mechanism of the pay telephone clicked into action and her nickel came rattling down into the coin chute.

She turned to the agreeable young man at the counter. 'How do I get to Hillcrest Drive?' she said.

'Go up to the first boulevard stop, turn to the left, go up the hill for four blocks, then turn to the left and follow that road around the hill. Keep an eye open for Hillcrest. It's one of the side streets that turns off about—oh, maybe ten or twelve blocks from where you make your second left-hand turn.'

'Thank you,' she said, and, walking determinedly out, got in the station wagon and started the motor.

She found Hillcrest Drive without difficulty. 1641 was a house very similar to what she had pictured in her mind as being the place where Paula was living.

The house was built on a side-hill. The front was one storey in height, the back, three storeys high. Because the lot was too steep for a

6

driveway to the garage, the garage was located behind the house, and access to it was from an alley which ran parallel to the main street. The service path to the back door was composed partially of a steep incline, partially of cement steps. The inconveniences of such a side-hill construction were offset by the marvellous panorama from every window in the house.

Down below, the ground fell sharply to a winding valley which was spotted with the dark green of orange trees.

Doris Kane had been smelling orange blossoms all the morning, bringing back to her senses the shock of Paula's sudden plunge into matrimony. It was a shock which had found the mother entirely unprepared.

Doris parked the station wagon in front of the house, walked along the short stretch of cement to the front porch and rang the bell.

There was a house on the south, a vacant lot on the north. A tall hedge grew along the property line, furnishing some measure of privacy for the front of the house, but, because of the steepness of the slope, it gave no privacy whatever towards the rear.

It was as Doris Kane was pressing the bell-button for the second time, that she saw something which filled her with disquiet. Over in a corner of the little porch was a pile of bundled newspapers, and on those newspapers, which were in the path of the morning sun, the outer pages had already

7

begun to turn yellow.

Doris frowned. Surely...

The corner of a slip of paper which appeared under the door caught her eye.

Doris Kane opened the screen door and retrieved the paper by a corner.

It was a scrawled note, and said:

No use leaving milk. It turns sour on the doorstep. Call me when you get back and want deliveries resumed.

THE MILKMAN

The mail-box was fastened to the inside of one of the posts which supported the roof over the front porch. Doris Kane found it was unlocked. She pressed a button on the side, and the sheet metal front of the box lifted.

There was only one letter in it.

The envelope bore the typewritten address: 'James L. Melvin, 1641 Hillcrest Drive, Madison City.' There was an embossed return address in the upper left-hand corner: 'Alfonse Baker Carr, Attorney at Law, 962 Monadnock Buildings, Los Angeles.'

The letter had been postmarked Los Angeles two days ago. It had apparently been placed in the mailbox some time yesterday. It was a thin letter, as though it contained a very small sheet of paper, perhaps a statement of an amount due for services rendered. The envelope was crackling crisp, with the feel of heavy bond

8

paper that had a large rag content.

Doris Kane held the envelope for a few moments, then reluctantly put it back in the mail-box. As she did, she heard the sound of metal scraping against metal, and investigated to see what had caused the sound. The key to the house was in the bottom of the mail-box.

Doris took tentative possession of the key. She turned towards the door, then hesitated.

As she stood there on the porch, she could hear sounds of activity in the place next door. Her nostrils detected the aroma of frying bacon and of freshly made coffee.

Mrs Kane hesitated for a few moments, while she debated the situation. Paula was a high-strung individual in every sense of the word. Almost imperceptibly, some of the sharp corners of her individuality would be rubbed off by life. But right now Paula would regard the unauthorised use of that key in Doris Kane's hand as unpardonable 'snooping'.

Doris Kane was still relatively young. She was attractive. She had many admirers of her own, and she and Paula maintained a certain brittle off-hand relationship, quite different from the old-fashioned mother-and-daughter attitude. Doris would be cordially welcome in Paula's home as a visitor, but it would be Paula's house, definitely.

Doris Kane knew she was going to use that key if she had to, but she wanted to have just a little more to work on before she did.

Still holding the key, Doris Kane walked back to the pavement, went down to the next house and rang the bell.

The woman who opened the door was well past middle age, a keen-eyed, thin-lipped woman with high cheek-bones and a certain bird-like quickness of motion.

'Good morning,' she said, the keen eyes sweeping Mrs Kane from head to foot. 'Are you selling something?'

There was a tone of latent hostility, ready to develop into a sharp-tongued dismissal and a slamming of the door.

Doris Kane smiled cordially. 'I'm trying to find out something about Mr and Mrs Melvin next door. They seem to be away. Could you tell me how long they've been away, or perhaps where they...'

'I certainly couldn't,' the woman snapped.

Mrs Kane tried her most disarming smile. 'Inasmuch as you're neighbours, I thought that perhaps...'

'Neighbours!' the woman snorted. 'They live next door to us, that's all. *Neighbours!*— Neighbours, indeed!'

'Well, of course,' Doris Kane said, 'I...'

The woman swept the conversational lead from Doris Kane. 'If you ask me, they're not the type of neighbours we want in this locality. This is a respectable community. Such goings-on you never did see! Parties until two and three o'clock in the morning, women

10

getting drunk, and then—well, anyway, *I* still say it was a pistol-shot. Humph! Neighbours, indeed! What do you want of them?'

'How long ago was this?' Doris asked, her face feeling as though the skin had been drawn tight as parchment across her cheek-bones.

'How long ago was what?'

'The party.'

'Parties,' the woman said. 'Lots of them.'

'And the pistol-shot?'

'That was last week—ten days ago, I guess. If you're selling something, it won't do you any good to be around there this hour of the morning. They don't get up until nine or ten, even when they're home, which they're not!'

'I'm ... I'm a friend of the family, and I ...'

'Well, I shouldn't be discussing things with you. Anyway, I've got work to do. Good morning!'

The door slammed.

Doris Kane had made up her mind now. She walked back to the house next door. Firmly, she fitted the key to the lock. She twisted the key, snapped back the catch, opened the door and went in.

The bedrooms were on the upper floor. From a hall, a wide staircase with wrought-iron banisters went down in a sweeping curve to the big living-room.

'Hello, Jim! Hello, Paula!' Doris called, and then added after a moment: 'Anyone home?'

The emptiness of the house swallowed up

11

her voice, emphasised the quaver in it.

Doris Kane marched firmly down the stairs. A light switch flooded the living-room with that sickly illumination which seems so hopelessly artificial when contrasted with the fresh sparkle of outer sunlight. Curtains drawn across the windows shut out virtually all daylight, but the electricity disclosed the living-room as being a huge, comfortable affair, with a big fireplace in the east end, French doors opening out to a wide balcony on the west, a door on the north leading to stairs which went down to rooms on a still lower level.

Off to the south was a dining-room, and behind that was a kitchen.

The living-room gave indications of convivial hospitality. There were glasses scattered about, trays with cigarette ends in them, and there was a stale aftermath about the close air of the place that held a typical morning-after atmosphere.

An insulated container for ice-cubes was on the table in the living-room. Doris raised the cover and looked down inside.

It was about a third full of water. Ice-cubes had been in there, had melted, and the water was now at room temperature.

Doris passed through the dining-room and went to the kitchen. Here everything was scrupulously clean. There were no dirty dishes in the sink.

Doris opened the ice-box, glanced inside,

12

moved into the pantry, opened the bread-box, felt the loaf and a half of bread that was inside. The bread was hard, dry and stale. She moved over to the kitchen table, drew her finger across one corner. The finger left a very distinct trail in the fine dust which had settled on the table.

Back in the living-room, she pulled a cord which swept back the heavy curtains that covered the windows. Bright daylight pouring in revealed the extent to which a film of fine dust had settled over everything in the room.

Doris switched off the lights, ran quickly up the stairs to the bedrooms.

The first one was evidently the master bedroom. There were twin beds, dressers, Paula's things on one, Jim's on another. The beds had not been slept in. A hurried inspection of the closets indicated that the clothes were in their proper places. If Paula had left, she had evidently taken very little with her. She could hardly have been planning any extensive trip.

Doris went through the bathroom into the communicating bedroom. Here also the bed was neatly made. Quite evidently a family guest-room, it was in a state of empty readiness.

The next bedroom was a large one, apparently intended for a guest who might not be a member of the family. It had a bath and . . . Doris Kane found herself standing in horror-stricken rigidity, the sound of the little scream

13

she had involuntarily given still echoing in her ears.

The surface of the bed was blotched and stained with a dark, reddish-brown something, so sinister in its incrusted appearance that Doris knew it instantly for what it was.

When she could get power back in her legs, she moved over to the bed, felt the dry stiffness on the coverlet.

The floor gave no indication of blood-drops, however. But in the bathroom there was another story. Here was a whole pile of blood-stained towels.

There had been an accident. Someone had, quite evidently, lost a lot of blood. Towels had been used to keep that blood from dropping to the floor, but the person had lain on the bed, perhaps waiting for a doctor and . . .

In Mrs Kane's mind the words of the next door neighbour repeated themselves ominously: 'Well, anyway, *I* say it was a pistol-shot.'

Doris Kane hurriedly left the bedroom. She went out through the front door into the morning sunlight, the odour of orange blossoms, the singing of birds, the laughter of children from the yard of a house half a block down the street.

She pulled the door shut behind her, so that the spring lock clicked into place. She opened the mail-box, replaced the key under the letter from Alfonse Baker Carr. She snapped the mail-box closed, walked with quick, nervous steps across to the station wagon, started the motor and drove away.

Her mind was a seething turmoil of confusion. Had Jim shot someone? Had a fire-arm been accidentally discharged? Was Paula hiding from the law? Or was Paula the victim? It was not like Paula to remain silent. Paula wouldn't run away. Paula was the sort who would face things. She'd always been like that. She never wanted to hide from anything or its consequences.

Almost aimlessly Doris Kane drove the big station wagon along the winding contour of Hillcrest Drive, until at length she came to a dead end, a wide place for turning, with the steep slope of a hill rising in front of the car.

She turned the station wagon, swung back down the road, followed the winding curves back to the main street of Madison City.

Here preparations for the *fiesta* were even more apparent than ever—men in tight-fitting cowboy-cut overalls, clumping down the street, many of them quite obviously unaccustomed to the high-heeled boots they were wearing. There were big, five-gallon hats very much in evidence, gaudy neck-wear, moustaches, whiskers and an occasional full beard. Store windows featured costume cowboy hats at '$2.98', vivid blue, gold or red neckerchieves, a 'popular' line of cowboy boots.

Everywhere was hilarity, a certain informality, a readiness to stop and visit while citizen appraised citizen, joking about the moustaches, about the cowboy regalia.

Madison City was preparing for a major celebration.

To Doris Kane it seemed a garish travesty. The sight of the dangling holsters served only to emphasise in her mind the reddish-brown stains which had dried into the bedding of the room in Paula's house.

CHAPTER TWO

Up in the court-house, Doug Selby, the district attorney, glanced casually at his reflection in the mirror in his private office, surveying himself dubiously.

Madison City had gone all out for the celebration and the vigilance committee was no respecter of persons. Citizens who failed to enter into the spirit of the thing were hustled away to encounter various disciplinary measures.

The county officials were by courtesy exempted from the extreme in cowboy garb, but Selby wore a red bandana around his neck in deference to the popular spirit, and a wide-brimmed cowboy hat hung on the rack beside the mirror.

Selby was turning back to his desk when his secretary tapped a perfunctory knock on the door of his private office, opened it and thrust in an inquiring head. 'Could you,' she asked, 'take time to run down to Sheriff Brandon's office for a minute, or would you prefer to have him come here? He says there's a woman with him, a Mrs Kane, and he's disturbed at the story she tells.'

'Is he on the phone?' Selby asked.

She nodded.

Selby picked up the phone. 'Hello, Rex.'

Sheriff Rex Brandon said: 'I didn't want to bother you, Doug, but there's something here that I don't like. What's the law about entering a house without a search warrant?'

'It's all right, if you can get the permission of the owner. All wrong if you can't.'

'There's no one home.'

'You'd better get a warrant, then.'

'You got a minute, Doug?'

'Sure.'

'I'm coming down.'

'Bringing the woman with you?'

'No. I'll come alone.'

Sheriff Brandon, some twenty-five years older than Doug Selby, was a grizzled cattleman, and while his head was streaked with white hairs, his eyes were keen and alert. The smooth ease of his motions indicated muscles that were like raw-hide. The cowboy clothes he was wearing in honour of the *fiesta*

17

seemed not a costume, but the only clothes that a man of his type would find really suitable.

Selby held the door of his private office open and Brandon walked in and sat on the edge of Selby's desk.

'It's Jim Melvin, Doug,' the sheriff said.

Selby stiffened to wary attention. 'What's the trouble, Rex?'

'The woman who's in my office is Jim Melvin's mother-in-law. She's worked herself into the jitters. Her daughter, Paula, let the mother's birthday go by without writing her or sending a wire.'

Selby grinned.

'And,' Brandon went on seriously, 'a little over a week ago Mrs Kane, that's Paula Melvin's mother, wrote Paula asking for some information about a book of recipes that Paula had been copying. She asked Paula to send her an answer by air mail. She got no answer to the letter. Then when she had no word on her birthday, she decided to come out and see what was wrong.'

'Anything else?' Selby asked.

'Lots of it, Doug. She went to the house. No one was home. There were papers piled on the porch and the milkman had quit delivering milk. The next door neighbour said no one had been there for about ten days, and that the last party they'd had broke up after the neighbours heard a pistol-shot.

'Mrs Kane looked in the mail-box to see if

her letters were there, and found a letter from Alfonse Baker Carr, and a key to the house. She went in. No one was home. It looked as though the place had been deserted in the middle of the party. There were bloodstains all over one of the upstairs bedrooms and in the bathroom that opened from it. She thinks her daughter's been killed.'

'Do you suppose it's a trap, Rex?' the district attorney asked.

'I'm darned if I know, Doug. It has me bothered.'

Selby said: 'If our enemies were setting a trap for us, Rex, this is just about the way they'd go about it. We'd get into Melvin's home. Melvin would catch us there. He'd claim we had gone in with a high-handed disregard for his property rights and were trying to exact a political vengeance. On the other hand, if we get a search warrant he'll claim we singled him out for persecution and the notoriety killed his deal on the parking device.'

There was a certain insistence about Brandon's silence.

'What time did she get into the house, Rex?' Selby asked.

'Somewhere around nine o'clock this morning, a little before, I guess.'

'And what's she been doing in the meantime?'

'Apparently biting her finger-nails and stewing herself into a lather. To hear her tell it,

19

she has more at stake than we have. If she makes a bum guess, Paula will never forgive her.'

Selby said: 'Let me take a look at her, Rex. Of course, it *would* have to be Jim Melvin. Why couldn't her daughter have married someone else?'

They walked down the long corridor. Brandon pushed open the door to his private office, said to Doris Kane: 'This is Mr Selby, our district attorney.'

Selby acknowledged the introduction and said: 'I was asking Brandon if you had explained to him how it happened that there was such a long interval between the time you made the discovery of this disquieting evidence you have told the sheriff about, and your report to us.'

She said: 'If you knew Paula, you'd realise my position, Mr Selby. If I'm wrong in—well, if Paula's all right—or if it should be that Jim is in trouble ... I don't know *what's* best.'

'Do you want to wait the thing out?'

'I can't. I've waited it out as long as is humanly possible.'

'You say there was a letter in the box from Alfonse Baker Carr?' Selby asked.

'Yes. Do you know him?'

'And *how* we know him!' Brandon grunted. 'He lives here.'

She looked at him in surprise. 'Isn't his office in Los Angeles?'

'His office is in Los Angeles,' Sheriff Brandon said, 'but he came out here and bought a country house a few years ago; says he's trying to retire, but his clients won't let him. You can't ever tell about Carr.'

'A criminal lawyer?'

'That's right. And he knows all the tricks. In fact, there was a while there in Los Angeles when crooks used to say there was a way of beating the rap that was simple as A.B.C.'

'Meaning A. B. Carr?'

'That's right.'

'I wonder what he would be doing writing to Jim?'

'You say it was a thin letter?'

'Yes. It seems as though there's only a very small sheet of paper in the envelope. It might have been a bill.'

Selby had been studying Mrs Kane while she was talking. Now he turned to Brandon and nodded, signifying his belief that Mrs Kane was genuine.

'All right, Rex. Let's go take a look.'

'A search warrant?' Brandon asked.

Selby looked at Mrs Kane. 'We'd need an affidavit, and ...'

'Oh, *please* don't make me do that, Mr Selby.'

Selby said to Brandon: 'I can appreciate her position.'

Brandon said: 'The key's in the mail-box.'

Mrs Kane looked hopefully from one to the

21

other. Selby made the decision. 'I think it's on the up-and-up, Rex. Let's go.'

CHAPTER THREE

Mrs Kane, opening the mail-box, gave a quick exclamation.

'What is it?' Selby asked.

'The letter. It's not here.'

'Is the key there?'

'Yes.'

'But the letter from Carr isn't there?'

'No.'

'Wait a minute,' Selby said. 'Let's be very sure there's no one home before we go into the house.'

Brandon rang the bell three times, then after a minute's wait rang it three times again.

It was nearly three minutes from the time the sheriff had first pushed the bell-button before Selby nodded to Mrs Kane. 'All right,' he said. 'If you want to take the responsibility of opening the house and inviting us in, we'll go in.'

'That's not a responsibility I'm willing to assume,' she said.

Selby promptly took the key from the mail-box, fitted the key to the lock and opened the door.

'I think first,' Selby said, 'we'll take a look at

the living-room. I wouldn't like to go prowling about the bedrooms if it should turn out there's someone in the living-room, and perhaps the bell wasn't answered for some reason or other. If anyone's home, we'll look to you to break the ice and start the explanations. Then the sheriff and I will take over.'

She nodded, led the way down the wide staircase, paused at the bottom step. 'Why, that's strange!'

'What's the matter?'

'Look,' she said.

Sunlight poured in through the western windows. The room was spick and span, dusted and swept. The ash-trays had been emptied. There were no glasses strewn around on the tables.

'That's not the way you left it this morning?' Brandon asked.

'Definitely not. Why, someone's been in here and cleaned things all up.'

Brandon said somewhat awkwardly: 'I'm afraid that we're intruding, Mrs Kane. I think you'll find your daughter has returned home. She's probably gone out again, but just for a minute or two.'

'Oh, I hope so!' Mrs Kane said.

Brandon was suddenly uncomfortable. 'Let's get out of here.'

As they started up the stairs, Selby said: 'Seeing we've come this far, we might just as well take a peek into the bedroom. You say one

23

of the neighbours said there had been a pistol-shot?'

Mrs Kane laughed nervously. 'Oh, I'm certain that's just something that the person said. A—a car probably backfired and—'

'Just the same,' Selby said, 'let's take a look in the bedroom. Which room was it?'

She pointed towards the door.

Selby walked down the corridor, followed by Rex Brandon. Mrs Kane held back, glancing apprehensively at the front door.

'I think,' Mrs Kane said, 'we should be *very* brief. I don't know when—well, when someone might come.'

Brandon opened the door, glanced inside at the bedroom, then turned to Mrs Kane. 'You say there was blood on the bed?'

'Yes.'

'Look here.'

She looked, and he heard her gasp.

'And you said there were bloody towels in the bathroom?'

'Yes.'

'Let's take a look.'

The bathroom was spick and span, clean in its white-tiled spotlessness. The trio looked, then marched back along the corridor to the front door.

'I guess that does it,' Brandon said bitterly.

Mrs Kane laughed nervously. 'That—that would seem to do it—whatever it is. I don't know how I can begin to express my thanks.

24

Can I—what I mean to say is—you gentlemen, naturally, won't...'

Selby silently held the front door open for her.

'The key in the mail-box,' Brandon reminded Selby.

Selby nodded.

Mrs Kane started across the threshold. Abruptly Brandon pulled her back and jerked the door shut.

'What is it?' Selby asked.

The sheriff's face was scowling. 'It's a trap,' he said. 'The jaws are closing.'

'Jim Melvin?' Selby asked.

'No. Old A.B.C.'

'What's the meaning of this?' Mrs Kane demanded.

'Don't be so innocent,' Brandon said.

Selby was more charitable. 'She was just the bait, Rex. Did he see you?'

'He saw her all right, and he was stopping his machine right in front.'

Selby said quietly: 'Well, we can't just stand here and let him ring the bell. Come on, Rex. We have to face it. Let's beat him to the punch.'

He opened the door.

Brandon placed his hand under Mrs Kane's elbow, guided her firmly through the door, followed immediately behind her, and was in turn followed by Selby, who pulled the door shut.

The spring lock clicked into place.

'Look at him,' Brandon grumbled, 'dressed up like a cowpuncher. That shyster! Wearing honest cattle clothes! Now I've seen everything!'

Alfonse Baker Carr had been standing in front of his big convertible, studying the house thoughtfully. Now he came moving towards the little group. His hand raised in a smooth gesture and removed the five-gallon hat which graced his head. 'Good afternoon,' he said in a richly resonant voice. 'Can you tell me,' he went on, addressing Doris Kane, 'if Mr Melvin is at home?'

'I don't think he is,' Brandon said.

Carr gave a quite perceptible start of surprise. 'Well, well,' he said, 'it's Sheriff Brandon!'

'Who'd you think it was?'

'I didn't know,' Carr said, interest in his voice. 'I was facing the sunlight and saw only the woman with the two men—and it's Major Selby, our district attorney. How are you, Selby?'

'I'm fine,' Selby said crisply. 'You've got a speech rehearsed. Let's hear it.'

Carr looked at him in surprise. 'I'm afraid I don't understand.'

'All right, do it *your* way,' Selby said.

'May I ask the reason for this visit?' Carr inquired, calmly ignoring the challenge of Selby's last statement.

'What visit?'

26

'Quite obviously you have been calling on Mrs Melvin, since, you say, Jim Melvin isn't at home.'

Selby laughed. 'I'm afraid your reasoning is at fault, Counsellor.'

'Indeed?'

'Oh, go ahead,' Brandon growled. 'Put on your act, Carr.'

'Mrs Melvin is not home either,' Selby said.

Carr's face showed courteous incredulity. 'Then may I ask...'

'Permit me,' Selby said, 'Mrs Kane, this is Mr Carr. Mr Carr is an attorney who has favoured our community by retiring from his active law practice to live in our midst.'

'*Favoured our community*,' Brandon echoed, with belligerent sarcasm.

Carr smiled. 'How do you do, Mrs Kane. I'm very pleased to meet you. I'm afraid that my young friend, the district attorney, is—shall we say, a little optimistic? Not only does the community show no signs of being favoured, to date, but my retirement has been largely academic. I find that my clients have a tendency to follow me, even into what I would like to consider the sanctuary of my country home. You are, perhaps, related to the Melvins?'

'I'm Paula Melvin's mother.'

'Indeed!' and Carr's voice showed the awakening of sudden interest.

The man was tall, rather slender, with the

27

lines of his face deeply etched. There was a vague hint of mockery in the twinkling grey eyes, and at times a sardonic smile seemed to flicker at the corners of the mouth. But he might well have been mistaken for a famous Shakespearean actor. His every move was made with studied grace. His hands were long-fingered and expressive. His voice had a rich resonance which indicated careful study and long training. About him was that consummate poise which Brandon always found so irritating.

As the sheriff had once expressed it angrily to Doug Selby: 'You come on A. B. Carr robbing a chicken-house, catch him in the act of sucking an egg, and he'd make one of those little bows of his, tap in the end of an egg, gracefully hand it to you and say: "Have one, Selby, you'll find they're very delicious!" And somehow, the way he'd do it would make it seem the most natural thing in the world. If you didn't watch out, you'd find yourself sitting there on the edge of the hen-roost, sucking eggs with the old shyster.'

'Are you acquainted with my daughter?' Doris Kane asked.

'Daughter?' Carr parried the question with his usual self-assurance. 'You'll forgive the triteness of the remark if I say that you hardly appear old enough to have a married daughter.'

'Thank you,' she said. 'And you do know

Paula then?'

'I've met her,' Carr said. 'A very attractive young woman, vivacious, up to the minute, a thoroughly modern young woman, and, therefore, exceedingly fascinating. You know, I feel at times that we fail to take into consideration the remarkable progress that youth has made in the last generation or two. We...'

'Okay,' Brandon interrupted, 'we've got our feet wet in this thing, so now we're going wading. We want to ask you a couple of questions, Carr. Never mind any more talk about the Gay Nineties.'

Carr faced him courteously. 'Something I can do for you, Sheriff? You are, of course, aware that you have only to call on me at any time and...'

'When did you last see Jim Melvin?'

'Why, I'm sure I couldn't tell you, Sheriff.'

'Recently?'

'Well, there again,' Carr said, the grave dignity of his manner seeming to deny any possibility that he might be merely sparring for time, 'it depends upon what one means by recently. There are...'

'Seen him within the last two days?'

'No. I don't think I have.'

'Within the last week?'

'Well, now, let me think. I'm sure I couldn't answer that question off-hand, Sheriff. I think quite probably I have, but I wouldn't want to

29

make that as a positive assertion until I had an opportunity to refresh my recollection somewhat. And now, may I ask what's the meaning of your questions?'

Brandon brushed the interrogation aside. 'How about Mrs Melvin? Seen her within the last two days?'

'No.'

'Within the last week?'

'I would say that the time interval would be the same in both cases.'

'In other words, the last time you saw Mrs Melvin, you saw Mr Melvin? Is that right?'

'They were together. Yes.'

'Where?'

'Here.'

'When?'

'In the evening.'

Brandon glanced inquiringly at Selby. 'How late were you here?' Brandon asked.

'I was here at a little gathering of friends.'

'All right,' Selby said. 'That's what we want to get at. What about the pistol-shot?'

'The pistol-shot?' Carr asked, raising his eyebrows.

'The pistol-shot,' Selby said with the quiet assurance of one who is absolutely certain of his facts.

For a moment, Carr gave the impression that he might have been caught off balance. He shifted his eyes quickly from the three people, glancing towards his automobile, as though he

30

wished he had remained in the car and kept on going.

'That pistol-shot,' Selby repeated. 'Come, come, Counsellor. You know whether or not you heard a pistol-shot.'

Carr faced him. He had once more fully recovered his composure 'No,' he said, 'there was no pistol-shot.' And then he smiled gravely. 'There was,' he said, 'a noise similar to the sound of a pistol report.'

'What was it?' Selby asked.

'The popping of a champagne cork.'

'Nonsense,' Brandon blurted. 'Do you mean to say the neighbours would mistake the popping of a champagne cork ...'

'The neighbours?' Carr asked. 'Well, well, this is indeed interesting. No, Sheriff, I feel quite certain that the popping of the champagne cork would hardly be loud enough to ... well, now, wait a minute. Perhaps I'm wrong on that. After all, the popping of a champagne cork in the dining-room might sound in the bedroom windows of this other house—and, I take it, those are the neighbours to whom you have referred. Come to think of it, gentlemen, I feel quite certain there is a distinct possibility the popping of a champagne cork *could* have been taken by sensitive people, by nervous people whose slumber had perhaps been interrupted, as the sound of a pistol-shot.'

'But *you* didn't hear any pistol-shot?'

31

'No.'

'Positive of that?'

'Yes.'

Brandon indicated the mail-box. 'You wrote Jim Melvin a letter. What was in it?'

'A letter?' Carr asked.

'A letter,' Brandon said. 'Come on, what was in it?'

Carr hesitated perceptibly, then said: 'Ah, yes. I believe there was some correspondence between my office and Mr Melvin.'

'What was it?'

'I'm afraid I can't help you there, Sheriff. I think that's a matter I wouldn't care to divulge. But I can assure you it has nothing to do with a pistol-shot. It would be what you would doubtless consider a very minor business matter. And now, if you will excuse me, inasmuch as the Melvins do not seem to be at home, I'll be on my way. Unfortunately, I'm having rather a busy afternoon, despite the fact that I'm trying to retire. I'm very pleased to have met you, Mrs Kane.'

'Just a minute,' Brandon said authoritatively as Carr turned away towards the machine he had left at the kerb.

'Yes?' Carr asked, pausing, only half turning.

Selby almost imperceptibly shook his head at the sheriff.

'What brings *you* here this afternoon, now?' Brandon asked.

32

'I wanted to see Mr Melvin.'

'Evidently on a matter of some importance?'

'My time is valuable,' Carr said significantly. 'I would hardly waste it upon a matter that was of no importance whatever.'

'You tried to telephone him?'

Carr smiled and said: 'Let's let the matter go as it is, gentlemen. I came to see him. It is a private matter, something that I couldn't divulge without tending to betray the interests of a client. At least, unless I know what is the cause of *your* visit.'

Carr waited expectantly.

'We,' Selby said, 'are investigating a pistol-shot.'

'Indeed! You have gone to the trouble of getting a search warrant merely on the strength of a popping champagne cork?'

Brandon said: 'It wasn't a champagne cork and we haven't got a search warrant.'

Carr's brows raised expressively. 'No search warrant? But surely, gentlemen, you have been making a detailed inspection of my client's house.'

'Intending to make something of it?' Brandon asked belligerently.

Carr smiled. 'My dear Sheriff. *I* make nothing of anything. My clients instruct me as to their wishes in various matters, and I try...'

'But,' Selby interrupted, 'you were here, Carr, at the time the sound of the popping champagne cork was mistaken for the sound of

33

a shot...'

'Tut, tut, Counsellor, there were several champagne corks. I definitely was not here ... now wait a moment ... I think perhaps I may know to what you are referring, but it's not a matter I am free to discuss.'

'You mean there was a shot?'

'Heavens, no! I mean merely there was a matter I am not free to discuss, but I think I can assure you, gentlemen, there was no sound of a pistol-shot emanating from the interior of this house. Definitely the neighbours are mistaken if they claim to have heard a shot fired anywhere in this house.'

'Well, tell us what you know about any shot, or any unusual sound that...'

'Tut, tut, Sheriff, I've already told you I can't do that, a matter of professional ethics, you know. And now, if you'll pardon me, I really am quite late for an appointment.' He made another sweeping bow, got in his car, started the motor and drove away.

'Well, there you are,' Brandon said. 'Try to get anything out of that fellow, and it's like trying to pull hen's teeth, but I'm beginning to think this isn't just a trap for us. I think Carr's worried.'

'For once in my life,' Selby said almost musingly, 'I've seen Carr confused. When we asked him directly about the pistol-shot, it gave him quite a jolt. Okay, Rex, we know now that there was a party here. Something must

34

have happened at that party. Let's find out who attended, what time it broke up, whether anyone heard a pistol-shot. Let's talk with the neighbours next door, and let's try and find out something about who came in here and cleaned up the house. And now, Mrs Kane, I think we may safely replace the key to the house in the bottom of the mail-box. We're going to make a complete and thorough investigation of this. Knowing Carr as I do, I would say that while there's nothing to worry about as yet, there's definitely something wrong. We want to talk with your daughter as soon as you find her, and I feel Carr will see to it that you find her very soon.'

'Want me to talk with the neighbours now?' Brandon asked.

'Not *right* now,' Selby said. 'We're just a little too much of a crowd. I think that if you'd come back alone and in your official capacity, Sheriff, and talk with the people next door, you might find out something. Sympathise with them a bit about their slumber having been disturbed. I think very definitely you'll get more information than Mrs Kane did this morning.'

CHAPTER FOUR

It was after seven o'clock that night when the phone in Doug Selby's apartment rang sharply.

Selby picked up the receiver and heard the sheriff's voice.

'That you, Doug?'

'That's right.'

'Suppose you could run down to the court-house for a minute?'

'Sure.'

'Come right up to my office, if you can, Doug. I've got something funny up here. I can't make it out. I'll be waiting for you in the entrance room. There's a man in my private office, but I want to talk with you before you see him.'

Selby got in his car, drove to the court-house and found Rex Brandon waiting for him in the sheriff's outer office.

The sheriff kept two night men on duty, and these men, seated near the telephone at the far corner of the office, merely nodded as Selby walked over to the table where Brandon was sitting.

The sheriff got up, took Selby's arm and walked over to stand at the window, looking down at the red, green, and purple lights which marked the stores of Madison City, the blaze of illumination which indicated the location of the Palace Theatre.

'You remember Milton Granby, Doug?'

Selby smiled. 'The one whose claim to fame is that he's the brother-in-law of Morris Sheldon, Mayor of Las Alidas?'

'That's the one.'

'What about him?'

'He's in my office in there,' Brandon said, nodding towards the private office. 'I want you to talk with him.'

'He certainly rides on his brother-in-law's coat-tails,' Selby said. 'One wonders what Granby would have done if he hadn't had a sister.'

Brandon said: 'I'm not sure but what we're wandering around in the same old maze of mirrors that we always encounter when we deal with old A. B. Carr.'

'In other words, you don't believe the story Granby told you?' Selby asked.

Brandon said thoughtfully: 'I think I believe it, but I don't know what it means. I want you to hear it.'

Selby, filling a crusted brier pipe and scratching a match into flame, said: 'Okay. Let's go in.'

Brandon opened the door of his private office and said: 'I want you to tell Doug Selby what you told me, Granby.'

Granby, a slender, small-boned man with a half-bald head, skin that was stretched tight across prominent cheek-bones, jumped up out of the chair he had been occupying, to pump Selby's hand. 'How are you, Mr Selby! It's great to have you back with us.'

Selby said: 'It's good to be here.'

'Sit down,' Brandon invited. 'Granby, I want you to tell Selby the story you told me. I want you to tell it in your own words. Begin at the beginning and go right through with it.'

Granby settled himself comfortably in the chair, obviously pleased with his position as a purveyor of important information.

'Well,' he said, 'I suppose you know there's a deal on over at Las Alidas for parking meters. Jim Melvin represents a new sort of device, one that pays off half again what the others do because of some kind of photoelectric cell that keeps one car from using up the unexpired parking time of a preceding car that stays only fifteen or twenty minutes.'

Brandon nodded encouragingly.

'Well, I met Jim Melvin and talked with him a few times. He didn't have much time for me until he found out that I was Morris Sheldon's brother-in-law, and then Melvin really started putting on the pressure.'

'We can skip most of that,' Brandon said. 'You've established the foundation. Now tell us about that party at Melvin's house here at Madison City.'

'Well, Melvin wanted me to come up, said that he was having a little get-together, just a sort of get-acquainted party. It was quite a shindig! He had people there whom he wanted to impress, and it was quite a mixture. People from here and some people from Los Angeles, some from Las Alidas.'

'And old A. B. Carr was there?'

'That's right.'

'Go ahead, tell what happened.'

'Well, there was a lot of champagne and other drinks, just about anything you wanted.'

'Tell about the pistol-shot,' Brandon prompted.

'Well, about one or two o'clock in the morning, I don't know the exact time, *I* thought *I* heard a pistol-shot.' Granby paused dramatically, looking from the sheriff to the district attorney as though proud of having a dramatic highlight for his story.

'Go on,' Brandon said briefly.

Granby went on with visible self-approval. 'One of the fellows to whom I talked said it was just a champagne cork in the kitchen, and another one said it was a truck that had backfired, but *I* said it was a shot, and they couldn't fool me on it!'

'Go on.'

'Well, the party went on about the same as usual, and then an hour or so later Jim Melvin came up to me and asked me if I could keep my mouth shut about something. Then he asked me to help him. He said he might need someone else, and looked around and caught the eye of

39

old Mr Carr, and asked him to help, and then led the way up the stairs.'

Brandon glanced at Selby, said to Granby: 'Okay, Granby, keep right on.'

'Well, we went up to one of the bedrooms. A man was lying on the bed. He had a bloody towel wrapped around his arm and twisted into a tourniquet. There was blood all over the bed and there was blood in the bathroom. This chap said he'd been at the party and had had too much to drink. He'd gone out to get some air and sober up, seen the garage, walked down to it and been pretty sick. He felt as though he didn't have an ounce of strength left and wanted to collapse.

'He went into the garage, opened the door of the automobile that was in it and was fumbling around getting into the car when he accidentally pushed the button on the glove compartment. The door popped open and there was a .38 revolver on the inside.

'The fellow said he took the revolver out and fumbled around with it for a while. He recognised that it was a dangerous plaything in his drunken condition, and was trying to put it back when somehow or other the thing shot him in the arm. He said he didn't know exactly how it happened.

'The effect of the shot sobered him. He went into the house to try and get to a bathroom and wash the blood off. He was bleeding badly. He twisted a tourniquet out of a handkerchief, got

40

up to the bathroom, staggered to the bed, fell down and went to sleep. While he was asleep, the tourniquet loosened and he lost a lot of blood.'

'So, what happened?' Selby asked, his voice and eyes showing his keen interest.

'Well, Melvin said he wanted to hush the thing up. In the first place, he didn't want anyone to know he was carrying a gun in the car, because he didn't have a permit and was afraid there might be some trouble. In the second place, he didn't want it to appear that a man had shot himself at a party at his house, because the newspapers would be apt to call it a brawl and publish a list of the guests. A lot of prominent men would be involved and things of that sort.'

'What did they tell you they were going to do?' Brandon asked.

'Well, the man said he was all right, that the tourniquet had stopped the flow of blood, that he was cold sober, that he'd get in his car and drive home, and that he was awfully sorry it had happened.'

'So what did you do?'

'We assisted him down the back stairs, out of the back door and around to the alley. His car was parked there. He said he didn't have to use his left arm at all, and that he felt perfectly able to get home all right.'

'Who was this man?' Brandon asked.

'Now there you've got me. I naturally didn't

ask for an introduction at a time like that. I didn't get the man's name and...'

'Hadn't you been introduced to him there at the party?' Selby asked.

'To tell you the truth, Mr Selby, I don't remember even having seen him at the party. There were a lot of people there. Quite a few of them were strangers to me. I know the local people, of course.'

'And why did Jim Melvin ask you to help?'

'You've got me. Maybe he thought the man was in worse shape than he really was. Anyway, I tagged along and walked down to the man's car with him.'

'What kind of a car?'

'There again, I can't tell you. It was a dark sedan and looked like a late model, but I just didn't pay any attention. I think it was one of the cheaper makes.'

'And, of course, you didn't get the licence number?'

'No.'

Selby looked at Brandon. The sheriff said: 'There you are, Doug. That's his story.'

'Do you remember where Jim Melvin was at the time the shot was fired?' Selby asked.

'I do,' Granby said. 'As it happened, I was standing right next to Melvin when the shot sounded. He was the one that said it was the popping of the champagne cork in the other room.'

'How about Carr?' Selby asked. 'Do you
42

happen to know where he was?'

'Sure,' Granby said, 'Carr was right there. He was the one who said it was a truck backfiring coming down the grade. He went on to explain something about what caused it. It was having a too lean mixture or something like that. I don't remember exactly what he said.'

'But you know both Carr and Melvin were right there when you heard the shot?'

'That's right.'

'Okay,' Selby said. 'I guess that's all.'

Granby seemed reluctant to leave. He was quite evidently impressed with his position as an important witness. 'I might be able to find out a little more about this chap for you,' he offered. 'I might ask some of the others.'

'No, thanks. We'll do our own investigating,' Brandon said.

'Well, if there's *anything* I can do for you, just let me know.'

'How about Morris Sheldon? Was he there?'

Granby drew himself up importantly. 'No,' he said, 'I was representing the family at the party. He'd been invited, of course, but—well, I was sort of—well, representing Morris—that is, sort of—well, you know.'

'All right,' Brandon said, 'don't tell anyone about having been up here or having been questioned about this. That's all, and thanks for your co-operation, Granby.'

When Granby had gone, Brandon pulled a

43

packet of cigarette papers from his pocket, fished out a cloth tobacco-pouch and sent golden-brown grains of fragrant tobacco rattling into the grooved paper.

'There you are,' Brandon said. 'It's the same old seven and six every time we cross old A. B. Carr's back track.'

'What do you make of it?' Selby asked.

'Well, in the first place,' Brandon said, 'this man, whoever he was, couldn't have been very badly hurt because he drove his car away.'

Selby nodded.

'And,' Brandon went on, 'Melvin went down and got Granby and Carr to help him get the chap out of the house, but the fellow didn't *need* any help. Now, if Melvin was really trying to keep the thing hushed up, why the heck did he go and get two witnesses just at the time the fellow left the house?'

Selby's pipe had gone out. He scratched a match on the underside of the table, held it to the pipe while he puffed thoughtfully at the tobacco for several seconds.

'Well?' Brandon growled. 'What is it, Doug? You look as thought you had an idea.'

'I have an idea,' Selby said, 'and that's all it is. Just an idea. How did the place get cleaned up?'

'I found out about that,' Brandon said. 'A negro maid comes in once a week and cleans up. Whenever Mrs Melvin is out, the key is left in the mail-box. The maid gets it and lets

44

herself in. When she finishes with the work she goes out. The front door has a spring lock.

'Last week Mrs Melvin phoned her not to come. This week Mrs Melvin *might* have tried to phone her again. The maid doesn't know. She'd been visiting friends in Los Angeles. She came back this morning and went directly to the Melvin house. She found the key, let herself in. She had her suitcase with her, changed her clothes there at Melvin's house and went to work.

'She found blood-stained clothes on the bed and towels in the bathroom. She figured it wasn't any of her business. She cleaned up and put fresh sheets, pillow-cases, clean blankets and a clean spread on the bed.'

'What did she do with the blood-stained stuff?' Selby asked.

'Took it home with her. She does the washing for the Melvins as well as the cleaning. She drives an old jalopy and she just chucked the stuff in, took it home and started washing it. She seems straightforward enough.'

Selby frowned. 'Last week Mrs Melvin phoned her not to come?'

'That's right.'

The men smoked in silence for a moment, then Selby said: 'It's a queer situation, all right.'

Knuckles sounded on the door. One of the night deputies opened it a crack and said: 'Sheriff, there's a man out here by the name of

45

Parlin who wants to see you. He gave me a card.'

Brandon said: 'I'm busy now, Dick. You'll have to find out what...'

'It's something about Jim Melvin,' the deputy said. 'Parlin's card shows that he...'

'Let's take a look at it,' Brandon said.

He took the card from the deputy, held it so Selby could see it. It was expensively embossed and read: 'HUDSON L. PARLIN, BUSINESS INVESTMENTS, RODNEY BUILDING, LOS ANGELES.'

'What does he look like?' Selby asked.

'Around fifty-five, a big, beefy chap with heavy colour and manicured nails. He's really dolled up in cowboy clothes.'

Brandon said: 'Keep him waiting a minute or so, then send him in. I don't want to seem too eager, but don't let him get away.'

The deputy closed the door. They smoked in silence for a few minutes. Then Selby said: 'Granby impresses me as bursting with a desire to talk, Rex.'

Brandon's nod was moody. 'That's the worst of dealing with tripe like that. He'll spread it all over town. He's so damn used to getting by on...'

The door opened and the deputy said: 'This is Mr Parlin.'

Hudson L. Parlin stood in the doorway, steely grey eyes under shaggy brows, making a lightning appraisal of the two men. Then he

46

smiled, a smile of frosty cordiality that was not overdone, but nevertheless showed a disposition to be friendly on the part of a man who was more accustomed to receive overtures than to make them.

'Come in,' Brandon said. 'You wanted to see us? I'm Sheriff Brandon. This is Mr Selby, the district attorney.'

'I'm glad to know you, gentlemen. I wanted to talk with you about James L. Melvin.'

'That's what the deputy said,' Brandon said. 'Sit down. Make yourself comfortable and tell us what's on your mind.'

Parlin sat down, the straight rigidity of his back emphasising the formality of his visit, making the sheriff's invitation to 'make himself comfortable' appear oddly incongruous. His cowboy costume seemed utterly out of place.

'Gentlemen,' Parlin said in close-clipped enunciation, 'I am a business-man.'

'All right,' Brandon said. 'Go ahead and talk business.'

'I finance inventions. Some time ago the inventor of a parking meter came to me. He wanted financial backing. His affairs were somewhat involved. I made a tentative investigation and decided much of his trouble had been inept salesmanship. I won't go into details, but eventually I bought the invention, lock, stock and barrel.'

'That's the thing Jim Melvin's handling?' the

47

sheriff asked.

'That's right. *Karpay* is the trade name for it. I invented that name myself and applied it to the device. I had my patent attorneys go over all the patent situation and arrange for large scale manufacture of the device. Then I went to work.'

'What about Jim Melvin?'

'I employed Jim Melvin on a basis of salary and bonus. If he reaches a certain quota, he is to have exclusive sales rights.'

'What territory does that arrangement include?'

'Southern district of California and all of Arizona.'

'Have you done any work in Arizona?'

'At the present time that territory is dormant. We are concentrating on two cities in this county and one city in northern California, which as it happens is out of Melvin's territory.'

'You wanted to see us about Melvin?' Brandon asked.

'That's right.'

'What about him?'

'In this business, Sheriff, I try to be broad-minded. I appreciate that there is a certain element of keen competition and that the element of politics must, naturally, enter into the situation. That means a certain amount of entertaining. I try to keep that within reasonable limits, so far as the financial investment is concerned. And I insist upon keeping it within reasonable limits, so far as the nature of the entertainment is concerned.'

'In other words, you're trying to tell us that you financed the party at Jim Melvin's house a week or ten days ago?'

'That is only partially correct. I'm also trying to tell you I didn't approve of it. Melvin told me he wanted certain things in the way of entertainment, and I okayed the expense.'

'Then what?'

'I understand you have been investigating that party.'

'Who told you?'

'I prefer to keep that to myself. In a community of this size, your investigation was bound to be known. I think you will agree, Sheriff, that it was only natural that one or more of the persons who was at that party would ring me up in something of a panic and insist that his name be kept out of the picture. You can see the adverse publicity that might well ensue from a situation of this sort.'

'If you want to prevent adverse publicity,' Brandon said, 'you'd better get the facts in my hands. Then I'll reach a decision.'

'Haven't you the facts now?'

'What makes you think I have?'

'Because I have heard the most glowing reports as to your ability, and I know that you did make an investigation.'

'What facts are you referring to?'

'What,' Parlin countered, 'is the reason for your investigation?'

Brandon detoured the question. 'Jim Melvin is working for you?'

'In a way, yes. He has the agency in the territory I mentioned, with a salary drawing account and a commission bonus...'

'Where *is* Melvin?'

Parlin hesitated.

'I want to talk with him,' Brandon said.

Parlin said: 'I want you to understand, Sheriff, that I am a business-man, a cold-blooded business-man, grasping, if you want to put it that way, but I'm fair, I'm honourable and I'm ethical. I don't approve of wild parties.'

'You paid for this one, didn't you?'

'I didn't think it was going to be one. I still don't think it was wild.'

'I want to talk with Melvin about it.'

'I have no objection to your talking with Melvin. My objection—well, of course, I won't call it an objection, because I am in no position to make one—but my protest is against calling in the various guests. A moment's reflection will show you what a disastrous effect that could have on the entire situation here.'

'Were you at that party?'

'No, sir, I was not. I don't mind telling you, Sheriff, that if I had been, the liquor would have been locked up and the party would have been over by midnight. There were fewer

50

guests than expected, and that meant a greater per capita consumption of liquor. Melvin, apparently, was so intent upon seeing that everyone had a good time he failed to take into consideration that in matters of that sort discretion is a most important factor.'

Brandon said: 'I want to talk with Melvin.'

'I take it, then, that when Melvin gets in touch with you, I can count upon a certain tolerance on your part, so far as the other guests are concerned. Many of these men are powerful politically. I see no need to dwell upon that point. I want to be able to assure some of these men who are telephoning me that there will be no summons to appear before you, no undue publicity in the Press. I take it you'll co-operate?'

Brandon said: 'Tell these people that I'm making an investigation. I'm going to keep on investigating until I've found out what I want to know.'

Parlin's steely eyes locked with those of the sheriff. 'You're in politics, yourself, you know, Sheriff,' he said quietly.

'I'm elected to do a job. I'm going to try and do it.'

'That's right,' Parlin said, 'you're *elected* to do a job.'

Brandon caught Selby's eye, made a little gesture towards the door of the outer office.

'Excuse me a minute,' he said. 'I want to talk with Selby about this thing. Just sit right where

51

you are, Mr Parlin.'

Brandon opened the door. Selby followed him into the outer office.

Brandon said angrily: 'That's the worst of these damn politicians. They elect you to do a job and then the minute you start doing it, and it involves anything they're interested in, they start hollering their heads off, wanting you to betray the interests you're sworn to protect, just in order to protect some damn politician. Is it okay by you if I get tough?'

Selby laughed. 'I hope you didn't call me out here just to see if I'd back your play, Rex.'

'If I'm going overboard politically, I don't want to drag you down with me.'

Selby merely motioned towards the closed door of the private office. 'Give him the works, Rex.'

They returned to the office. Brandon said: 'There are two ways of getting the facts—the hard way and the easy way. The easy way would be to have James L. Melvin tell me about them. I'll be here until ten o'clock tonight.'

Parlin said smoothly: 'And until he gets here—that is, while I'm locating him—I take it for granted there will be no further...'

'You can't take a thing for granted,' Brandon said. Parlin pushed back his chair. 'I have to be in Los Angeles at eleven-thirty tonight. It's a two-hour drive.

'Before I keep my appointment, I will have

to change the bizarre clothes which the fashion dictates of your Chamber of Commerce require all persons to wear if they wish to do business in Madison City.

'I shall have time to put through one or two telephone calls, and that will be about all. If I can reach Jim Melvin I'll ask him to be here by ten. I promise nothing. Good night.'

'There goes a man who isn't accustomed to being pushed around,' Selby said, as the door closed behind Parlin.

Brandon leaned forward and picked up a spectacle-case from the floor.

'Now, where did this come from?' he asked.

The sheriff opened and closed the spectacle-case. 'Just a plain dark brown spectacle-case,' he said. 'And there's no stamped name of an optical company in it. Now, why would a man drop a spectacle-case in here, Doug?'

'Do you remember whether Granby was wearing glasses when he came in?' Selby asked abruptly.

'No. Why?'

Selby indicated the assortment of papers on the sheriff's desk. 'Anything in those papers that concerns Granby?'

'Not a thing,' Brandon said.

'Or anything having to do with Melvin?'

Brandon's shake of the head was a quick, decisive negative.

'Of course,' Selby pointed out, 'Granby couldn't be expected to know that until he'd

53

looked. Could anyone else have dropped it?'

'It wasn't lying there on the floor before Granby came in. I'm sure of that,' Brandon said.

Selby was thoughtful. 'I know he was wearing glasses when I met him.'

Brandon said: 'Lots of times men about that age can get along without glasses except for close work, but when they once put 'em on, they're apt to forget and leave 'em for a while. I don't know as it's particularly important except that I don't like the idea of him snooping around my office. He's an officious little nuisance.'

'Why not hang on to the spectacle-case and say nothing?' Selby suggested. 'Then when he finds he left it here, he'll be in a panic for fear you'll take him to task for prowling in your papers.'

'Good idea,' Brandon said, dropping the spectacle-case into his coat pocket. 'We'll let him squirm a bit. What do you think of his story?'

'There are certain peculiar things about it, Rex. No one *saw* the wound, only the bloody towel around the man's arm. No one apparently knows who the man is. Granby says he hadn't seen him at the party. Now just suppose that there *was* a pistol-shot. Suppose old A. B. Carr knew that he had to account for that pistol-shot. Suppose he planted a stooge there on the bed with the bloody towel and then...'

'But Carr didn't know anything about it. Melvin called Carr over *after* he'd got hold of Granby.'

'Exactly!' Selby said, smiling. 'And when you think *that* over, Rex, you realise that's exactly the way old A.B.C. would have arranged the thing *if* it had been carefully planned. Granby was the one person who could account for the whereabouts of both Melvin and Carr at the time the shot was fired.'

Brandon came bolt upright in his chair. 'Good heavens, Doug! Do you think that...'

Selby interrupted: 'Let's not think too much before we get more facts, Rex. I'm simply pointing out that *if* this man had been a ringer who was planted with a blood-stained towel wrapped around his arm, it would have been a typical Carr trick.'

'Damned if it wouldn't!' the sheriff agreed.

CHAPTER FIVE

Having taken a cabin at a motor court on the main highway east of Madison City, Doris Kane fought off sleep while she waited for a report from the sheriff's office. But the strain of her all-night drive, the comfort of the chair in which she relaxed, gradually lulled her into a state of dozing quiescence.

55

Reality became mixed with dreams until her sleep-sodden senses were unable to discriminate between the real and the unreal. Paula had been murdered ... Paula had killed Jim ... Paula and Jim had...

She sat up, startled into sudden wakefulness by a noise at the door. The moonlight showed the outline of a dim figure. There were fingers fumbling at the screen door, at the knob.

She fought back a desire to scream ... and then recognised the man's figure.

She ran to the door, opened it and found Jim's reassuring arms around her. His muscles gave her a sense of strength, his laugh was so contagious, his kiss on her cheek, the aroma of tobacco all so splendidly matter-of-fact that her doubts disappeared in gladness at seeing him, at his very apparent gladness at seeing her.

She was pouring questions at him almost before he had released her. 'Jim, what on earth? How did you find me? Where's Paula? How ...?'

'Hey ... wait a minute,' he laughingly interrupted. 'One thing at a time. I found where you were because Sheriff Brandon told me. He suggested I'd better drive by and pick you up.'

The memory of her part in instigating an official investigation stabbed her consciousness. 'Oh, Jim, I'm *so* sorry! I went there to the house, and ...'

And then suddenly she realised that Jim didn't know.

The sheriff would have told him something of necessity, but how much? There was that in his face, in his attitude that told her Brandon hadn't said too much.

'I know,' Jim said, laughing, 'you found the papers in a pile, the note from the milkman, and you appealed to the authorities to find out if I'd been in an accident. That started an investigation. Probably it's as well. It had to come some time. The snooping neighbours did all they could to make trouble. You see, Doris, there was a party there at the house ten days or so ago, and one of the guests got tight. He went out to get some air, staggered into the garage, opened the door of my car, fumbled around in the glove compartment and found a revolver I'd been carrying the night before when I had to carry a lot of cash.'

'What happened?' she asked in quick alarm.

His laugh was as soothing as the hand which was patting her shoulder. 'Nothing very serious. He sent a bullet through an artery in his arm. But he recovered all right, stopped the bleeding, sobered up and drove home.'

'Who was it, Jim?'

'No one you know. No one I know very well. He was a gate-crasher, one of the tribe that always horn in whenever they know there's to be free liquor. He was a typical friend-of-a-friend. I've been trying to think of his name, but for the life of me I can't remember it. I remember seeing him there at the house, pouring liquor down himself as though he was trying to put out a fire. The chap was never really introduced, although I heard his name—I think it was Merton or Martin— something like that—I never even heard his first name. He was from Hollywood. He managed to sound vaguely important. But that doesn't mean anything. They all manage to sound vaguely important. That's their stock in trade.'

'But, Jim, the man was really shot?'

'Just a wound in the arm.'

'And he did it himself?'

'That's right. It was a typical piece of drunken stupidity. However, it's nothing to worry about. I've been telling the authorities all about it until I'm tired of the whole thing. Anyhow, Doris, we're certainly glad we found you. You see, I had to leave very abruptly for Las Alidas, a prosperous little city over here in the county. I thought it was going to be for only a few days. But the deal I'm working on keeps dragging and we're still there, believe it or not. We've been fortunate in getting a house where we could do some entertaining. On the sort of deal I'm working on, a hotel would be out of the question. Gosh, but you're looking fine!'

Doris laughed in relief. After all, it was all so simple, and Jim was so *very* tangible.

'I phoned Paula,' Jim went on. 'Heaven

knows what happened to the birthday telegram we sent. It must have miscarried somewhere ... Well, come on, get your things together. We've got lots of room over there at Las Alidas. We're living in a regular barn of a house.'

Jim smothered her objections, perfunctorily made, that she was an unexpected guest, that she could stay at an auto court or hotel. He laughingly rushed her into packing, and within a few minutes was loading her baggage into her station wagon.

'You're to follow me,' he instructed her. 'I'll keep watch in the rear-view mirror, so don't worry about getting lost. If you *should* want to stop for anything, just blink your lights. Come on. Paula's dying to see you. She's missed you. And *I'm* dying to have you bake one of your famous bread-puddings. Promise me that you'll do that for us.'

'It's all right,' she laughed. 'I'll bake you two.'

'That's a deal. Come on. Let's go.'

He held the door open for her, waited until she had the motor started, and then walked over to his own car.

Doris was tired, and it seemed an interminable interval before Jim's car slowed for the outskirts of Las Alidas. They crossed through the business district, waited for a traffic signal, then were in a high-class residential district, and Jim was signalling her by flashing his brake light on and off. She followed him in a left-hand turn and then midway in the block he motioned she was to turn into the drive-way and put her car into the garage.

A reaction had set in by the time she switched off the ignition and the lights. She felt she simply couldn't summon the strength to face Paula. The sheriff quite evidently hadn't told Jim any of the details, and Jim wouldn't ask any searching questions. Paula would be different. The dangerous factor in the situation was the lawyer who had seen Doris emerging from the house. Doris knew she must find some way to meet that man and silence him. She was almost too weary to recall his name—A. B. Carr. She must remember it.

Jim helped her with her overnight bag and suitcase, closed the garage door and left his own car parked in the drive-way.

She said: 'Jim, I'm absolutely all in.'

'Sure, you are,' he said soothingly. 'We'll do our talking tomorrow. We'll just say "Hello" to Paula and let all the talking go for a while.'

Weary as she was, she half-consciously recognised a note of relief in his voice, but was too fatigued to take the time to try to figure out why he was relieved.

Paula was waiting for her, and Doris Kane, who had found herself dreading the interview with her daughter, suddenly realised that she had nothing to be afraid of. Paula was more on the defensive, less certain of herself than Doris

Kane had ever seen her.

Paula was looking wonderfully well. There was a new maturity about her. She had always affected an attitude of extreme poise, but there were times when the fact that it was merely an act had been quite apparent. Now Paula seemed to have welcomed her new responsibilities as a wife.

There were greetings, embraces, and then for a moment a half-awkward silence, then Jim saying: 'Doris is all in. She drove all night last night and didn't get any sleep today. She wants to go beddy-bye. You two can do your talking in the morning.'

Paula said: 'We'll put her in the upstairs room on the east, Jim.'

Jim picked up Doris Kane's suitcase and bag, started for the stairs, then stopped. He turned and looked back inquiringly at Paula.

Paula said quickly: 'We have another house guest, Mother. You'll meet her tomorrow, a delightful girl. You'll have to share the bathroom. Try not to make any more noise than necessary when you go up the stairs, and be as quiet as you can in the bathroom. She hasn't been sleeping well.'

Doris Kane nodded mechanically. It wasn't until she was half-way up the stairs that it suddenly occurred to her there had been a tell-tale crispness to Paula's words. When Paula talked rapidly that way and had that air of assurance, that ... oh, well, it could all wait until morning.

Doris walked up the stairs, saw the invitation of a soft white bed, knew that no matter what else might be wrong, Paula was safe.

She stretched and yawned, said to her son-in-law: 'Thanks ever so much, Jim, for being so nice.'

He grinned at her, an awkward, boyish grin.

And then some aftermath of her reaction to what Paula had said prompted her to ask: 'What's peculiar about your house guest, Jim?'

The grin faded from his face. 'She's okay. Look, Doris, you've been driving all last night. You're tired. You'd better go to bed and...'

'Yes, of course,' she said. 'Good night, Jim.'

''Night.'

Doris Kane undressed slowly, a vague fear gnawing at the back of her mind. There was something definitely and decidedly wrong with Jim Melvin's house guest. Paula's manner, as she gave that little speech—the way Jim Melvin's eyes had suddenly grown hard when she mentioned the house guest.

Doris got into bed, but the weariness which had gripped her earlier in the evening now had been displaced by a nervous tension. She lay taut, physically and mentally weary, yet nervously apprehensive, distinctly worried and with a mind that persisted in racing endlessly over the events of the day.

After almost an hour of turning and

twisting, she was just getting relaxed sufficiently to feel that sleep might be possible when she heard the sound of someone moving around in the bathroom. Then the knob turned. The door to her room gently opened. A ribbon of light gradually widened, and then remained stationary as the door was held in position, open some three or four inches.

Doris Kane sat up abruptly in bed. She fought back an impulse to feel frightened.

'Who is it?'

'Oh, I'm so sorry. I wakened you, didn't I?'

'Who is it, please?'

The woman's voice said: 'I'm Eve Dawson. I know all about you. You're Doris Kane, Paula Melvin's mother. I—I was too nervous to sleep. I thought I heard you tossing around in bed and felt perhaps...'

'I'm trying to get to sleep,' Doris said firmly.

The door opened wider.

'May I talk to you for *just* a moment? Just a minute or two. Honestly, I'll not stay over five minutes.'

Eve Dawson entered the bedroom, pulling a fluffy *négligé* about her, apparently so desperate for human companionship that she was quite willing to run the risk of a curt rebuff.

Doris saw her face for a moment, as the light from the bathroom illuminated one side of the girl's features against a halo of blonde hair. She was lovely in a full-blown way, and Doris Kane, shrewd judge of character that she was,

was able to make a quick classification.

She came over to sit on the edge of Mrs Kane's bed.

'I'm cooped up here where I don't have any visitors,' she said. 'I don't have anything in common with the Melvins. I just stay there in my room and think, think, think. At times it seems I'll go mad.'

'Don't you read?'

'I don't like to read. I want people. I want action. I've been very ill. I guess for a while they thought I wasn't going to make it.'

'I should think, under the circumstances, you'd acquire a taste for reading.'

'I don't like reading and I can't learn to like it. As Paula Melvin's mother, you know all about me, of course. The way you timed your visit forced them to confide in you. I'm kept here very hush-hush, and I'm terribly tired of it.'

Doris Kane felt herself stiffen. This young girl was being kept in her daughter's house, and her presence was very hush-hush.

'You've known Paula long?' she asked.

'Heavens, no. I just met them the night— well, the night it happened. And while they've been perfectly swell, still it isn't like having your own friends around.'

Mrs Kane nodded.

'Of course,' Eve Dawson went on, 'inasmuch as you're one of the family, I don't need to hand out any line to you. I can let my

64

hair down.'

'You've been ill?' Doris Kane asked.

The girl's laugh was mockery. 'You don't need to beat around the bush with me. Perhaps you'd like to see just how ill I was.'

Eve Dawson raised a hand, stripped back the *négligé*. Doris Kane found her horrified eyes looking at an angry, red, circular scar in the girl's side. Even with the half-lighting which trickled into the room from the bathroom light, it was impossible to mistake the nature of that wound.

'You ... you've been shot!' Doris Kane heard herself saying.

Eve Dawson regarded her quizzically. 'Of course,' she said. 'What else did you expect? Why did you think they took this house? Do you mean to tell me they didn't let *you* in on the ground floor?'

'I didn't know.'

'Look here. Are you handing it to me on the square? Don't you know?'

'They hadn't told me the details as yet. I guess they were going to wait until tomorrow.'

The *négligé* was drawn hurriedly back over the puckered red welt in the flesh.

Eve Dawson rose abruptly. 'I guess,' she said, 'I've been talking out of turn again. Can you cover for me?'

Mrs Kane smiled.

'You look like a good guy,' the Dawson girl said. 'I thought you knew all about me, and

65

thought it would be a swell chance to have a little talk with someone who knew her way around enough to tell me what to do. I've got to reach a decision tonight. Your daughter is just a little young and sort of—well, she hasn't been around too much. Oh, I don't mean it exactly that way. I meant I'd like to have a visit with some older woman that I'd be free to talk to. Forget all about it, will you?'

Mrs Kane found herself nodding vaguely.

'I suppose I could catch hell for this,' Eve Dawson said. 'However, I'll be out of here in another week. All I need to do now is get my strength back. I guess it was touch and go for a while.'

Doris Kane said: 'Do you mean to tell me that you stayed here in this house, that you were in a critical condition from a bullet wound and they didn't even have a doctor?'

'Sure they had a doctor,' Eve Dawson said. 'If I'd croaked, it would have been a hell of a problem for all of them. Oh no, they couldn't take a chance on that! I bet I had the best doctor money could buy, but I don't know who he was, and I never will know. You can bet money on that. He wasn't anyone who lived in this hick town, you can bet on that. I tried to look out of the window once to get a glimpse of the licence plate on his car, but they caught me at that, and I never had another chance. They saw to *that* all right. Oh, they were solicitous enough about bringing me through, but that's

66

all they were concerned about. Say, I am talking a hell of a lot, aren't I?'

'I thought that was what you wanted to do.'

Eve Dawson was suddenly reticent. 'I guess,' she said bitterly, 'I talk too much. I'm sorry I interfered with your sleep. Ever get so you can't sleep, night after night?'

Doris Kane shook her head.

'Don't do it. It's a terrible feeling. I've got some sleeping-tablets to take, if I have to. I've been trying to swear off of them. I don't like to develop a habit for anything. I'm all jittery tonight. I feel apprehensive as hell. I'm going to have to make a decision within the next hour. I wish I knew what was the best thing to do— afterwards I'll take a *real* dose of sleep medicine.'

'Don't take too many,' Doris Kane warned.

There was a light laugh, a laugh that somehow seemed to hold a note of mockery. 'Don't worry. I'm in too sweet a position to rub myself out now—only I wish I knew a little more about how to play my cards.' Then the bathroom door closed. After a moment, the light was switched off.

For a few minutes, Doris Kane lay there, tense and thoughtful. Then fatigue caused her attention to wander. Her apprehension dissolved in lassitude. A delicious sense of warmth steeped her limbs. Her eyes fluttered closed, opened and closed again, and remained

67

closed. Her breathing became rhythmic and regular.

CHAPTER SIX

It seemed to Doris that she had been sleeping for only a short interval when she was awakened by the sound of the bathroom door once more.

Every shred her sleep-drugged senses could muster registered indignant protest at having her slumbers once more disturbed by a brassy blonde who had not as yet learned that there was no 'easy way'; that the roads of life which seemed so perfectly paved on a gentle downhill slope invariably ended on rough detours.

Mrs Kane raised herself on one shoulder. In a voice thick with sleep, she said: 'Go back to bed. Don't bother me again tonight.'

She was vaguely conscious of the motionless figure silhouetted in light from the bathroom, a dark bundled figure that paused for a thoughtful moment, then hastily withdrew. She heard the bathroom door very definitely close, and with the sound of the clicking latch, Doris Kane, as though needing no more than that to give her the feeling of security that would induce sleep, settled into a deep, untroubled slumber which was finally penetrated by a knife-edged scream of sheer terror.

Doris Kane's eyes fluttered open. Sunlight streamed warmly and reassuringly in through the eastern windows to make patterns of the lace curtains on the floor.

Running steps were coming towards her from the room on the other side of the bathroom. It was Paula who was screaming, Paula who explosively jerked the bathroom door open and stood white-faced and shaken.

Mrs Kane reached for the robe at the foot of the bed. 'What is it, Paula?'

Paula tried to tell her, but now a nervous reaction had set in, making the girl's lips quiver, so that the first words were merely unintelligible sounds.

Mrs Kane, her robe around her, her feet in slippers, was moving towards Paula, all of her motherly instinct reasserting itself.

And then suddenly Paula was herself once more. At least the outer semblance of poise had returned. She said, as calmly as though she had been announcing that breakfast was ready: 'Eve Dawson seems to have died during the night.'

Mrs Kane followed her daughter into the bedroom on the other side of the bath.

The blonde was a grotesque lump of inanimate flesh lying across the bed. The flaxen hair streaming down over the edge of the bed looked like golden grain stalks in the sun.

The handle of the big carving-knife protruding from the left side of her chest gave

69

mute evidence of what had happened, and Doris, looking at it with fear-widened eyes, found herself wondering how in the world so small a body could have made such a great pool of red on the bed, on the floor, over the rug.

There was another door leading to the corridor, and in front of this door was a tray and the remains of a breakfast strewn over the hardwood floor, scrambled eggs, brown toast, a shattered coffee-cup and saucer.

Doris noticed, as little insignificant trifles register on the brain at such times, that steam was still coming up from the coffee where it had spread out over the floor.

'I was bringing her her breakfast,' Paula said by way of explanation.

Mrs Kane said firmly: 'All right, Paula. We must get out of here, ourselves, and see that no one comes up here. Where's Jim?'

'He's gone to work.'

'We're alone in the house?'

'Yes.'

'We'll go down and telephone the police immediately.'

'Mother, I . . .'

'What?'

'I don't think Jim would want me to . . . you know the police . . .'

Mrs Kane said quietly: 'I think you've been listening to Jim's ideas about not calling the police a little too much, Paula. If you'll show

70

me where the phone is, I'm going to put through a call to the sheriff.'

Paula said resignedly: 'Yes, I suppose so. I wish I knew where I could get in touch with Jim ... I'll put through the call.'

Mrs Kane said with determination: 'Call Sheriff Brandon. He knows who you are.'

'How does he know who I am?'

'I told him yesterday. I had him help me—looking for you—checking the hospitals, seeing if there had been a car accident and...'

'Checking the hospitals!' Paula interrupted. 'Why in the world didn't you come here?'

'For the simple reason,' Mrs Kane said quietly, 'that I had no idea where you were.'

'You mean—you didn't get my letter?'

'I haven't heard from you for more than two weeks.'

The two women stood for a moment, looking at each other, Mrs Kane quietly certain that between her and Paula there was going to be no more subterfuge.

Paula's face showed that her mind was suddenly orienting itself to some new situation, then quietly, casually and with that calm poise which at times lately Mrs Kane had found to be a barrier between herself and her daughter, Paula said: 'All right, Mother. Get into your clothes and I'll do the telephoning. Sheriff ... what did you say his name was?'

'Brandon. Rex Brandon, dear.'

'I'll telephone him. Thank you, Mother. Get

71

your clothes on and come down. You can use the other bathroom which opens off our bedroom. You'll find Jim's shaving things littering the place, but I guess you'll find room. I'll telephone.'

Doris Kane dressed, went to the big bathroom which opened off the master bedroom. She could hear Paula telephoning. Cleaning her teeth, she suddenly realised that she had been hearing Paula's voice over the telephone on several occasions during the past few minutes. Paula was doubtless trying to locate Jim.

CHAPTER SEVEN

Sheriff Brandon's siren cleared the way, Doug Selby bracing himself against the turn as the big county car swung around the corner from the courthouse.

Brandon said: 'Thought you'd like to go along, Doug. It seems to be a continuation of what we had yesterday.'

'What is it?' Selby asked.

Brandon didn't answer for several seconds, concentrating on piloting the car through the traffic of Madison City. Then he cleared the more congested district and relaxed somewhat.

'First,' he said, 'I received a call from a Mrs Melvin. I didn't place her for a minute, and then she said that she was Paula Melvin, and that I had talked with her mother yesterday.'

Selby nodded.

'Paula Melvin,' Brandon went on, 'seemed to be calm and collected. She said she'd had a friend staying with her, and the friend seemed to have been stabbed during the night. She thought I should come right out. The friend was dead.'

'Anything else?'

'That was about all. I told her not to let anyone in the place until I got over there, and to see to it that no one touched anything in the room where the body was.

'I called your apartment,' Brandon went on, 'and got no answer. I thought probably you were at the Palace Café. I rang there and they told me you'd had breakfast and had just left. I thought perhaps you were headed up to the court-house, so I told the courthouse operator to let me know as soon as you came in.

'I felt that a few minutes wouldn't make *too* much difference, so I sat there at the phone, waiting. I'd made up my mind I'd give you ten minutes. If you hadn't shown up within that time I'd have gone without you.

'While I was waiting, the phone rang again. This time it was Mrs Kane on the phone. That woman seems to be a pretty square shooter.'

'What did she want?' Selby asked.

'She said she thought I should know the woman who had met her death during the

73

night had been nervous and apprehensive; that she had been living in the house with Jim and Paula Melvin apparently while recovering from a bullet wound.'

'A bullet wound!' Selby exclaimed.

'That's right,' Brandon said grimly.

'Well, good for Mrs Kane!' Selby said. 'Did her daughter know she was telephoning?'

'Apparently her daughter was standing right there at the time,' Brandon said. 'I could hear her saying something to her mother. She sounded angry.'

'I can imagine,' Selby said, grinning. 'Well, Rex, I guess that was the pistol-shot the neighbours heard. The man who was found lying on the bed with the bloody towel twisted around his arm was apparently a stooge old A.B.C. had dragged in to account for the shooting.'

'I'd like to pin that on him,' Brandon said.

'Who wouldn't? But it's an odds-on bet he's covered his tracks so well we won't stand a chance. Of course, with this new development and the fact that Jim Melvin now finds himself in a spot, we may be able to give old A. B. Carr a few uncomfortable minutes. Bet the old fox is out covering his trail right now.'

'This is one time,' Brandon said, 'when I'd like to be triplets or quadruplets. I'd like to be in four or five places at the same time, and one of them is in the breakfast-room of Carr's house. But we've got to be mighty certain we

74

don't overlook any bets on this death. She was stabbed with a carving-knife.'

'You notified the coroner?' Selby asked.

'Yes, I got Harry Perkins personally. Told him to come on out. There's a local photographer in Las Alidas who's done pretty good work on some of our cases, and I've made arrangement with him to come in and take photographs as soon as we're ready ... There's a car bobbing along right behind us, Doug.'

Selby turned in the seat to look through the rear window. 'Seems to be a Press car, Rex. Looks like Sylvia Martin driving the *Clarion* car. Now how do you suppose *she* got tipped off?'

Brandon glanced somewhat sheepishly at Selby and grinned. 'I wonder,' he said.

The big county car ate up the miles between Madison City and Las Alidas. They entered the city and the sheriff swung the car in a screaming turn around a corner, turned down an old residential street shaded with huge pepper trees, and then brought his car to a stop.

'This is the place,' he said. 'Hello, there's Jim Melvin. I guess they managed to locate him all right.'

'Hello, Melvin,' Brandon said. 'What seems to be the trouble?'

Melvin said gravely: 'I was waiting for you folks. There's trouble, all right, but it only needs to be as big as you fellows want to make

75

it. And I suppose,' he added bitterly, 'that, under the circumstances, that'll be plenty big.'

'Don't yell before you're hurt,' Brandon said. 'What happened?'

'A woman committed suicide in my house last night. She stabbed herself. She'd been despondent for a long time.'

'No one stabbed her?'

'Of course not. There was no one here to stab her.'

'You were here, weren't you?'

Melvin's face darkened. 'I'd expected you'd raise all the stink you could, but don't think you're going to frame...'

'Keep your shirt on,' Brandon interrupted. 'You were here, weren't you?'

'Yes. Asleep. My wife was also here, and my mother-in-law.'

'Who was the woman who was killed?'

'A house guest. She wasn't killed. She committed suicide.'

'What was her name?'

'Eve Dawson.'

'How long she been with you?' Brandon asked.

'Around ten days.'

'Ever since you left Madison City?'

'Yes.'

'Friend of yours?'

'Why, yes, of course.'

'Known her long before she came to live with you?'

76

Melvin said: 'I think you'd better take a look at the room. We've left it just as...'

'Known her long before she came to live with you?' Brandon repeated insistently.

'Not very.'

'How long?'

'I—I couldn't tell you the exact time.'

'More than a day?'

Melvin said sulkily: 'Perhaps not.'

'All right,' Brandon said, 'try to cover up and it'll be worse for you. We'll take a look.'

They entered the house.

'Right this way,' Melvin said.

'Just a minute. Before we go up there,' Brandon said, 'tell us a little more about this woman. How did it happen she was staying with you?'

'She—she had an accident,' Melvin said.

'What sort of an accident?'

'I don't know the details. I assumed it was a car accident.'

'How did it happen?'

'I don't know.'

'Why don't you know?'

'I never asked her and she never told me.'

Brandon reached out and took hold of the lapels of Melvin's coat. He spun the big man around and pushed him against the wall. 'Now I'm going to tell you something, young fellow,' he said. 'There's a murder here. We're going to investigate it. We're going to make a real investigation of the whole background. If you've got anything to say, you'd better start saying it quick.'

Melvin said: 'I—well, to tell you the truth, the thing happened—well, I don't know how it happened. I was asked to take this woman...'

'Who asked you?'

'A friend of mine.'

'Who was it?'

'I'd rather not mention his name.'

'Well, you'd *better* mention his name.'

'It's a personal matter. It has nothing to do with this suicide.'

'How do you know it doesn't?'

'I'm certain it doesn't.'

'Who killed her?'

'I tell you she killed herself.'

'Suppose she didn't. Then who killed her?'

'I don't know.'

'Then how do you know this other business doesn't have anything to do with it?'

'I ... I don't think it does.'

'All right,' Brandon said, '*I'm* here to do the thinking. *You're* here to do the talking. Who asked you to take this woman?'

'A friend,' Melvin said.

'You keep talking like that and you'll be in the county jail before night,' Brandon said. 'Who told you to take this woman and keep her here?'

Melvin's eyes avoided those of the sheriff. He clamped his lips, merely shook his head.

'Suppose I make a guess at it. Was it a lawyer

by the name of Alfonse Baker Carr?'

Melvin was visibly shaken.

'Was it?'

'I've said all I'm going to say.'

Brandon impatiently pushed Melvin to one side. 'All right, my boy,' he said, 'you've had your chance. You muffed it. From now on you'll be dealing with us at arm's length. You don't get any of the breaks. You understand?'

'I didn't expect any,' Melvin said. 'Ever since I took the position I did on the recall matter I was told your office would be laying for me. I was warned to watch my step.'

'Bosh!' Brandon said explosively. 'You report a death by violence. I ask you routine questions about the corpse and you refuse to answer. I suppose that means I'm persecuting you.'

'This thing can entirely ruin my chances of putting across the deal I'm working on here in Las Alidas,' Melvin said.

The sheriff was sarcastic. 'Well, *isn't* that too bad!'

'And I suppose you'll revel in seeing that it does,' Melvin said bitterly.

Selby said quietly: 'As far as my office is concerned, Melvin, you'll be treated just like any other citizen. However, you'd better make up your mind to tell us more about how this woman came to live in your house if you don't want to find yourself answering questions in front of a grand jury. Now take us up to look at

79

the corpse.'

Half-way up the stairs, the county officials heard a frantic ringing at the door-bell. A moment later, as Paula Melvin opened the front door, Sylvia Martin's voice was audible as she said crisply: 'I have a very important message for the sheriff. Will you take me to him at once, please?'

'Just a minute,' Paula Melvin said. 'He's upstairs.'

They heard the quick patter of Sylvia's feet on the stair treads behind them.

Brandon turned to Doug Selby and grinned.

'Oh, hello,' Sylvia said.

'What's the important message?' the sheriff asked sternly.

She flashed him one of her smiles. 'The important message,' she said in a low voice, 'is that *The Clarion* wants the dope on this case.'

Brandon's manner held the paternal indulgence of a man who is personally fond of a protégée, coupled with the recognition of a county official for a newspaper which has given him ardent support through the carnage of mud-slinging political campaigns.

'Look, Sylvia, you can go as far as the door of the bedroom. You can stand there and look inside, but don't enter the room. Is that a promise?'

'It's a promise.'

They climbed the stairs to the front room. Brandon opened the door.

The wreckage of the breakfast which Paula Melvin had spilled was still strewn over the floor. The body lay just as it had been discovered, on the bed.

Selby heard Sylvia say with a quick gasping intake of breath: 'My, but she was beautiful!'

Selby made low-voiced comment to the sheriff. 'Notice that the windows are all tightly closed, Rex.'

'How's that?' Brandon asked.

Selby said: 'A person going to bed at night in a mild climate such as this, and particularly in the early autumn, will open at least one of the windows. The fact that the windows are *all* closed may be significant.'

'It was a fairly warm night last night, too,' Brandon said thoughtfully.

Melvin said: 'You'll notice there's no faintest sign of any struggle. She had slept in the bed, or tried to sleep. Then she became despondent, got up and killed herself and fell back over the bed.'

'Peculiar angle for the knife,' Brandon said.

'She could have done it easily that way, by using both hands.'

'Where did she get the knife?'

'I don't know. I haven't even looked at it closely. She could have got it from downstairs … she could have bought it. I don't know.'

'Have you looked downstairs to see if a knife was missing?'

'Not yet.'

Sylvia Martin said: 'Doug, may I come in the room for just a second, just to look at something?'

'Better not,' Brandon said.

'I think perhaps I can help you.'

'What do you want?'

'I want to look at the girl's face.'

'Come in so you can look at it,' Brandon said. 'Keep right in the middle of the room. Don't touch anything.'

Sylvia Martin tiptoed over to the corpse.

'Mean anything to you?' the sheriff asked. 'Do you know her?'

'It isn't that I recognise her,' Sylvia said, 'but if you'll notice, she has her make-up on.'

'Well?' Brandon asked.

'Don't you see?' Sylvia Martin said. 'A woman doesn't leave all of that stuff on when she goes to bed. She has lipstick, and it's unsmeared. She has rouge and powder. See, she wanted to look her best. That means either that she was meeting someone, probably a man, or that she—well, that she did it herself and—well, you know I've seen that happen before. Women who are committing suicide want to make themselves look as attractive as possible. It's a last gesture of vanity to the body they're about to destroy.'

'A messy way of suicide,' Selby said. 'Women usually go for poison. Men are more apt to shoot themselves. Notice anything else, Sylvia?'

'Just the make-up,' she said. 'Of course, if I looked around, I might...'

'Just stay right there for a minute,' Brandon said.

He bent forward and with gentle fingers parted the *négligé* the dead girl was wearing.

The scar made by the bullet showed plainly.

'She's been shot!' Sylvia exclaimed.

'Probably about ten days ago,' Brandon said. 'It's pretty well healed up now.'

Melvin said: 'That's the scar from a car accident.'

'It left a peculiarly round hole.'

'Something punctured her. It *could* happen that way.'

'A nice neat puncture. Just like a bullet,' Brandon said.

Melvin said nothing.

'She tell you how it happened?' Selby asked Melvin.

Melvin's 'No' was curtly succinct.

A car drew up outside.

Brandon said: 'That'll be Harry Perkins, the coroner, Sylvia. Better get back out in the corridor.'

Sylvia dutifully backed out to the corridor. Melvin went down to let the coroner in.

Brandon said: 'Now I'm not going to touch anything, Doug. I've got a deputy who is pretty good on finger-prints and photography. I'm going to get everything in here photographed before we touch the body or move a thing. Now let's all get out.'

CHAPTER EIGHT

Brandon and Selby engaged in low-voiced conversation at the foot of the stairs. Brandon said: 'You were right about what happened at that party. The man with the wounded arm was just a ringer.'

Selby said: 'You'll remember, Rex, that Mrs Kane said there was a letter from A. B. Carr in Melvin's mailbox.'

Brandon nodded. 'Sure. That was Carr's bill. Jim Melvin got in a jam over that shooting. We haven't got the true story about it yet. We may have some trouble getting it, but Melvin hired old A. B. Carr to get him out of a spot. Carr told him what to do and then sent him a bill. Melvin will send Carr a cheque and...'

'I'm just wondering,' Selby said, 'if perhaps it may not have been the other way round. I'm wondering if Carr didn't hire Melvin.'

'What do you mean, Doug?'

'The contents of that letter Carr sent Melvin might have been a cheque.'

Brandon raised his eyebrows. 'What gives you that idea, Doug?'

Selby said: 'Let's put two and two together, Rex. This Dawson girl must have been shot at that party Melvin gave some ten days ago. Carr

84

started an immediate cover-up. That included getting a place for the girl to stay and that in turn necessitated finding a house in Las Alidas where she could be kept.

'All of this took a lot of work and a lot of pull. It seems to me the person who could command all that must have drawn a lot of water. Jim Melvin doesn't seem to answer that description.

'Therefore, if he isn't the man for whom the services are being performed, he must be the one who is being paid in one way or another. And that's why he's so terribly afraid to answer questions.'

'Could be, all right,' Brandon said, 'but Carr will never let us know what was in that letter.'

Selby said: 'Suppose we make a quick round-up of the two banks here in Las Alidas. Jim Melvin may have gone to his house in Madison City yesterday and got that letter out of the mail-box. If it had a cheque in it he might have cashed it here. If he did, we might get some evidence that would help us unscramble this mess.'

'You're on,' Brandon said, suddenly excited. 'It's worth a try. And we've got to go up town and notify the police here. If we don't, and it should be murder, we'll be roasted by every paper in the county. I know we can count on Harry Perkins to keep everyone out of that room until the finger-printing is all done.'

'Let's go,' Selby said.

They left Harry Perkins in charge and drove to police headquarters.

Sam Freeland, the genial, heavy-set city marshal and ex-officio chief of police of Las Alidas, greeted them warmly. 'Come on in and sit down, boys,' he invited. 'What's new? Looks as though you're tearing around on official business.'

They settled themselves in chairs. Brandon explained the situation to Freeland, and the three of them went to the Farmers' & Merchants' Bank, where they drew a blank.

Then they went to the First National Bank. The president listened to their story and summoned the cashier.

'Why, that's right,' the cashier said. 'Mr Melvin came here yesterday and wanted to open an account. He deposited a cheque in an amount of one thousand five hundred dollars, We didn't credit his account, but took the cheque to put it through for collection. It was on a Los Angeles bank.'

'Has that cheque gone out?'

'Just a minute,' the cashier said. 'As a matter of fact, I think we're ... yes, it went out. It went to our correspondent bank. We can call up and get the data on the cheque.'

'Do that,' Brandon said.

The cashier put through a call to the bank in Los Angeles which acted as his correspondent. He explained what he wanted, held the phone for some two minutes, then said: 'Yes. Okay ...

86

All right. Now read it to me, will you, and I'll repeat it to the sheriff here. Yes, the sheriff is interested in it ... No, I don't know why. Just let me have the data.'

Doug Selby took out his pencil. The banker handed him a pad of paper. 'Go ahead,' Selby said.

'Go ahead,' the cashier repeated into the phone.

The cashier's voice droned out the information as he relayed the data given him by the Los Angeles banker.

'Cheque number seven six two three,' he intoned. 'Drawn on the Merchants' Seaboard National of Los Angeles. Dated October 25, 1947, in an amount of one thousand five hundred dollars, payable to James L. Melvin. Endorsed on the back, James L. Melvin and then a rubber stamp: "Pay to the order of any bank or banker, First National Bank of Las Alidas. October 27, 1947." Signature on the cheque, Alfonse Baker Carr ... Okay. Thanks. Just a minute.

'Anything else?' the cashier asked Brandon.

Brandon said: 'Tell the Los Angeles bank to call in a photographer and photograph that cheque immediately, and then put it through in the usual banking channels.'

CHAPTER NINE

Driving back to Madison City, Selby said: 'Well, Rex, we get a pattern. Eve Dawson was the victim of a shooting. Whoever shot her took her into Melvin's house and put her on that bed that Mrs Kane found all soaked with blood, then ran to old A.B.C. in a panic.

'A.B.C. did some fast thinking. Probably that's why he collects the fees he does. He's fast on his feet.

'He knew that the guests had heard a revolver-shot and that neighbours had heard it. That shot had to be accounted for. Carr telephoned the people who lived in that house in Las Alidas and told them to get out, that he intended to use their house for two or three weeks. Then Carr got a stooge who could account for the shot. You can see the dangerous power of a man who has enough on people to give orders like that and to get people out of predicaments like that, Rex.'

'Damn it,' Brandon said irritably, 'what can we do against brains and power of that type? He insinuates himself into a community, and the first thing you know has a strangle-hold on it. That's what makes Carr powerful, Doug. He's got the brains, and he's got the connections.

'When he first came here, he was a pariah, an

outsider. But now he's the power behind everything that goes on. Carr gets the big shots out of their difficulties, and he has plenty on them afterwards. Carr uses all those connections to build himself up and get more and more power.'

Selby indicated a cardboard box on the seat of the car. 'Well,' he said, 'we've got the knife that did the job. It still has the cost mark and selling price of the store that sold it written with a grease pencil on the blade—the letters of the cost price are T-E-M and the figures $7.65. We're going to have to trace that knife.'

'You can trust old A. B. Carr to have the answer to that one,' Brandon said bitterly. 'He'll have half a dozen witnesses who will swear they saw her buying a knife in a hardware store.'

'I know,' Selby said, 'but he'll have to get the right store.'

Brandon turned the county machine into the parking square at the court-house reserved for the sheriff's cars, from long habit backing the car into its stall so that in the event of an emergency call he could jump in the car and go tearing out.

They entered through the back door of the courthouse and were starting up the stairs to the Sheriff's Office when they heard the sound of quick, light steps, and Sylvia Martin, her finger on her lips in a sign for silence, came around the bend in the corridor and beckoned to them.

The two county officials detoured, to follow her down the corridor to where she had been waiting for them near the door of the Assessor's Office.

'What is it, Sylvia?'

She said: 'A man broke all speed laws getting here, and I think he's the doctor.'

'What doctor?' Brandon asked.

'The one who treated the girl there at Las Alidas.'

'Oh, oh,' Brandon said. 'Would that be a break!'

'Wait a minute,' Selby cautioned. 'I'm not so certain it is a break.'

'What do you mean?' Brandon said. 'If we can get ahold of that doctor we'll...'

'We aren't getting hold of him,' Selby said, 'he's getting hold of us. You know, Rex, it looks very much as though that's one of A. B. Carr's moves.'

Brandon shook his head. 'Carr would try his darndest to keep us from getting hold of that doctor.'

'Ordinarily, perhaps,' Selby said, 'but suppose the doctor tells you that the girl had suicidal complexes. Then what?'

The sheriff's face puckered into a portentous scowl.

'Get the sketch here,' Selby said. '*Our* hands are tied by law. Before we can convict anyone of murder, we have to prove that there was a murder. We have to prove every element of the case beyond all reasonable doubt. Old A. B. Carr is smart enough to know that. He's apt to start tinkering with the facts so we'll never be able to get past that first hurdle. If he can trip us on that, it won't do any good to go ahead and work up a case involving motivation and opportunity.'

Sylvia said: 'I have something else for you, Doug.'

'What?'

'I—well, in a way, I tried to steal a march on you, but it was all in the line of duty.'

'How come?'

'I wanted an interview with old A. B. Carr.'

'Who doesn't?' Brandon said grimly.

Sylvia said: 'He wasn't anywhere around Madison City. No one seemed to know where he was. I rang up his office in the city, putting through a station-to-station call. I asked his secretary, who answered the phone, where I could get in touch with Mr Carr, and, naturally enough, she wanted to know first rattle out of the box who was talking.'

'And you told her it was the Press?' Brandon asked, consternation in his voice.

Sylvia Martin shook her head. 'I lied like a trooper.'

'What did you say?' Selby asked.

'I said it was Paula Melvin on the phone.'

Brandon gave a low whistle.

'And the secretary said that Carr might not

91

be in for two or three days, that he was on a motor trip to the northern part of the state. And,' Sylvia went on, 'in my phony capacity as Mrs Jim Melvin, I threw a fit and said that I *had* to reach him right away, and where would be the first place he'd stop at where I could reach him? And the girl said he'd gone to Highdale. Does that mean anything to you?'

Selby and Brandon both looked blank.

'I see that it doesn't,' Sylvia said. 'But I'm willing to bet it means something to this case.'

'Anyhow,' Brandon said, 'we want to talk with Carr. Knowing where he is, is a help.'

'We don't want to talk with him yet,' Selby said.

Sylvia asked Sheriff Brandon: 'How about a photograph of the dead girl?'

'We're having some prepared, Sylvia. They'll be retouched to show her with her eyes open. I hope we can get a pretty good likeness. So far no one has been able to tell us where she comes from or who her relatives are. However, we're going to try a lot of angles.'

'When will you have the pictures?'

'My deputy's back here now, developing the photographs he took.'

'Okay, Sheriff, remember if that's the doctor who's waiting for you upstairs, I want a report.'

'Go you one better on that,' Brandon said. 'If that's the doctor, you be waiting for him when he comes out of the office. Tell him you

92

want an interview. See what he says. What gives you the idea he's the doctor?'

'The registration on the car he was driving shows he's a Los Angeles doctor. I'll bet ten to one it's the same doctor.'

'What's the name?'

'Dr Sparton Capaldo, and his office is in the Greenberry Building.'

Brandon grinned, and said: 'I wish the county would give me enough money to put you on the payroll, Sylvia. You'd make a great detective. Now, since you've been nice to us, I'll give you a tip.'

'Shoot.'

'The knife that did the job was a brand new knife. It had never been used. The blade still had the cost and selling price pencilled on it in grease pencil—T-E-M—$7.65 It's a carving-knife with a synthetic stag-horn handle. Now, suppose you get busy around the county and see if you can get a line on any hardware store that's selling such a knife and has a cost code that would call for the letters T-E-M on an article selling for approximately seven dollars and sixty-five cents.'

Sylvia's soft-leaded pencil flew over the folded newsprint she took from her purse as she made notes of the sheriff's conversation. 'I'll get to work on it right away, Sheriff.'

'We'll be working on it, too,' Brandon said. 'Let me know if you find out anything, and we'll do the same for you.'

93

'I'll phone in to the paper and start them working,' Sylvia said. 'Personally, I'm going to be right here waiting for Dr Capaldo when he's finished his interview.'

'You should find him pretty well softened up,' Brandon said with a grin. 'Come on, Doug, let's go take a look at him.'

They climbed the stairs to the Sheriff's Office.

The man waiting for them was a dark, suave individual, attired in a grey double-breasted suit, with clean-cut, intellectual features and a wealth of dark, wavy hair. He sized them up with keen grey eyes, then let his face light up in a cordial smile. 'Permit me to introduce myself,' he said in the effortless voice of a glib talker, 'that is, if I have the honour of addressing the sheriff and the district attorney of Madison County, and I assume that I do.'

'That's right,' Brandon said.

Selby moved forward, hand outstretched. 'Dr Capaldo, I presume,' he said, 'I'm Mr Selby and this is Sheriff Brandon.'

The doctor stiffened with startled surprise. 'You know my name?' he asked.

'Certainly,' Selby said, nudging Brandon's leg with his knee. 'We were just about to get out a subpœna for you.'

'For me? But you didn't know who I was! You didn't know...'

'Of course we know who you are, Doctor,' Selby said, 'You're the man who treated Eve

94

Dawson for the gun-shot wound. Do come in.'

Brandon held the door of his private office open. Dr Capaldo, looking completely ill at ease, entered the room. His suave, professional manner had for the moment completely deserted him.

Sheriff Brandon indicated a chair, and Dr Capaldo seated himself, crossed his knees, touched the tips of his fingers together in his best professional manner, and took a deep breath, apparently seeking to regain his composure.

'Why didn't you get in touch with me before this?' Brandon demanded.

Dr Capaldo's delicately arched eyebrows raised in an expression of well-bred astonishment. 'But, Sheriff, I literally burned up the roads as soon as I learned of what had happened to my patient.'

'Why didn't you get in touch with me before something happened to her?'

Dr Capaldo shook his head. 'I'm sorry, Sheriff, but my ideas of professional ethics won't permit of any debate on that point.'

Brandon said: 'Go ahead, you've got your story all planned out. Probably you've rehearsed it. Let's hear it.'

Dr Capaldo said: 'Early in the morning of Saturday, October eighteenth, I was called to come to Las Alidas, to treat Eve Dawson for a very serious injury she had sustained.'

'You went?'

'Yes.'

'How did you happen to go that far at that hour of the morning?'

'Because she was my patient.'

'In other words, she'd consulted you before?'

'Yes.'

'When?'

'I couldn't say—perhaps two or three weeks earlier.'

'What was wrong with her at that time?'

'She was suffering from despondency, with suicidal complexes.'

'Oh, oh,' Brandon said to Selby, 'here it comes.'

'I'm afraid I don't understand,' Dr Capaldo said, with exaggerated dignity.

'You understand, all right,' Brandon said. 'Go right ahead, let's have the rest of it.'

'Eve Dawson consulted me. She was nervous, apprehensive, and despondent. I gave her a tonic, suggested some vitamins and tried some psychological treatment.'

'Then what happened?'

'She came back the next week and her condition showed improvement. I particularly warned her against alcoholic excesses because of the feeling of despondency which so frequently occurs the day after drinking. I remember at that time I talked with her somewhat about changing her mode of life.'

'What was wrong with her mode of life?'

'She was,' Dr Capaldo said, separating the tips of his fingers and then touching them together at regular intervals, as though keeping time to the cadence of his words, 'what I believe might be called a party girl.'

'What do you mean by that?'

'She went out occasionally on missions of entertainment. That is, she was considered a good sport, a person who could liven up a party. Understand, gentlemen, I do not necessarily imply any immorality, I am talking merely about her environment—the fact that her hours were exceedingly irregular, her diet even more so, and her exposure to the temptation of alcoholic beverages a regular occurrence. I remember that I suggested to her she must be more regular in her hours and above all get a certain minimum amount of sleep every night.'

'And then what?'

'The next I knew, I received this telephone call.'

'Who placed the call?'

'I don't know. Someone said the call was being placed on behalf of Eve Dawson, that Eve Dawson had been in a very serious accident and wanted me at once.'

'And what did you do?'

'Naturally, when I considered the distance, I was loath to come. I asked a few questions and then found that the accident consisted of a self-inflicted gun-shot wound and that the girl

97

was in a serious condition.'

'So then you came?'

'That's right.'

'Where did you go?'

'To the house in Las Alidas.'

'Who gave you the address?'

'The person who telephoned.'

'Man or woman?'

'Woman.'

'Did she give you a name?'

'No, simply stated she was calling on behalf of Eve Dawson.'

'You went there, and what did you find?'

'I found Eve Dawson in bed. She had lost considerable blood. She had received a self-inflicted gun-shot wound.'

'Who told you it was self-inflicted?'

'She did.'

'What did you do?'

'I treated the wound.'

'Did you report at any time to the authorities?'

'I did not.'

'You knew it was a gun-shot wound?'

'That's what she told me and that's what the wound appeared to be.'

'Aren't you accustomed to reporting gun-shot wounds to the authorities?'

'I am not, under circumstances such as this.'

'What about the circumstances in this case? What made it so exceptional?'

'I knew something of the background of Eve

Dawson. She was despondent, she felt that she was unworthy of her mother's love; she felt that she had not made the most of her opportunities, that she was a failure in the world and, generally, she was building herself up quite an inferiority complex. Under the circumstances, I felt that any newspaper notoriety would have a very unfavourable result. I was asked to keep the confidences of my patient inviolate, and I kept those confidences. Any publicity, any notoriety would have been the same as signing the girl's death warrant.'

'Her condition was serious?'

'Very. There was every possibility of peritonitis.'

'And you continued to treat her?'

'I did.'

'Were you paid for that treatment?'

'No, sir.'

'Rather a long ways for a doctor to drive to treat a charity patient, isn't it?'

'I had taken a keen professional interest in the case. I decided to do everything in my power to bring it to a satisfactory conclusion.'

'Did she tell you anything about the circumstances incident to the shooting?'

'She told me all about it.'

'What about it?'

'On the evening of Friday, October seventeenth, she had gone to the residence of James Melvin in this city, on the occasion of a party there. She had had a few drinks and become despondent. She had gone out to the garage in order to be by herself and escape the unwelcome importunities of a guest who was slightly alcoholic. She climbed in James Melvin's car. There was a gun in the glove compartment. She took it out and on a sudden impulse decided to end it all.'

'Did she say who the alcoholic guest was?'

'No, she was always very, very discreet about mentioning names. During all of my treatment I was never able to get any information from her concerning names.'

'You know her address?'

'No, sir. I do not.'

'Look here,' Selby interrupted impatiently. 'You apparently came here just to give us a run-around.'

'I'm afraid I don't understand.'

'You want to be certain that all the information that would point to death by suicide is made available to us, and, I assume, will be made available to the Press. But when it comes to giving any information that will facilitate *our* investigation, you become exceedingly vague.'

'I am sorry, gentlemen, but that's the way it was. Miss Dawson was an office patient. She gave me a hotel address. I ascertained this morning by means of the telephone that that address was fictitious. I see nothing particularly unusual in this. Many patients

100

situated as she is take elaborate precautions to remain somewhat anonymous. They are particularly anxious to conceal their family connections.'

'Anything else?' Brandon asked.

'I think that about covers it, gentlemen.'

'Who sent you here?'

'Shall I say my professional conscience?'

'Your professional conscience!' Brandon repeated sarcastically.

'By any chance,' Selby said, 'are you acquainted with Jim Melvin?'

'No, sir.'

'Hudson L. Parlin?'

'No, sir.'

'But you are acquainted with A. B. Carr, the lawyer, aren't you?'

'Mr Carr? Oh yes. Yes, indeed!'

'Know him well?'

'I've met him several times, yes.'

'Is he *your* lawyer?'

'Why would I need a lawyer?'

'Haven't you ever needed one?'

The doctor was silent.

'You have needed one, haven't you?'

'I *have* had occasion to employ counsel in the past, yes.'

'And the lawyer you employed was A. B. Carr?'

'I fail to see what possible significance that has in the present case.'

'Didn't Eve Dawson tell you she was

consulting you at the suggestion of A. B. Carr?'

'I don't remember.'

'She may have told you that?'

'I have a faint recollection that she told me she was acquainted with some friend of mine, or some patient, or that someone had recommended me. Really, I can't say, gentlemen. I have so many patients and my time is so thoroughly taken up that I can't remember all of these little insignificant details.'

'How did you know Eve Dawson was dead?'

'I was advised over the telephone.'

'How did that happen?'

'I called to see how my patient was getting along.'

'You called the house in Las Alidas?'

'Yes.'

'Who answered the phone?'

'Mrs Melvin.'

'And what did she tell you?'

'She told me that Miss Dawson had stabbed herself fatally, that the county authorities had been notified.'

'So what did you do?'

'I tried my best to cooperate,' Dr Capaldo said in a tone of martyrdom. 'I thought that my information would be welcome. I postponed an operation at the hospital in order to drive here at once, in order to give you the background of the case.'

'You don't know where Eve Dawson lived,

you don't know who or where her folks are, and you don't know the names of any of her relatives.'

'I have an address that proved to be fictitious. I assumed that any attempt to elicit other information would have been similarly ineffectual. I believe she came from somewhere near Fresno.'

'When did you talk to A. B. Carr last?'

'I really can't say, gentlemen.'

'Recently?'

'I haven't seen him for some time.'

'How about the telephone?'

Dr Capaldo shook his head.

'Got a card giving your telephone number?' Selby asked.

Dr Capaldo took a card from his card-case, handed it to Selby, then extracted another and handed it to Sheriff Brandon.

'Any time,' he said, 'that I can be of any assistance, don't hesitate to call on me. I'm very, very sorry this happened. I was hoping that I could cure this young woman. You'd really be surprised, gentlemen, how many similar cases come to my office, young women who have arrived in Hollywood with high hopes of a picture career. Then comes the period of bitter disillusionment, then the times when it is necessary to make certain sacrifices of the ideals in order to cope with life's practical, economic problems—then a feeling of futility and failure, the desire to end life. It is tragic, particularly as one sees it in a medical office. The lure of the films, the love of glamour is ...'

'Like a flame,' Selby interrupted, 'against which the poor moths beat themselves into singed futility.'

'You've taken the words right out of my mouth,' Dr Capaldo said.

'I thought so,' Selby remarked dryly. 'All right, Doctor. Thank you very much for having volunteered your information. I'm sorry you didn't see fit to let us know at the time when you were called to this county to treat a patient suffering from a gun-shot wound.'

'At that time my professional ethics stood in the way.'

'Yes, I see,' Selby said. 'You may hear from us further on that factor, and may I suggest that, in the event this gets to be a habit, there are most unpleasant consequences in store for you?'

'What gets to be a habit?'

'Being called into this county by a Los Angeles lawyer to treat a patient suffering from a gun-shot wound and saying nothing about it!'

'Surely, gentlemen, you don't think this is a routine part of my practice?'

'I just don't want it to get to be a habit,' Selby said.

'In other words, tell A. B. Carr to get

104

another doctor,' Brandon growled. 'And you aren't, either one of you, out of the woods on this.'

'I certainly did not come here at the suggestion of A. B. Carr,' Dr Capaldo said. 'I have told you that the telephone call was received ...'

'Yeah, I know,' Brandon interrupted. 'That's the window-dressing. I'm just telling you, Don't let it happen again! That's all for now.'

Dr Capaldo strove to make his exit dignified, but it was a self-conscious bit of acting which deceived no one.

Brandon waited until the door had closed, then said to Selby: 'Well, that's just about the way you figured it, Doug.'

Selby nodded slowly, thoughtfully.

For some half-hour they sat, talking over the various phases of the matter. At length Brandon said: 'I hate to give up, but faced with that doctor's testimony, we're licked. Everything now points to suicide—and all that about Eve Dawson telling him the gun-shot wound was self-inflicted!'

Seyby was about to reply when the phone rang.

Brandon picked up the receiver, said: 'Hello ... Yes, Sylvia, he's right here. I'll put him on.'

He handed the phone to Selby. 'For you. Sylvia Martin calling.'

Sylvia's voice was excited. 'Doug. I want to

105

get a personal background on this dead woman. I think she came from Highdale. The postman remembers she gave him a letter to mail that was addressed to Highdale. I'm satisfied that old A. B. Carr is up there gumshoeing around for no particular good.'

'Elementary, my dear Watson,' Selby said, laughing. 'Did you interview Dr Capaldo?'

'Did I! He fairly spilled professional confidences into both my ears. He is very anxious to have it published that the girl had suicidal complexes.'

'So I gathered. Well, what about Highdale, Sylvia?'

'You remember Howard Comstock, the nephew of my publisher?'

'Yes. In aviation during the war, wasn't he?'

'That's right, and we have a four-place plane that was army surplus. The suggestion has been made that I fly up to Highdale and—well, Doug, *The Clarion* would like very much to take you along as its guest.'

'When do we leave?' Selby asked.

'As soon as you can get a good, clear picture of that dead girl.'

'Get your plane serviced,' Selby said, glancing at his wrist-watch. 'We'll be started in half an hour.'

CHAPTER TEN

It was late in the afternoon when Howard Comstock circled the big plane over a small country town.

'There you are,' he said. 'There's Highdale. We can't land here. The nearest landing-field that will take this baby is fifty miles away. We'll have to land and drive back. We've arranged for a Highdale taxi to meet us at the field. This will give you an idea of the city, such as it is.'

Selby studied the town. The plane was some three thousand feet up, and from that elevation it was easy to see the tumbled mass of mountains to the east, the river which had worn a canyon through these mountains, roared out in white turbulence and then spread into a placid stream, from which irrigation ditches carried water to the thirsty lands behind Highdale.

Farming lands, which appeared as green checkerboard squares, dotted the country around Highdale. The business district consisted of a scant six blocks strung out on one street. The roofs of residential houses peeped up at the plane from the shadows cast by huge shade trees. Everywhere were evidences that this town was no civic up-start, but a California town that had been rich in history even when those shade trees had been young. Selby remembered reading somewhere that Highdale had been one of the more important outfitting points for prospectors in the gold rush of '49, rugged pioneers who sallied forth into the high mountains in search of adventure and gold.

'That gives you an idea of the place,' Comstock said. 'Here we go.'

He straightened out the plane, and gunned the motor.

A few minutes later Selby saw the slight haze which surrounded a big city, caught a glimpse of buildings and a crowded business district with buildings of the rural 'skyscraper' class jutting up high above their more sedate neighbours. Then the plane was gliding down to an airport, and it had no sooner taxied up to a hangar than a man came running towards them.

'You the folks that telephoned for the car to take you to Highdale?' he asked.

'That's right,' Howard Comstock said. 'You take the girl and this man. I'm staying here with the plane to check things for the return flight and report to the authorities. Go ahead, Sylvia. I'll get all the red tape straightened out. But I don't want to fly back before tomorrow morning. I want to keep contact all the way. I'll be ready from seven o'clock in the morning on. Come back any time you want.'

'We may be delayed,' Sylvia said, smiling. 'We might want to have the Chamber of

Commerce delegate us as a special reception committee to meet old A.B.C. when he arrives.'

'How long will it take to get to Highdale?' Selby asked the cab-driver.

'About an hour and fifteen minutes.'

'There's a hotel there?'

'Oh, sure. A couple of hotels. Nothing fancy, you understand, but nice places.'

'Let's go,' Sylvia Martin said.

The airport was on the outskirts of the city and the driver was able to hit a state highway boulevard, and almost immediately pushed the speedometer up to fifty miles an hour.

'You live in Highdale?' Selby asked the driver.

'That's right. That's where this phone call came asking to have a car down to meet the aeroplane. You folks got business in Highdale?'

Selby winked at Sylvia Martin. 'Yes. Do you know where a Mrs Dawson lives in Highdale?'

'Dawson?'

'That's right.'

He shook his head slowly, 'I don't know any Dawson. Can you describe her?'

'Probably around forty-five to fifty-five,' Selby said. 'I don't know any more than that.'

'Lived in Highdale long?'

'Several years I would say.'

'Don't know her.'

Selby took from his brief-case the picture of Eve Dawson.

'Wouldn't happen to know this young woman, would you?'

The driver slowed the car, pulled to one side of the road. 'Let's take a look.'

Selby passed him the photograph.

The cab-driver studied it, shook his head, started to hand back the picture, then suddenly pulled it back to look at it again. 'Say, she's got her hair done different and there's something funny about her eyes, but she looks a lot like a girl from here who went to Hollywood. Eve Hollenberg, her name was ... Say, wait a minute, I heard she was using the name of Eve Dawson. Does this tie in with what you want?'

'You bet it does,' Selby said. 'That young woman was killed last night.'

'The devil! A car accident?'

'No, a murder.'

The driver brought his car to a full stop. 'Can you beat that!'

Selby kept quiet, and after a moment the man started his motor-car. 'You want to see Mrs Hollenberg?' he asked.

'That's right. If you know where we can locate her.'

'Murdered!' the man said. 'That's what I call a darn, dirty shame! Eve was a mighty fine girl, and her mother is the salt of the earth.'

'You know them?'

'Sure, I know them. I drove Eve down to the depot when she took the train. She didn't say so, but I knew what she had in mind. She was

110

headed for Hollywood. Always expected to see her in the pictures. To tell you the truth, after she left I started reading the motion picture columns in the paper. You know, the ones where they mention new actresses.'

Selby nodded gravely.

The driver slowed the car some five miles an hour, half-hitched around in the seat so he'd be able to talk to better advantage. 'Now that girl,' he said, 'had something. She certainly had looks. She was a regular queen. I never will forget how pretty she was when I put her on the train.'

'How long ago?'

'About two years ago. She had a blue dress and jacket effect, something that she hadn't worn around Highdale. Harriet Hollenberg— that's her mother—drove down to see her off. She pretended to Eve she was going to ride back with me, but just as soon as the train pulled out she told me she was walking back. Saving money, you see. Well, I just told her nothing doing. I told her she was going to ride back in style, and it wasn't going to cost her a cent. Poor woman, she was so proud you could see it in her eyes. And then she was lonesome, too, but she didn't cry. She just kept her head up all the way home. She knew Eve was going to make good.'

'She never did get in pictures, did she?' Sylvia asked.

'She didn't have time,' the driver said

loyally. 'You can't bust into those things in a day. I guess there's lots of pretty girls in Hollywood, and it takes a little time. What happened? How did she get killed?'

'I couldn't tell you all the details,' Sylvia said, 'but she was stabbed. I guess they have no idea who did it.'

'Well, whoever did it ought to be—hanging's too good for him!' the driver said with emphasis. 'Eve was one of the sweetest little girls that ever came out of this town.'

There was silence for a moment; then the driver said:

'You want to go right to Harriet Hollenberg's house?'

'That's right.'

'Now, let's see,' the driver said, 'what line of work are you in? What...'

'We're investigators,' Sylvia said.

'You mean the police?'

'Not exactly.'

The driver said meaningly: 'I guess we're *all* sort of investigators—of one kind and another.'

The silence from the back of his car advised him he was going to get no farther with his passengers. Reluctantly he swung back in the seat so that he faced the road, and pushed down the accelerator.

Sylvia said in a low voice to Selby: 'I think ideas are going to germinate in that mind of his, Doug.'

112

The driver, apparently considering his passengers 'unneighbourly', indicated the extent of his indignation by pushing the car into even greater speed, as though anxious to get the business in hand over with as soon as possible.

By the time he arrived in Highdale, however, he had once more thawed out.

'Now this here is probably the best hotel,' he said. 'There's another one a block down the street that's just about as good, but if I was you folks and was going to stay overnight, I think I'd come here to the Riverview Hotel.'

'Thanks,' Selby said.

'Now I'll take you right around to Mrs Hollenberg's place. It's a pretty good little house. She managed to hang on to it after her husband died. He left her a little insurance, and she does some sewing and occasionally a little housework, but she ain't too strong. However, she gets by all right.

'This here's the business district. We're due for some new construction when costs come down a little bit. The plans are all fixed for a building over there on that corner. Store-rooms downstairs, offices upstairs. May even have an elevator in it. But things are too high right now.

'That drug-store over there is where Eve used to work. Ran the soda-fountain for a while after she got out of high school. A darn nice kid—I always liked to go in and have her

113

fix me an ice-cream soda—used to put just a little more chocolate in it than the rules called for, too. She was always nice that way. Now we turn to the left here, and—you want me to wait while you're talking to Mrs Hollenberg?'

'You might as well,' Sylvia said. 'We'll let you drive us to the hotel.'

'Now here's the house, right down here in this next block on the left-hand side, the one between the big trees there. I remember when Jim Hollenberg built that place.'

The driver swung the car in a circle and said: 'If you want, I'll go in and tell Mrs Hollenberg that you're here. She...'

'No, thank you,' Selby said firmly. 'We prefer just to walk in on her.'

The driver said: 'Guess I'll sit on the front porch while I'm waiting. It's a little more comfortable and...'

'On second thought,' Sylvia Martin said firmly, 'we have decided that it wouldn't be worth while for you to wait. We may be here some little time. We'll walk to the hotel from here.'

The driver regarded them with the hurt eyes of a wounded deer.

'I'll pay you now,' Sylvia said, 'if you'll tell me how much it is. You can leave our bags at the hotel.'

'Well, I had a round trip and...'

'I know you did. How much is it?'

'It makes right around a hundred miles. I'll

114

have to charge you fifteen dollars. There was a little waiting time and...'

Sylvia Martin handed him a ten, a five and two ones. 'The extra dollars,' she said, 'are for cigars.'

The driver pocketed the money, said somewhat wistfully: 'I'm not so very busy now, and if you folks wanted me to wait...'

'No. It may be some time,' Selby said flatly.

'Well now, she just might not be at home,' the driver said. 'I'll just stick around to see if you get in all right. And if you'd like to have me...'

Selby held the gate open for Sylvia Martin. They walked together up the shaded walk to the spacious front porch of the house. Selby rang the bell.

The driver shut off his motor, rolled down the window on the right-hand side so he could hear everything that was said.

Selby winked at Sylvia Martin, took a card from his note-case, and when a woman in the late forties opened the door, Selby merely handed her his card. 'May we talk with you for a few moments, Mrs Hollenberg?'

She studied the card for a moment, then said: 'Why, certainly. Of course. You're from Madison City. Come right in. Come right in.'

'And this,' Selby said, 'is Miss Martin.'

'Come right in,' Mrs Hollenberg invited cordially.

She looked out at the car, said: 'Who

brought you here? Why, it's Gib Spencer. How are you, Gib?'

The driver jumped out of the car, came hurrying up the walk. 'Harriet,' he said, 'I want to tell you how sorry I was to hear about—about Eve.'

'I know,' she said simply. The two shook hands.

Gib Spencer stood awkwardly for a moment, glancing at his passengers. Then he said somewhat lamely: 'They want to see you about her,' and then walked back to his car, got in and drove off.

'Now you just come right in here and sit down,' Mrs Hollenberg said. 'I'd like to know all the particulars I can about Eve. She was the only child I had. The only thing I had left. But you can't help things, I guess. I wired the coroner to send the body up here. I think Eve would like it better if she came home to rest.'

She led the way into a somewhat stiffly conventional parlour, which evidently was kept only for state occasions. Her eyes showed that she had been crying, but she kept herself quietly under control.

'I don't want my grief to stand in the way of doing whatever has to be done,' she said.

Selby said: 'I hadn't expected you'd have heard about it as yet, Mrs Hollenberg. When I left Madison City the sheriff was trying to locate the girl's relatives.'

'I know,' she said. 'He called the sheriff's

116

office here to try and locate an Eve Dawson. The deputy here in town knew Eve. That Dawson name was one she took for pictures. It sounded better than Hollenberg. The deputy told them all about her and your sheriff said to notify me. And he said to tell me you were on your way up here.'

Selby said uncomfortably: 'We don't like to intrude on you at this difficult time.'

'I know you don't, but what's happened has happened. We can't change that. Having someone to talk to is going to help me, and I'd like to know the details.'

'We haven't many details,' Selby said. 'You heard from your daughter frequently?'

'She let me hear from her regularly. She was awfully nice that way, always thinking of me.

'I wish you folks could understand that I'm so proud of my daughter. It makes it a lot easier for me to face this thing. Eve was a mighty fine girl. She kept writing to me all the time she was away. She came home a couple of times to visit, and she always sent me money. Sometimes it wasn't much money, and I had an idea she needed it more than I did, but she kept sending me money.

'And then along towards the last, when she began to really make a success, I'm telling you the money amounted to something! She sent me over three hundred dollars in one month.'

Selby started to look at Sylvia Martin, then suddenly averted his eyes.

117

Sylvia Martin said: 'I don't want any misunderstanding, Mrs Hollenberg. I'm a newspaper woman. I'm representing the *Madison City Clarion*. Whatever facts I get, I want to publish. Mr Selby is the district attorney. He's investigating the death. If there's anything you want to tell him in confidence, anything you don't want to have published—well, I don't want to take any advantage of you or of the situation.'

'That's mighty nice of you,' Mrs Hollenberg said. 'No. There isn't a thing that I wouldn't just as soon have right in the papers. Land's sakes, I guess the papers here will be full of it. I didn't get much information from the sheriff down in Madison City over the telephone, but I understood he thought it might have been a burglar that killed her.'

Sylvia said: 'I think your daughter must have had an enemy, Mrs Hollenberg.'

'Well, I don't know how anyone could have been an enemy of Eve's. She just made friends right and left.'

'Someone had shot her about ten days ago,' Selby said. 'Did she mention anything in her letters?'

'Shot her!' Mrs Hollenberg exclaimed incredulously.

'Yes,' Selby said, and then hastened to add: 'Of course, it *could* have been accidental. We don't know anything about the circumstances yet.'

118

'She was in a motor-car accident and was hurt just a little bit,' Mrs Hollenberg said. 'She wrote me that she'd gone to a private hospital, but it was nothing serious. It was a car accident. Perhaps someone got mixed up about it and told you it was a...'

'That's entirely possible,' Selby conceded, 'only it looked very much like a bullet wound, and the doctors think that's what it was. Did your daughter ever intimate she might be considering suicide?'

'Suicide! Heavens, no! Don't ever think Eve killed herself. She was happy and she was just getting successful, just beginning to make the grade in Hollywood.'

'Did she ever write you exactly what she was doing?' Selby asked.

'No, not exactly. It was something in connection with pictures. I don't know what it was. She wrote me that I wouldn't be seeing her on the screen for some time, but that she was beginning to get in with picture work, that what she was doing was technical. But I think she was really getting ready to go places when ... when this happened.'

Selby nodded.

'Eve,' Mrs Hollenberg went on, 'was a *good* girl.'

Again Selby nodded.

'She always thought of her mother, always kept in touch with me. Lots of girls go to the city, and the city swallows them up. Then they get to feeling sort of superior and citified, and, first thing a body knows, they're half-way ashamed of their parents.'

'I suppose you've kept her letters?' Selby asked.

She shook her head. 'No, Mr Selby, I didn't.'

'None of them?'

'No. I'm not a hand to keep things like that.—Of course, I wish now that I had, but I've never kept any personal letters that way. I get them and hold them until I answer them, and as soon as I answer them, I burn them up.'

'When she sent you money, how did she send it—by money order or cheque?'

'Money order.'

'How about pictures? Did she ever send you photographs?'

'One, yes.'

'Did you burn that up?'

'No, I sent it back to her.'

'When?'

'Just a few days ago. She wrote and told me about this car accident and asked me to send the picture back to her at her Los Angeles address—the Freemantle Apartments on Adams Street.'

'You sent it?'

'Yes.'

'Did she say why she wanted it?'

'Yes. One of the men in the party wanted to have it copied. It was a picture taken aboard a private yacht. It showed Eve and another girl and four or five men, prominent motion picture people, I guess. Imagine Eve being out on yachting parties right along with real celebrities!'

'Did you recognise any of them?'

'Land's sakes, no! Eve tells me the big actors on the screen are just a small part of Hollywood. It takes adapters, producers, readers, and all sorts of high-priced executives to keep the thing going.'

'Yes, I guess it does. So you have no letters, no photographs?'

'Just some portraits Eve had taken last Christmas. I can let you have one of them.'

She got up from her chair, went to the desk, returned with an inscribed picture so heavily retouched, so theatrical in pose, that the subject looked like a movie star.

Selby studied it, then returned it. 'You keep this,' he said. 'It won't help us. We won't intrude any further right now, Mrs Hollenberg. We may be back later.'

They got to their feet. Mrs Hollenberg went to the door with them, stood watching them anxiously until they reached the tree-shaded pavement. Then she gently closed the door.

Sylvia Martin turned to Selby. 'Does that picture mean anything, the one on the yachting trip, Doug?'

'It means something,' Selby said, 'but I don't know what. Her daughter wanted it back. That means she was told to get it back.'

Sylvia said: 'Well, let's start looking over the list of men who were at Melvin's party and find who has a yacht ... Well, well, look who's here!'

A car pulled into the side of the street. Gib Spencer said: 'Hop in, folks. Just happened to be driving around. I'll be glad to take you to your hotel. Well, did you get what you want?'

'So far we're doing fine,' Selby said.

'Anything you want to know around here, just ask me,' Spencer said. 'I keep pretty well posted driving a car around the way I do. And lots of times people who are riding with me talk to me about things, not that I want you to think that I'm any hand to gossip, because I ain't.'

'I can see that,' Selby said, holding the door of the car open for Sylvia.

'I took your bags to the hotel and reserved a couple of rooms for you,' Gib Spencer went on. 'I told them you were pretty important people investigating that Dawson murder, to get you the two best rooms in the house.'

'There's nothing like having a local man as a public relations director, when you're trying to make a quiet investigation,' Selby said.

'Well, that's the way I figured it. I sort of know the ropes, and you folks are nice people. Anything I can do for you, well, I'll be glad to do. What did you find out from Mrs Hollenberg? Anything?'

'Just confirmed what you had already told us,' Selby said.

122

'That's fine. Glad you had a talk with Harriet. Now there's a mighty nice woman, a mighty nice woman.'

Selby leaned forward. 'Gib,' he asked, 'what're your rates by the day?'

'Steady driving?'

'No, you probably wouldn't have to drive over eight or ten miles all day.'

'Make you a flat two dollars an hour,' Gib said.

'You're hired,' Selby told him.

'Doing what?'

'You're going to help us.'

Spencer slowed the car in front of the hotel. 'Now you're talking!' he said. 'I reckon there ain't a thing goes on in this town that I either don't know about or can't get some way of finding out about. Not that I'm nosey, you understand, but I just get around.'

Selby said: 'A man will call on Mrs Hollenberg some time either late tonight or perhaps early tomorrow morning. He's a tall, grave, rather distinguished-looking man, past middle age with grey hair. He carries a walking-stick and gloves, and is very, very impressive in appearance. He has a deep, resonant voice. His name is Carr.'

'Okay. What do I do?'

'You park your car in front of the Hollenberg residence,' Selby said. 'You keep it there. Whenever Carr comes to call on Mrs Hollenberg, you notice the time he arrives, you notice how long he stays, and then you follow him until after he leaves town. As soon as he leaves town, that's all. Then you make a report.'

Spencer said gleefully: 'Buddy, I'm on my way.'

'And this mission, of course, is highly confidential.'

'You leave it to me,' Gib boasted. 'I sure know how to keep my mouth shut. When it comes to information, I can sure be a one-way street. You ain't made no mistake in getting me. No sir-ree!'

'That,' Selby said, 'is fine.'

'What did you say your name was?' Spencer asked.

'Selby, but be very careful not to mention my name, and I don't want anyone to know you're keeping an eye on the Hollenberg house. You understand?'

'Sure. I got it. I gotcha the first time,' Spencer said, grinning. 'What time you got now?'

'It is now exactly twelve minutes of five,' Selby said.

'I'll give you the twelve minutes,' Spencer said. 'I'll throw that right in. I'm on the job right now. Call it five o'clock. Now I'll have to lay off a few minutes around six o'clock to get a little something to eat, just go get a bite and ...'

'That's right,' Selby assured him gravely, 'but make it as brief as you can, and get back

124

on the job as soon as possible.'

'Don't worry,' Spencer told him, 'I'll be there.'

CHAPTER ELEVEN

At eight o'clock in the morning, Selby, waiting in the lobby of the Riverview Hotel, finished reading the account of the murder in the local daily.

Eve Dawson, he learned from the account, was one of the most beautiful and respected of the local girls who had gone to the city and made good. She was about to startle her friends with an appearance in a star role in a Hollywood production, but her untimely death, which authorities felt certain was due to an attack by a prowling burglar, had cut short the promising career.

The newspapers went on to decry the sensationalism of the Press in the southern part of the state, which had sought to interpret a scar resulting from injuries, which had been received some ten days earlier in a motorcar accident, as having been made by a bullet wound. The local paper announced with dignity that it had 'indisputable proof' that the injury in question was received in a minor motor-car accident.

Selby cut the account of the murder from the

paper, went over to the desk. 'Would you mind ringing Miss Martin's room?' he asked.

The clerk obligingly made the connection, nodded towards a telephone on the desk.

Selby heard Sylvia Martin's voice over the wire.

'How are you coming?' he asked.

'Doug, I overslept. I wanted to be up early. Have I missed anything?'

'Not so far. How soon will you be ready for breakfast?'

'Just two minutes. I only have to put on my face.'

'That's fine,' Selby told her. 'We'll eat here in the hotel.'

Selby hung up the telephone. The clerk broke the switchboard connection and said to Mr Selby: 'What are you finding out, Mr Selby?'

'Oh, so, so,' Selby said.

'A mighty nice girl! It's certainly too bad it happened.'

Selby nodded.

'I understand, on good authority, that she was to play opposite one of the real big actors.'

'Is that so?'

The clerk nodded. 'I had it given to me in confidence,' he said. 'I guess it's quite a blow to Mrs Hollenberg.'

'It must be.'

'Well,' the clerk said, 'I hope you get what you're looking for, Mr Selby. You couldn't get a better man than the one you have to help you.'

Selby raised his eyebrows.

'Gib Spencer,' the clerk said. 'He's full of energy and right on the job. You don't need to worry about passing up any bets locally. Gib will see you don't miss a thing.'

'I'm satisfied he will,' Selby said gravely.

Sylvia Martin came running down the stairs to the lobby.

Selby escorted her into the little dining-room. There a waitress studied them with that covert curiosity which is reserved in a small town for celebrities, detectives, actresses, and glamorous fallen women.

Sylvia asked: 'Think we can leave here by noon, Doug?'

'I hope so. Old A. B. Carr certainly should show up before then. I want to see what he does when he goes to Mrs Hollenberg's and finds that we've been up there ahead of him.'

'Think he'll show his hand?'

'It's hard to tell. He'll probably hunt us up. He ... oh, oh,' Selby said. 'Don't look now, Sylvia, he's just come in. He's going up to the desk.'

'Alone?' she asked.

'Apparently alone. What a surprise he's going to get when he finds the whole town buzzing with news of a murder. He doubtless wants to implant the suicide idea.'

'Doug, I wonder if Carr will say something

127

to the mother, something that will disillusion her and...'

'I don't think so,' Selby said. 'He's pretty cautious. I have an idea old A.B.C. will go call on Mrs Hollenberg. He'll only talk with her a few minutes before he'll find out that we were there yesterday, that she hasn't saved Eve's letters, and had returned the one photograph she had.

'Then old A.B.C. will do either one of two things. He'll either wipe his trip off the books as being a total loss, get in his car and go back; or he'll look us up and try to pump us. If the latter, we'll know that the evidence we have is mighty important—either to old A.B.C. or one of his very influential clients.

'Old A.B.C. wouldn't be making a trip up here just for the scenery. When he does anything in a hurry you can gamble he does it for money, and big money.'

'You think someone who is wealthy is mixed up in this, Doug?'

'Either someone who is wealthy, or else old A. B. Carr is mixed up in it, personally. He's going out now. Looks as though he stopped in here to make inquiries about reservations. Finish your breakfast, Sylvia, and we'll drift out and see if we can pump the clerk.'

'Don't put it that way,' Sylvia said, 'or I'll choke my breakfast down. Couldn't you go out and ask the clerk some casual question and...'

Selby pushed back his chair. 'Okay, Sylvia,'

he said. 'Excuse me for a moment. I guess I'm just as curious as you are.'

Selby approached the clerk. 'What time do we have to let you know about giving up the rooms?'

'Oh, any time during the afternoon. Any time up to five o'clock. We try to be accommodating here. Another man was just in here, Mr Selby, working on the same thing you're working on.'

'Indeed?' Selby said.

'Yes. A chap who's representing one of the newspapers. Wanted to know how to get out to Mrs Hollenberg's house.'

'You told him?'

'Yes.'

'Well,' Selby said very casually, 'I suppose there'll be a lot of people around. Something like this appeals to readers. An element of mystery, a beautiful young woman, a crime of violence. Newspapers have to give their readers what the readers want.'

'I suppose so. Yes. Seems a shame to have all this hit poor Mrs Hollenberg right at a time when she's suffering as much grief as she is. She was all wrapped up in Eve. Really proud of her.'

'The reporter didn't say what paper he was with, did he?' Selby asked.

'No. Just said he was with one of the metropolitan dailies. I didn't think of asking which one. I told him I wished they'd get their

129

facts straight, that it was all foolishness to say Eve Dawson had been wounded by a bullet. She'd been in a motor-car accident. I know that for a fact. You can read it in the local paper. It's right there in print.'

'I noticed the article,' Selby said. 'Well, thanks a lot. I'll get back to my breakfast. I just wanted to be sure what time we had to give up the rooms. I'm trying to make my plans accordingly. Thank you.'

Selby went back to join Sylvia Martin. 'Okay, Sylvia. You can take it easy. He's a newspaper reporter, representing one of the metropolitan dailies, and he wants to go out and interview Mrs Hollenberg.'

'The old buzzard!' Sylvia said. 'Remember, Doug, I want to interview him for *The Clarion*, but we'll give him lots of rope first.'

Selby stirred his coffee. His eyes were fixed thoughtfully on the slowly rotating spoon. 'Hang it, Sylvia! There's something strange about this. I can't imagine old A.B.C. waiting this long if he's after something like that picture, or Eve's letters.'

'He's afraid of aeroplanes,' Sylvia said. 'I know that for a fact. He won't get in one of them. And this was a job he had to do personally.'

'Yes, so I understand,' Selby said.

He looked at his watch. 'We'll wait here just in case old A.B.C. should show up and want to talk. I feel certain he'll come to the hotel before

130

he leaves and try pumping the clerk about us.'

They finished breakfast and sat waiting in the lobby.

Twenty minutes stretched into half an hour. Then a car pulled up hurriedly in front of the hotel and Gib Spencer jumped out and came striding into the hotel, his face positively beaming.

He flashed the clerk a glance, then crossed over to Selby and Sylvia Martin.

'Let's come over here,' he said in a whisper, 'over in the corner where we can talk. The clerk's watching us.'

One of his hands rested on Selby's elbow, the other on Sylvia's arm. He guided them over to the far corner of the hotel, ostentatiously seeking extreme privacy. Then he lowered his voice to a hoarse half-whisper. 'He's gone,' he said.

'Gone!' Sylvia exclaimed in dismay. 'Oh, but he *couldn't!* I want an interview.'

'He's gone,' Gib declared positively.

'Something must have frightened him,' Selby said.

'Nope. He acted just like a man who accomplished what he wanted to do.'

'There goes my interview,' Sylvia said. 'Oh, Doug, they'll pan me for that when I get back.'

'Perhaps we can get something better than an interview,' Selby said. He turned to Gib Spencer.

'You spotted him all right?'

'Sure I spotted him all right. Just like your description. He went to the house and rang the bell. Harriet Hollenberg answered the bell, and he raised his hat just as courtly as could be.'

'He alone in the car?' Selby asked.

'No. There was a young woman with him. Redhead, twenty-one or two, lots of class. She got out and went in with Carr. They stayed about ten or fifteen minutes, and then they came out.'

'Jumped in his car and left town?' Selby asked.

'No, he didn't. He got in his car and drove up to the main street. He parked the car and then he and the young woman got out and they went directly into Tom Kittson's hardware store. They were in there about five minutes, and when he came out he was carrying a package. Then he got in his car and they started right straight out of town, driving fast, making a bee-line for the state highway South. I followed them about a mile just to make sure they were on their way, and then came back to report, just like you told me.'

'Kittson's Hardware Store,' Selby said, puzzled.

'That's right.'

'And he bought something there?'

'Yes. He came out carrying a package.'

'What did the package look like?'

'Long, thin, wrapped in hardware brown paper. Shucks, Mr Selby, we can go right

132

across to Kittson's place and find out. Old Tom Kittson will tell us anything we want to know.'

'You've known him long?' Selby asked.

'I've known him just about all my life. Tom Kittson's a fixture here.'

'Let's go talk with him,' Selby said.

Followed by the eyes of the curious clerk, the trio left the hotel, crossed the street and walked down a shaded pavement until they came to a hardware store, the sign over the door proclaiming: 'TOM KITTSON. HARDWARE — SPORTING GOODS — REFRIGERATORS — RADIOS.'

Gib Spencer held the door open for them, ushered them into the store with something of a flourish.

A man was bent over a ledger, so that at first they saw only a head of white hair. Then, as the sound of their steps on the board floor attracted his attention, he looked up, a man well past sixty with a wiry frame, and keen grey eyes that peered out from behind steel-rimmed spectacles. He first sized up Sylvia Martin and Selby, and then turned to Gib Spencer.

His face softened into a smile. 'How're you, Gib?'

Spencer led the others up to the counter. 'We're working on something, Tom,' he said. 'Can't tell you what it is, but I guess if you read the papers maybe you have an idea. This is something pretty big. These people are from

133

down South. Now we want a little information. There was a man in here with a redheaded girl about ten or fifteen minutes ago. He bought something. He...'

'The name,' Kittson said, speaking with a high-pitched, sing-song voice, as though he had been reciting something he had learned by heart and was painfully conscious to get his articulation distinct and the words accurate, even at the expense of all expression, 'is Alfonse Baker Carr. He wanted a carving-knife of a certain description. Had to be just a certain make and style of knife.'

'You remember what you sold him?' Selby asked.

'Certainly I remember what I sold him. Nothing wrong with *my* memory, young man. This was only ten minutes ago. I'm certainly not going to forget things *that* soon.'

'How did you know his name?' Selby asked.

'Told me his name. Told me he wanted a sales slip made out showing the purchase and that he'd made it here.'

Selby was plainly puzzled. 'Do you,' he asked, 'have a duplicate of the knife the man purchased?'

'Nope, I sold him the very last one I had in stock.'

'A carving-knife?'

'That's right. Imitation stag-horn handle, stainless steel blade. Sells for seven dollars and sixty-five cents. It's been a good number. I could have sold half a gross of 'em if I'd had 'em. This man, Carr, wanted to take over my entire stock. He was disappointed when he found I only had one left.'

Selby, conscious of Sylvia Martin's fingers digging in his arm, tried to keep excitement out of his voice. 'I'm not trying to pry into your business, but were the cost figures on that knife—'

'Now, just a minute, young man. I'm not going to tell people about my cost prices. I have a living to make, same as anyone else.'

'Not the amount,' Selby protested, 'just what appeared on the knife. Did the letters that represented your costs read T-E-M?'

'Well, now,' Kittson said, 'you seem to know something about these knives. You aren't selling 'em, are you? I'll give you an order for...'

'No. I'm trying to find out something about them. I'd like to know about your method of keeping track of costs.'

'What about it? Something I've worked out myself,' Kittson said. 'I've had it for just about fifty years. Letters represent my cost, and figures represent my selling price. Now, I don't want to go blabbing around about my costs openly. If you're investigating this Hollenberg case, and want to know something about costs, why, that's all right. I'll tell *you*; but I'm not going to tell Gib. Gib's all right, but his tongue is hinged in the middle and clacks at both ends.

He can't keep anything to himself any longer than a kid can keep a candy bar.'

'Now, Tom, you ain't got no right to say anything like that,' Gib protested. 'I'm just like a clam when things are important. Only unimportant things...'

'You just go on out and sit in your motor-car,' Kittson said, 'and I'll tell this man about my cost code.'

'Now that ain't fair,' Gib said. 'I ain't the least bit interested in your costs. I don't care a thing in the world about them. Lord knows your selling prices are high enough.'

'You just go on out in your car,' Kittson said. 'If you ain't interested in my costs, you won't be missing anything.'

'Well, I just ought to stay here to see if there's anything I can help Mr Selby on.'

'He don't need an interpreter,' Kittson said. 'He can speak English good enough so I can understand him.'

Selby said: 'I think this is very important, Gib. I have the greatest confidence in your discretion myself, but, after all, Mr Kittson can take such reasonable safeguards as he desires to keep his cost system from becoming public.'

'Becoming public!' Gib protested. 'That's the thing that makes me mad, thinking I'd tell anybody. Why, I'm just a one-way street when it comes to information like that.'

'You're a one-way street, all right,' Kittson said in his precise sing-song voice, 'but you get too danged much travel to suit me. You go on out and sit in your car.'

Spencer, still protesting, reluctantly withdrew.

'Now, then,' Kittson said, 'there ain't anything particularly complicated about a cost system. You just have it so you can take a look at things and know how much they cost, and in case you have to mark 'em down a little bit you don't need to go looking up a lot of invoices.'

Selby nodded.

'All you require,' Kittson said, 'is something you can remember. Some combination of ten letters, all of 'em different. Now, when I started in business almost fifty years ago, I took the words *"party women"*, and I arranged them this way. P-A-R-T-Y—W-O-M-E-N, and underneath each one of those letters I put the figures, starting with one and going right on up. 1-2-3-4-5-6-7-8-9-0.

'You take this knife, for instance. You've got the letters T-E-M up at the top, and then $7.65 down below. Now that T-E-M means that knife cost me, laid down here, four dollars and sixty-five. I'm selling it for seven dollars and sixty-five. I probably could stand just a *little* more margin of profit on that knife, but people look at it and like it, and that knife's got good steel in it. It's a real humdinger of a knife, not just any old, ordinary carving-knife.'

'You have sold several of these?' Selby asked.

'I'll say I have. I've been selling 'em right along. People like 'em. It's a nice knife.'

'How long have you been handling this particular number?'

'Well, I bought three dozen of 'em a month ago. I sold the last one today.'

'Could you remember the people to whom you have sold the knives?'

'I can remember some of them. Now, some of them, I think, were strangers. And then I've got a clerk that comes in afternoons. I run the place mornings and the clerk comes in about noon when I go to lunch and stays during the afternoon, and he's here all day on Saturdays. He's made some of the sales. Understand, when I say *I've* sold them, I mean the store has sold them.'

'I take it there's no reason why Gib Spencer can't come back now?' Selby asked.

Kittson chuckled. 'Let him stay out there for a while. He's straining his ears wondering what's going on.'

Selby said: 'Well, perhaps I can give Spencer an errand to do.'

He walked outside the hardware store to where Gib Spencer was standing on the pavement. The man was seething with indignation.

'Kittson,' Gib announced, 'is a damn fool! Just an old woman. The idea of thinking that I couldn't be trusted with a little confidential information. He makes me sick.'

Selby said: 'Well, perhaps you could get some more confidential information for me while we're waiting in here.'

'What's that?'

'Suppose you run around to the Hollenberg place and see how Carr introduced that young woman.'

Spencer moved with alacrity. 'I'll get around there right away, Mr Selby. I'll find out all about it and be back at the hotel to make you a report.'

'And when you've made it,' Selby said, 'I think we'll be ready to start back for our aeroplane.'

Spencer, now thoroughly mollified, bustled over to where he had left his motor-car, and Selby walked back to the hardware store.

'Some time during the day,' Selby said to Kittson, 'do you suppose you could talk things over with your clerk and make a list of all the local people to whom you remember selling these knives?'

'I reckon I could,' Kittson said, 'but I'll tell you one thing. Two or three of them were sold to strangers. I sold a couple of 'em myself.'

'Thanks,' Selby said. 'When you get that list worked out, would you mind sending it to me?'

Selby gave the man one of his official cards.

'And,' Selby went on, 'it might be just as well if you didn't mention what has happened here this morning.'

Kittson said: 'Okay by me. I'm able to keep
139

my mouth shut. I'm like Gib Spencer—just like a clam.'

And he chuckled with wry humour at his own joke.

Selby and Sylvia Martin returned to the hotel. Twenty minutes later, Gib Spencer was there with his report.

'I got the information you wanted. This man, Carr, is representing one of the Los Angeles papers, and the girl that was with him apparently was what they call a sob sister. Only, of course, he didn't tell Mrs Hollenberg that, but I knew what she was from the reading I've done. I was able to spot her just as soon as Mrs Hollenberg told me about her and...'

'What's her name?' Selby asked.

'Well, that's a funny thing. When you get right down to it, they didn't give Mrs Hollenberg any name for the girl. It was sort of an informal affair all around. Carr introduced himself and said that he was a feature writer and that the girl handled specialised romantic and human interest angles. I think that is what she said Carr told her. Mrs Hollenberg's pretty smart. She's got a pretty good memory for things people say that way and...'

'What did he want?' Selby asked.

'He made her an offer of a thousand dollars, cash money, for all the letters she had from Eve and any and all photographs.'

'And what did Mrs Hollenberg say to that?'

'She told him that she wasn't going to
140

commercialise on her daughter's memory, in the first place; and in the second place, she didn't have a thing.

'Well, Carr questioned her, but she finally convinced him that she didn't have what he wanted.

'She got a little suspicious of Carr because, when she told him about not having a thing, Carr seemed to be pretty well satisfied, just as though he'd been able to get possession of the letters. That made her think something was wrong.

'And when they left, she shook hands with them and said to the girl: "And what is your name?" and the girl just smiled at her and said: "Daisy," and then they walked out very quickly to the motor-car.'

'Well,' Selby said, 'I guess that's that. Carr seems to have run true to form. All right, Gib. Let's load the baggage and we'll be on our way.'

They checked out of the hotel. Gib Spencer, even more than usually loquacious, said: 'I guess this man Carr's sort of mixed up in this thing. Ain't he?'

'Oh, I don't know,' Selby said. 'He probably just wanted to get photographs.'

'Yeah, what did he want to get 'em for? Seems to me that's a lot of money for the newspaper to pay for photographs and a few letters.'

Selby made himself comfortable in the car

141

and closed his eyes.

'*You* folks don't seem very talkative,' Spencer said.

'No,' Sylvia told him. 'We're like you. We talk a lot about little things, but when it comes to the big things that are really important, we know when to keep quiet.'

'You can trust me,' Gib said in a hurt voice.

'Of *course* we can,' Sylvia told him, 'but it just becomes a habit with us to keep quiet about things.'

'Say, I'll bet you're with the F.B.I. Aren't you?'

Sylvia laughed.

'I'll bet old Tom Kittson makes plenty of profit on his merchandise,' Spencer ventured after a while. 'He's got a regular gold-mine there, been running that store for forty years or so, and I'll bet he's got the first nickel he ever made. He's tight as the bark on a tree—not that I care a hang about his old cost system. My gosh, some people think a man has nothing to do except meddle in other people's businesses.'

Sylvia said nothing.

After a few miles Spencer said tentatively: 'I suppose they have to make about twenty-five per cent, don't they?'

'It depends on what you mean by twenty-five per cent,' Selby said.

'Well, if you sell something for a dollar and it only cost you seventy-five cents, you've made twenty-five cents profit. I guess that's twenty-five per cent, ain't it? After all, Mr Selby, I ain't dumb.'

'But,' Selby pointed out, 'your cost price was only seventy-five cents. Therefore, if you've made twenty-five cents, you've made one third of your cost price, so that your profit is actually thirty-three and a third per cent, less expenses.'

Spencer thought that over for a while, and then slowly nodded his head.

They drove for another ten miles in silence, Selby and Sylvia Martin keeping their eyes closed, Spencer venturing sidelong glances from time to time.

At length Selby opened his eyes, glanced at his wristwatch and said to Sylvia: 'We should be back early this afternoon. I hope the plane's all ready.'

A car coming up behind them blared its horn for the right of way, went sweeping on past with a burst of rocketing speed that swayed Gib Spencer's lighter car on its springs.

'Damn speed fiend,' he said. 'He . . .'

'Hold everything,' Selby said, upright in his seat. 'Wasn't that Carr that just passed us?'

'I . . . well, it could have been. I . . .'

'Give it everything this car's got,' Selby said. 'Get after him! Hurry up! Step on it, Spencer!'

Spencer pushed the throttle down to the floor-board. 'Now listen,' he said, as the car motor roared into vibrating action, 'this car hasn't got that much speed under the hood, and it ain't safe . . .'

143

'I guess you're right,' Selby said wearily. 'I'm quite certain that it was Carr, however, and he was alone in the machine.'

'It looked like the same motor-car all right,' Spencer said, 'but I didn't get *too* good a look.'

Selby said thoughtfully: 'He must have doubled back or something. We didn't pass him on the road anywhere or meet up with him, and yet he had left from fifteen to twenty minutes before we did, perhaps half an hour... You followed him down the road a ways, Gib.'

'He was sure going,' Spencer said. 'And I sure saw he was started out of town when I was following him there.'

Selby said: 'Look here, Gib, Carr has disposed of the girl who was with him. Now either he put her in some motor-car and turned her over to another driver, or he turned his machine around and went back to Highdale. Or perhaps he turned off on a side road. What other town is there around here where Carr could have gone ...?'

'There's a little place called Dunton Oaks about six miles off the main road here.'

'How big is it?' Selby asked.

'Oh, I'd say it was about—oh, let's see, perhaps a thousand or fifteen hundred. I'm not too good at judging populations. It isn't a big place. Want to swing around there and see if you can find...'

'No,' Selby said. 'Keep going. I want to get back to my plane.'

144

'*Okay*,' Gib said reluctantly, 'just as you say. But I *could* drive you over to Dunton Oaks and ask a few quiet questions around. I know a lot of people there.'

'Doubtless you do,' Selby said, 'but it's hard to ask questions in a town of fifteen hundred people without people knowing that you're asking questions.'

'I'm the boy that can do it,' Gib said confidently.

'I'll bet you are!' Selby agreed, winking at Sylvia. 'And, I suppose, keep quiet about it afterwards.'

'On things like that I'm a one-way street,' Gib Spencer assured him earnestly. 'The idea of old Tom Kittson thinking I'd care a hang about knowing his cost code!'

CHAPTER TWELVE

Rex Brandon was waiting for Selby at the airport in Madison City; Sylvia Martin went with Comstock in Comstock's car, which he had left at the airport, leaving Selby to drive with Brandon. The district attorney reported in detail on the results of their trip while Brandon drove to the court-house.

'Good work, son,' Brandon said when Selby had finished telling about Carr's purchase of the knife. 'This is apt to be the break we've been

145

waiting for. Incidentally, a call came through for you from Highdale—a man named Spencer wants to talk with you and wants you to pay for the message. Says he has to talk with you personally. No one else will do.'

Selby threw back his head and laughed.

'Who's Spencer?' Brandon asked.

'A he-gossip. Most nosey guy I ever ran across. He ran the car that met us at the plane and took us around Highdale.'

'What do you s'pose he wants, Doug?'

'He may have some information on this girl who was with Carr. I'll accept the call as soon as we get to the court-house.'

Brandon urged the county machine into speed, and within ten minutes Selby, at the court-house, was listening to Gib Spencer's excited voice on the telephone.

'Mr Selby! Hello, hello. Yes, this is Gib Spencer. I'm sorry to be calling you collect this way, but I found out all about that red-headed woman Carr had with him, and I thought you'd like to know.'

'That's fine,' Selby said. 'How did you find out about her, Gib?'

'Well, to tell you the truth, I didn't have very much to do after you left. That is, I thought perhaps I could find out a little something there in Dunton Oaks, and it wasn't much out of my way driving back. So I just took a swing through there and asked a few people if they'd seen a car like this one driven by the man that I

146

was shadowing, and whether they'd noticed a red-head. You see, I could describe her perfectly because I'd seen her and knew just what she had on and...'

'I understand,' Selby said. 'What did you find out?'

'I didn't have any trouble locating her at all, or finding out who she was. She's Eleanor Harlan. They call her "Babe" there in Dunton Oaks. She lived there for a while, worked in the picture-show as cashier and ticket-taker. She's got a brother living there in Dunton Oaks, a Roland Harlan. She came up to visit him about two weeks ago and stayed with him for two or three days. Then she went back, and this time when she came up with Carr she stopped off to visit her brother again. Just made a quick trip.'

Selby said: 'That's very interesting, Gib, but I'm afraid now everyone will know we're trying to find out about her...'

'Now don't you worry about that,' Gib said hastily. 'I've covered things perfectly. I just talked around about how much class she was and—you know, just swapped a little gossip. I've covered my tracks so nobody could...'

'Yes, I imagine,' Selby said dryly.

'And,' Gib rushed on, 'you haven't heard anything yet, Mr Selby. When I got back here to Highdale, I dropped in to see Tom Kittson. I didn't have anything in particular on my mind, but I was just talking. Of course, we talked about you. Well, what do you think? On the list of sales of carving-knives he's making out for you appears the name of Roland Harlan. That's Eleanor's brother. Kittson knows Harlan right well. Harlan does most of his shopping there in Highdale ... Now I've found out something else for you. This Eleanor Harlan just made a flying trip to see her brother and she's taking a bus to Fresno. She's due out of there on the plane that leaves San Francisco around ten o'clock and arrives just a little after midnight there at Los Angeles; and you could pick her up at that plane if you wanted her.'

'That's fine,' Selby said. 'Now, I think that winds up everything there at Highdale. I'm very grateful to you, Gib, but I *would* like to handle this investigation my own way, and I'm afraid that if you do anything more up there, you'll have the whole town talking.'

'Not me!' Gib said. 'I'm inclined to visit with folks when things don't amount to anything, but when things are really important, I'm close-mouthed.'

'I know,' Selby said wearily, 'like a clam.'

'That's right,' Gib told him. 'Like a clam.'

'Well, thanks a lot for calling,' Selby said.

'I thought you'd want to know, Mr Selby.'

'I do,' Selby said.

The district attorney hung up, turned to Rex Brandon and said: 'Now we've got the pattern, Rex. Carr is mixed up in this thing right to the eyebrows.'

'What have you got?' Brandon asked.

148

Before Selby could answer, the telephone rang again. Central said: 'I'm holding another call for Mr Selby. Just a moment, please.'

This time the voice that came over the wire was the smoothly modulated voice of old A. B. Carr.

'Good afternoon, Counsellor. How are you?'

'Fine,' Selby said cautiously. He cupped his hand over the transmitter, said to Brandon: 'It's Carr, Rex. Get on an extension.'

The sheriff all but upset his chair scrambling to the phone in the next office.

'I think perhaps I can be of some assistance to you in that murder case you're investigating,' Carr went on.

'How?'

'Well,' Carr said smoothly, 'I have an interest in the matter which I'm not exactly free to explain. But my client is anxious to see that the character of Eve Dawson isn't smeared in the newspapers. Intimate revelations, diaries, pictures, all that sort of thing.'

'Who is your client?' Selby asked, conscious of a faint click which announced the sheriff's extension had been plugged in on the line.

'I'm afraid I can't tell you that. But there's one piece of information I *can* give you which I think will have a most important bearing on the case.'

'What's that?'

'While I was in Highdale earlier in the day,'

149

Carr said, 'I wanted to get a screwdriver for my car. The screw on the visor above the windscreen had worked loose, and I went into the local hardware store to pick up a screwdriver. I was casually looking over things in the display counter, and imagine my surprise when I happened to notice a carving-knife apparently exactly identical to the murder weapon in the Dawson case. And damned if it didn't have exactly the same cost mark and selling price on it that was on the murder weapon.

'I thought of you immediately, Selby, and promptly proceeded to buy one of these knives and had the man make out a sales slip in my name so that I could be a witness later in case you wanted to call me. I have that knife as a little present for you, Selby, an exact duplicate of the murder weapon, together with the exactly identical grease pencil marks on the blade, showing the cost price and selling price. I think you will find it is a very valuable piece of evidence. I am driving down. I hope to get as far as Fresno tonight, but I'll be in your office with it shortly after noon tomorrow. And in the meantime I wanted you to know that the murder weapon must have been purchased in Highdale from a store operated by a man named Kittson. The place is referred to as the Kittson Hardware Store.'

There was a long silence over the line. 'Hello. Are you there?' Carr asked.

'Yes,' Selby said.

'You heard me?'

'Yes. I was thinking things over. How did you know the mother of Eve Dawson lived in Highdale?'

Carr's laugh was melodious.

'How *did* you?' Selby insisted.

'Tut, tut, Counsellor. I told you I had a client.'

'And how did you know what the murder weapon looked like?'

'Come, come, Selby, you must remember the public Press. There was a wire-photo in the newspapers this morning.'

'How many such knives did Kittson have, Carr?'

'This was the last.'

'And when will you be here?'

'Some time tomorrow, early in the afternoon. I'm driving down and I must get on my way if I'm to make Fresno tonight. Goodbye, Counsellor. See you tomorrow.'

And Carr, with courteous finality, hung up the phone at his end of the line.

Rex Brandon rejoined Selby in the private office.

'Now,' Brandon said, 'I *have* seen everything. He's stuck his head in a noose and then he hands us the rope!'

CHAPTER THIRTEEN

Doug Selby said: 'That looks like our party, Rex, the one in the brown suit. Second from the end.'

'I guess so,' Brandon said. 'Gosh, she's an upstanding little filly, isn't she?'

Selby moved back into the shadows. 'Let's see if anyone's meeting her before we make a move.'

The girl emerging from the midnight plane walked towards the passenger exit, head high, shoulders back. With her slim waist and straight long legs her walk was a glide that carried her swiftly ahead of everyone else.

Inspector Ormond, of the Metropolitan Police, shifted his cigar, said: 'Stands out like a sore thumb. Don't need to be a detective to spot *her*. Now what do you boys want *me* to do?'

'Simply furnish the official contact,' Selby said.

'You want me to do the questioning?'

'You start in,' Brandon said, 'and we'll take over if we think of something.'

'Okay,' the inspector said. 'Looks like no one's going to meet her.'

His broad shoulders pushed their way through the little knot of spectators who were gathered to greet the incoming passengers. His hand touched the woman on the shoulder. 'Your name Eleanor Harlan?'

She whirled to face him. For a moment, she seemed tense, as though the inspector's light touch on the shoulder had started off a chain of reflexes that released springs of emotion.

Then she smiled up at the inspector's six feet of authority. 'Yes,' she said.

'I want you to step over here and meet a couple of people,' Inspector Ormond said.

'Isn't it rather late for that?'

'Not for these friends, it isn't.'

'I'm sorry, but I don't know you, and...'

The inspector said: 'A few people are looking at us. If I pull back the lapel of my coat and show you the star, it's just going to make you feel conspicuous.'

She met his eyes. 'Make me feel conspicuous then.'

'You're asking for it,' Ormond said, and pulled back his coat lapel, showing her the gold shield.

'Just a minute,' she said as he folded the coat back, 'I want to get the number of that ... All right, I've got it. Now what do you want?'

'I want you to meet the Sheriff and the District Attorney of Madison County. They're up here from Madison City. They want to talk with you.'

'I take it this is an order.'

'It's official, if that's what you mean.'

'All right,' she said, 'let's have it over with.'

153

The spectators at the airport who had seen the by-play, the tapping on the shoulder and the flash of the official badge, had rapidly communicated their discovery to bystanders, feeling a vicarious importance as they explained in audible tones: 'Look, that girl's being arrested.'

As a result, some two dozen morbidly curious eyes followed Eleanor Harlan as Inspector Ormond piloted her to a corner of the waiting-room where Rex Brandon and Doug Selby had been watching what had happened.

'Sit down,' Ormond said.

'Thank you. I prefer to stand.'

'This is Rex Brandon. He's the sheriff. And Doug Selby, the district attorney.'

She inclined her head in a frigid gesture of acknowledgment.

'You knew an Eve Dawson, didn't you?' Inspector Ormond said.

'That's right. We shared an apartment.'

'Why didn't you come forward and say so, when you learned what had happened?'

'Was I supposed to?'

'Why not? Why didn't you want the officers to find out?'

She said: 'It was a shock to me. I've lost a friend. I didn't feel like going to the police and saying: "I know that girl. She rooms with me. Please come up to the apartment, blow cigar smoke all over the place, drink up what little

154

liquor I have, and make passes at me." The police had the girl's identity. They knew her mother's address, and...'

'And?' Ormond prompted belligerently.

She met his eyes defiantly. 'All right,' she said. 'Eve had been in trouble. I didn't have anything to do with that trouble, and I didn't want to be dragged into it.'

'What sort of trouble?'

'I don't know. I know now she'd been shot. I didn't know it then.'

'What *did* you know?'

'I knew that Eve telephoned me and said she was going to be away for a while, that she was in a little trouble and she wasn't feeling well; that she had to lie low and would I please not say anything to anyone.'

'She was your friend, and yet when she told you she was in trouble and was going to have to lie low, you didn't ask any questions and didn't make any investigation?'

She said: 'Eve is free, white and twenty-one. I'm free, white and twenty-one. Under similar circumstances, I wouldn't have thanked her to have asked a lot of questions or done any snooping. I said: "Okay, Eve, I'll keep the place going. The rent is due on the first," and hung-up.'

'Even at a time like that, your first thought was of the rent!'

She looked him up and down coolly. 'I don't know what *your* salary is, but I know what

155

mine is. I took Eve Dawson in with me because the apartment was too expensive for me to carry by myself. I suppose that badge gives you a right to push me around at this hour of the morning. But don't think you're going to make me like it.'

Brandon, in his slow drawl, said: 'There's only a couple of things I'd like to know, Miss Harlan. And when I tell you what they are, I think you'll agree that this was the only way to get the information.'

She turned to look him over. Slowly the defiance faded from her face. The corners of her mouth relaxed somewhat in a smile. 'All right,' she said. 'What's *your* story?'

Brandon said: 'I'm not beating around the bush, Miss Harlan.'

'Don't,' she said. 'I don't like it.'

'I'm going to hand it to you straight.'

She nodded.

Brandon said: 'Eve Dawson was stabbed with a carving-knife. There's reason to believe that carving-knife was sold by the Kittson Hardware Company in Highdale.'

Her eyes widened, and Selby, watching that expression of her face, for the life of him couldn't tell whether it was something that had been rehearsed deliberately, or an actual reaction of genuine surprise.

'And,' Brandon went on, 'you have a brother, Roland Harlan, who lives in Dunton Oaks. He does some of his shopping in

156

Highdale. A couple of weeks ago he bought the knife that stabbed Eve Dawson, or else a knife that was the exact counterpart of that knife.'

'Roland?' she said, and then added after a moment: 'I'm afraid that's utterly impossible, Sheriff.'

'It's what we're trying to check on.'

'Why not check with Roland, then?'

'We will.'

Her face held the frowning concentration of someone who is trying to recall something, then she said: 'Wait a minute. Roland gave me a knife the last time I was up visiting him. I'd almost forgotten about it. I really didn't have any great use for it. Usually, I eat out, or else we open a can of something. Most of our cooking is done in a frying-pan.'

'Then why did you take the knife?' Brandon asked.

She laughed then, and as she laughed, the beauty of her face became brittle. There was no melody and no mirth in the laughter. It was merely a nervous reflex. When she laughed, one could after a fashion see the whole interior mechanism of her personality.

'Go on,' Ormond said. 'Quit stalling.'

She stopped laughing. 'I guess Kittson just sold my brother the carving-knife. Talked him into taking it, I mean. Roland didn't have any particular use for it, and when he brought it home, Fay, that's his wife, said *she* didn't have any place to put it, and wanted to know what in

157

the world he had bought another knife for. Roland told her it was a very fine knife, that it had exceptionally good steel in it and the blade would take an edge like a razor. Fay's inclined to be sarcastic at times. She asked him if he'd bought it to shave with. Then Roland turned to me and said: "No, I bought it for Babe. She needed a carving-knife and I thought it would make a swell present for her."'

'What did you do?' Brandon asked.

She said: 'I played up to him. I knew that's Roland's weakness. He goes into a store and sees something, and he wants it. It doesn't make too much difference whether he has any use for it or not. He isn't what you'd call a wise or a careful buyer.'

'You played up to him,' Selby said. 'Just how do you mean?'

She turned to give Selby a rather careful appraisal then, and her eyes grew more confident. She said: 'I pretended that a carving-knife was the one thing on earth that I wanted most. He gave it to me. I wrapped it up and put it in my suitcase and took it home with me, and to tell you the truth, that's the last I thought about it.'

'Then,' Ormond said, 'it'll be in the suitcase right now, won't it?'

'I presume it will.'

'That's what these folks are interested in.'

She said: 'Would you like to have me call you as soon as I get to the apartment and let

158

you know?'

Ormond grinned, shifted his cigar once more, said: 'Oh, we don't want to put you to that much trouble, sister. Come on, we'll take you home.'

'In a police car?'

'That's right.'

'Well,' she said, 'after all, saving a dollar bus fare and another six bits for a taxi is the silver lining on this particular cloud. Let's go.'

It was Selby that she smiled at, Selby at whose side she walked as the district attorney led the way to the place where Ormond had left the police car.

Ormond, dropping behind with Brandon, said: 'Look at her walk. Look at those hips. She'd be a movie queen if it wasn't for that laugh. When she laughs, her face busts wide open and you can see what she is.'

'What is she?' Brandon said.

Ormond looked surprised. 'Don't you know?'

'Not yet,' Brandon said with firm finality.

Inspector Ormond removed the soggy end of the cigar from his mouth, tossed it into a brass cuspidor and said musingly to himself: 'If it wasn't for that laugh...'

Selby held the car door open for Babe Harlan. He followed her into the rear seat. Brandon sat in front with Ormond.

'You got that address?' Ormond asked.

'The Freemantle Apartments,' Eleanor

Harlan said.

'Okay, let's go,' Ormond said.

'Can't we spare the population the annoyance of the siren?' Babe Harlan asked.

'Don't you want to get there fast?'

'Not that fast.'

'We do,' Ormond said, and snapped the switch which turned on the siren, started the official red spotlight snapping on and off.

'People who have lots of weight like to throw it around,' Eleanor Harlan said, and settled herself comfortably in the corner of the seat.

The big police car rocketed through frozen traffic towards its destination. Babe Harlan, turning to Selby, said: 'After all, it was only a question of time.'

'What was?'

'Until Eve rubbed herself out.'

'What do you mean?'

'Don't you know?'

'No.'

'Eve kept thinking about her mother and her future.'

'What does that have to do with it?'

'She wanted to get it all at once.'

'From whom?' Selby asked.

Babe laughed then. 'Once you've decided to be on the make,' she said, 'you don't care where it comes from, just so it comes. Then when it doesn't come, you've nothing to fall back on— except oblivion.'

A drunken driver shot across the front of the

car at a street intersection. Inspector Ormond slammed on brakes. For a moment, Selby and the girl were thrown around in the back of the motor-car, then the car straightened, shot on once more to speed.

'Yes,' Selby said, 'you were saying?'

'I wasn't,' Babe Harlan said.

'I thought you were.'

'You mean you thought I was going to.'

'Well, isn't that the same thing?'

She smiled and shook her head.

'How do you know these things?' Selby asked.

'Perhaps I read a book or saw a movie,' she said noncommittally.

Selby studied her, trying to devise some way of getting her to throw off the fit of morose silence which seemed to have smothered the mood for friendly chatter.

'I understand Eve Dawson sent money home quite frequently,' Selby said.

'Did she?'

'I thought she did.'

'What gave you that impression?'

'Oh, just something one of the witnesses told me. In a case of this kind, you meet so many people and hear so many stories, you have a hard time keeping them segregated.'

'There's nothing wrong in sending money to her mother, is there?'

'No. Certainly not. I just thought it was an index to her character.'

161

'Well, it was, wasn't it?'

Again she was silent.

Inspector Ormond switched off the siren, kept the red light on, said over his shoulder: 'It's only three or four blocks.'

The car eased into slower speed.

Babe Harlan said suddenly: 'In this racket, you learn how to be a good sport. You take things as they come. You make contacts. Most of the time the contacts aren't worth anything except a good time. But you always stand a chance. You may strike pay dirt that's really worth while. But the only way you can cash in is to have a record of having played it clean.'

'You work?' Selby asked.

'Of course I work. I am trying to build up a background so that when I do make the right contact I can do something with it. That's where Eve made her mistake. She...'

Inspector Ormond slid the car to a stop. 'Here we are.'

'Yes, go ahead,' Selby said to Babe Harlan.

'That's all,' she said. 'I've said it. She left herself only one way out and she had to take that.'

Inspector Ormond opened the door.

'Now look,' Eleanor Harlan said, 'will you fellows be decent and take your hats off and not try to put on the hard-boiled act? I don't want the neighbours to think the law is bringing me home.'

She whirled in the seat, gave them a flash of

legs that could have graced an art calendar anywhere, and then slid out through the door of the car and walked swiftly to fit a key in the door of the apartment house. Inspector Ormond pushed the door open as soon as the latch clicked. They went in, crowded into the elevator and rattled up to the fourth floor.

The girl led the way down the thinly carpeted corridor to the door of her apartment, inserted the latch-key, opened the door, and then was crowded to one side as Inspector Ormond shouldered his way into the room and clicked on the lights.

The apartment was a picture of dull mediocrity. The old and worn furniture was neither comfortable nor home-like. The place was clean, with the cleanliness of a commercialised antiseptic. The carpet was worn and faded. The pictures on the wall were conventionalised prints in cheap pine frames that had evidently been on the walls for years.

'You girls don't seem to try to make the place too attractive,' Inspector Ormond said.

'Why should we?'

'Don't people come to see you?'

'People come to see us,' Babe Harlan said, 'and then they take us out. Have a place that's comfortable and home-like, and the first thing you know you'll be cooking for a bunch of bums who will paw you over and leave you with a sink full of dirty dishes. Every time they see you after that they'll want to know when you're going to cook them another dinner.'

Inspector Ormond laughed.

Brandon said: 'You know where that knife is?'

'I know where it should be. I can't guarantee that it's there. I don't stay here all the time, and after all you can see that any lug with a pass-key could walk right in. We haven't anything particularly valuable here, anyway.'

'Let's take a look,' Ormond said.

She opened the door to the bedroom, switched on lights, walked past twin beds to a closet, opened the door, went inside and pulled out a suitcase.

'Hand me my purse, will you?' she asked Doug Selby. 'I'll get the key out.'

It was an expensive suitcase with her initials stamped in gold under the lock.

'Nice baggage,' Ormond said.

'A birthday present,' she commented dryly.

She took keys from her purse, selected one and unlocked the suitcase.

'What's the idea of keeping it locked?' Ormond asked.

'It makes a nice place to keep things,' she said. 'Things you don't want the maid prying into. Take a look at the bureau drawers and then tell me how you'd lock those.'

She unfastened the clasps on the suitcase. Inspector Ormond's big hand reached over her shoulder. '*I'll* look for it.'

'You keep your paws out of there!'

164

Ormond dragged the suitcase out into the middle of the floor, under the light.

'Say, what do you think this is?' she demanded.

Ormond opened the suitcase.

There were nylon stockings, silk underwear, letters, an address-book, photographs and feminine lingerie neatly packed in the bag.

Ormond's hand reached down under the lingerie.

Babe Harlan slapped the hand. 'Keep your big paws out of here. Your hang-nails will snag my stockings.'

She slid her hand expertly under the folded garments, groped around, said: 'As a matter of fact, I'd clean forgotten about ... Here it is.'

She pulled out a long parcel wrapped in newspaper, untied the string, unwrapped the newspaper and extended for their inspection a carving-knife on the blade of which was marked in black grease pencil T-E-M $7.65.

'This it?' Inspector Ormond asked Selby.

'That's it,' Selby said, handing the knife to Brandon.

Selby picked up the newspaper. It was a copy of the *Highdale Register* dated October 7th.

'Want to take it along?'

'Say,' Babe Harlan demanded, 'what do you boys think you're doing? That's *my* knife.'

'It may be evidence.'

'Evidence of what?' she asked scornfully. 'Don't be a sap. As long as I've got that knife,

165

you can't pin anything on my brother, and you can't pin anything on me. You walk out with it and how do I know what's going to happen? That knife stays right here, gentlemen. If you don't like that arrangement, I'll get my lawyer on the phone.'

'Who *is* your lawyer?' Selby asked.

She met his eyes. 'A. B. Carr. Ever hear of him?'

'You took a trip with him, didn't you?'

'Oh, so you know about that?'

'That's right. What was the idea of the trip?'

'He was driving to Highdale. He asked me if I wanted to go along. He thought perhaps I'd like to see my brother.'

'That was all of it?'

'What do *you* think?'

'I'm asking.'

She said: 'I wanted to come back with him, but I couldn't get enough time off. I got another girl to take my place, but I have to be on the job at seven o'clock in the morning.'

'You know Carr well?' Ormond asked.

She smiled at him. 'I'd recognise him anywhere, Inspector. Put him in a line-up and I'd pick him out instantly.'

'That isn't what *I* meant,' Ormond said.

'Well, that's what I meant.'

'You know Carr pretty well?'

She said: 'Look. Carr is a slow, careful driver. He's staying in Fresno tonight. I know where I can reach him. He doesn't like to have

166

his sleep disturbed, and I wouldn't want to do it, but if I have to I can. If you want to ask him questions, you can go right ahead.'

Inspector Ormond glanced at Rex Brandon.

Brandon said: 'I guess that's all right. If she wants the knife, it's hers. After all, we know these knives were sold by the Kittson Hardware Company at Highdale. If you ask me, it's quite a coincidence that Eve Dawson's room-mate should have the duplicate of a knife with which Eve Dawson was murdered.'

Babe Harlan said quickly: 'It's a shame you don't know your way around traffic lights a little better, Sheriff. Eve bumped herself off. I'm sorry, but that's the way it was.'

'*We* think she was murdered,' Selby said.

'*You* would,' she told him, snapping the suitcase closed and locking it.

'You boys want to take a look around through Eve Dawson's things while you're here?' Ormond asked.

Selby nodded.

'Have a heart,' Babe Harlan said. 'I have to be at work at seven o'clock in the morning, and I don't want to look like . . .'

'Where are Eve's things?'

'The bottom two drawers of the dresser,' she said. 'The top two are mine.'

Ormond went over and pulled a drawer out of the dresser.

'You won't find anything,' she said. 'I packed up a suitcase for Eve that had about

167

everything she wanted in it, all of her intimate personal stuff. All you'll find in there is clothes.'

'And what did you do with the suitcase?' Brandon asked.

'Left it right slap-bang in the middle of the floor, just where Eve told me to leave it.'

'And then what happened to it?'

She said: 'It disappeared. Of course, I'm not a professional detective, but *I* would say that Eve gave the key to her apartment to someone, and that someone came in, got the suitcase I'd packed up and took it out to her wherever she was staying.'

'And who do you think that someone was?' Selby asked.

Her eyes grew wide. She raised her hand and snapped her fingers. 'I know,' she declared with enthusiasm. 'Santa Claus!'

The officers went through the bureau drawers, finding nothing but clothes. They inspected the side of the closet which was Eve's and found the usual assortment of clothes on hangers, of shoes on trees.

'That's all of her stuff?' Ormond asked.

'That's all of it.'

'Do you realise there isn't so much as a scrap of paper? Not a letter, not a picture, not a thing?'

'If you say there isn't, I'll take your word for it. *I'm* not inclined to be sceptical.'

'Isn't that unusual?'

168

'I don't know,' Babe Harlan said. 'I haven't made a practice of searching through the personal belongings of dead girls. You're the one who's had all that experience.'

'Well, *I'll* tell *you* it's unusual.'

'All right, then it's unusual.'

'You wouldn't have gone through all of her things and taken out anything that might have been incriminating, would you?'

'Me?'

'Yes, you.'

'Don't be silly. Suppose a boy friend came to get her suitcase. He could have done it, couldn't he?'

'That's supposing he came to get the suitcase.'

'Yes.'

'You don't know that he did?'

'I don't know that he didn't.'

'So what?'

'So I'm asking you, if Eve Dawson gave a boy friend the key to her apartment and told him to come here and get the suitcase, if he couldn't have gone through the drawers and taken out any documents he wanted to take out.'

'Do you know whether anything is missing in the bureau drawers?'

'If you'd known Eve, you'd have known that the very nicest way to smash a beautiful friendship into ten million pieces would have been to have looked into one of the bureau

169

drawers that were set aside for her. I lived my life. Eve lived hers. We shared the apartment. We split the rent. We had some contacts together. Eve was playing the game one way; I was playing it the other. She was suspicious of me, and I think a little jealous of me. She was shrewd, and she always had her eye open for the dollar. She wanted to be a succeess in the world, and she wanted to send money to her mother. Now then, I want to take a bath, and I want to know what I'm going to do about the rent when it comes due on the first.'

'I'd suggest you'd better pay it,' Ormond said.

'With what?'

'With money.'

'What about Eve's share of the rent?'

'Perhaps your friend, A. B. Carr, will pay it,' Inspector Ormond said.

She said: 'You ought to be ashamed of yourself. You, a policeman, and smoking hop while you're on duty.'

'Won't he?'

'Don't be silly!'

'Well, he's your lawyer. Ask him what you're going to do.'

She said, somewhat bitterly: 'Yes, he's my lawyer. He's spending the night in Fresno. He wouldn't shake a leg and drive right on through. He could have been here by this time. Old A.B.C. is a good egg, but he drives like an old woman. He doesn't like night driving against the headlights, and he doesn't want to get up before eight o'clock in the morning. That leaves me with a nice aeroplane ride to get here.'

'But he *did* pay for your plane ticket, didn't he?' Selby asked.

She met his eyes and said: 'He did pay for my plane ticket, Mr Selby. Does that violate some section of the Penal Code?'

Selby smiled, glanced at Brandon and Ormond, said: 'Come on, let's let her get her beauty sleep.'

'The bath first,' she said, smiling. 'Do come again, *gentlemen*.'

CHAPTER FOURTEEN

Sheriff Brandon thrust long legs which were slightly bowed from years in the saddle out in front of him and moodily inspected the worn toes of his boots.

'Well, Doug, *The Blade* really crucified us.'

Selby nodded.

'You just can't put your finger on what makes you so darned mad about the thing,' Brandon went on. 'I can't sling lingo and don't know too much about the way it's done. But I guess it's the calm way an editorial writer acts, as though his judgment was the thing that was running the universe.'

Selby smiled and said: 'It's hard to take, Rex. You've put your finger on it. There's an assumption of omnipotent superiority. You have the tendency to forget that you're reading words that have been penned by a hostile lame-brain and feel that perhaps the chap really is superior after all. Just listen to this.'

Selby picked up *The Blade* which lay on the sheriff's desk and read a section from the editorial:

'It was to be assumed that once the court-house ring was again firmly entrenched in power, the arch leaders of that ring, Sheriff Brandon and District Attorney Selby, would engage in a programme of persecuting their political enemies.

'We distinctly remember, when this possibility was mentioned during the initial stages of the recall campaign, that Selby's friends greeted the charge with hoots of derision, branding it as libellous campaign propaganda.

'Now, with Selby's new tenure of office hardly ninety days old, we are treated to a spectacle of county authorities deliberately ignoring the overwhelming weight of evidence indicating that a young woman, whose bruised feet had stumbled along the primrose path until she became bitter and disillusioned, had finally chosen "the easy way out". We find the sheriff and the district attorney trying to torture this suicide into a murder case.

'The sole purpose in doing this is to launch an *"investigation"* with taxpayers' funds which will, under the expert innuendo of our district attorney, succeed in smearing the characters of some of the people who are prominent politically in this county and who were unfortunate enough to have felt conscientiously that the court-house ring should no longer be perpetuated in power.

'The pay off, fellow citizens, will come at a time when the officials, having used this suicide as a means for a smear, try gently to ease themselves out from under. Let's have no mistake about this, Mr Sheriff and Mr District Attorney! If the death of Eve Dawson was a murder and not a suicide, then IT IS UP TO YOU to get the murderer and get a conviction. Please, let's not have the taxpayers' money dissipated in a mudslinging investigation and then have you back out. If it's a murder, make an arrest. And when you have made an arrest, get a conviction. If it's a suicide, quit your yammering and quit your attempts to crucify persons who have opposed you politically. In other words, gentlemen, either fish or cut bait. If you're infallibly competent as your supporters led the voters to believe, you can solve this murder

173

case in your stride. If you're corrupt enough to use your office to twist a suicide into an excuse for political persecution, let's see that the voters know what's going on.'

Selby crumpled the newspaper and threw it into the waste-basket.

Brandon said: 'They've sort of got us walking a tight rope, Doug.'

Selby nodded.

'I don't think Eve Dawson killed herself,' Brandon went on, 'and there certainly has been too much skullduggery about that bullet wound. And I don't think she inflicted that herself, regardless of what that crooked doctor says.'

Again Selby nodded.

'But,' Brandon said, 'the minute we start to do anything, we find ourselves up against the legal rule that we have to prove someone guilty beyond all reasonable doubt, and if the jury has even a reasonable doubt as to whether the thing was a suicide—well, there we are, Doug.'

'How about alibis?' Selby asked. 'Have you checked up on ...'

'You can't very well have an alibi for one o'clock in the morning,' Brandon said.

'Was it one o'clock?'

'As nearly as the autopsy surgeon can fix the time, it was. He puts it as between midnight and two-thirty, but he figures it right around

174

one o'clock.'

'We can't place anyone in the vicinity at that time?' Selby asked.

'Jim Melvin,' Brandon said dryly, 'sleeping in twin beds. His wife claims she is not a particularly heavy sleeper and swears she would have heard him if he had left the room. Then, of course, there's Paula Melvin! If you want to be perfectly impartial, there's also Doris Kane.'

'No sign that the house had been entered from the outside?'

Brandon shook his head. 'Melvin says he locked the doors before he went to bed. There's a spring lock on the front door, a catch that clicks into position as soon as the door is closed. But it's a good lock and it would be hard to pick. The right sort of skeleton key might work it all right. The back door had an old-fashioned bolt on it in addition to a lock. The windows on the lower floor were all closed and locked.'

'How about Granby? Where was he?'

'He says he was at home in bed. He's a widower, living alone. A housekeeper comes in by the day. Hudson Parlin, who might be pretty much interested, left here that Monday night for Los Angeles.'

'Any proof that he got there?'

'Plenty of it,' Brandon said grimly. 'He witnessed a car accident at one o'clock in the morning. He'd kept his appointment in Los

Angeles and was on his way back to the hotel when he saw this accident at a street intersection. They subpœnaed him as a witness. I've talked with the lawyer for the plaintiff. He says Parlin is the only disinterested eye-witness and his testimony is so clear-cut that the insurance company is going to make a settlement. Obviously, he couldn't have been in Los Angeles at one o'clock and got back to Madison City in time to have committed a murder. And he couldn't have been in Madison City and committed the murder and been in Los Angeles by one o'clock. So there you are.'

'How about Morris Sheldon, Granby's brother-in-law?'

'He says he was home. You can't prove it and you can't disprove it. His wife was away on a visit. There are no children, and he was alone in the house.'

'And Carr?' Selby asked.

Brandon stroked his chin. 'I'd like to find out about Carr myself. I'm going to give him the works this afternoon when he comes in with the knife.'

Selby said: 'Be careful, Rex. Carr knows all the answers.'

'Well, I'm going to ask him all the questions,' Brandon promised savagely.

'Suppose he gets on his dignity, takes offence at something we say, and refuses to answer any further questions?'

'Then we'll drag him in front of the Grand Jury,' Brandon said. 'He'll...'

Abruptly the sheriff ceased speaking.

Selby raised his eyebrows. 'What is it, Rex?'

Brandon growled: 'They've got the Grand Jury into their camp, Doug.'

'Who has?'

'I don't know. Morris Sheldon, I think. And, of course, there's his stooge, Milton Granby. There's a lot of powerful political influence in the background of this thing. There are people who aren't anxious to have the details of what happened at Melvin's party dragged out into the open. There's been a lot of whispering to the Grand Jury.'

'Do you suppose Mrs Kane could give us any better description of that figure she saw there in the bathroom door?' Selby asked.

'No, I've talked with her again. She thinks it was a *dark* figure, silhouetted against the light; that indicates pretty positively there was someone in the room with Eve Dawson. Eve was wearing a *négligé*. Of course, she *could* have had a visitor and then killed herself, or been murdered after the visitor left.'

'How did the visitor get in?'

'She must have let him in. You'll remember that Mrs Kane said Eve Dawson told her something about having a decision to reach within the next hour or two.'

Selby nodded.

The telephone rang.

177

Brandon picked up the receiver, said: 'Hello, Sheriff Brandon talking.'

He listened for a few seconds, then said laconically: 'Okay, that'll be fine. We'll be waiting for you.'

He dropped the receiver back into position. 'A. B. Carr telephoning,' he said dryly. 'Long distance. Says he'll be able to be here at one-thirty this afternoon and will have the evidence with him.'

CHAPTER FIFTEEN

Promptly at one-thirty in the afternoon, Alfonse Baker Carr entered Rex Brandon's office.

'Good afternoon, Sheriff,' he said, then turned to Selby. 'And how are you, Major Selby?'

'Doug Selby.'

'Yes, yes. You're scrupulous about not keeping the military title. That's your privilege, but a title becomes you.'

Carr seated himself, crossed his long legs, took a cigarette-case from his pocket, extracted a cigarette and tapped it gently on the edge of the cigarette-case.

'Quite by accident; gentlemen,' he said, 'I stumbled upon the fact that the knife with which Eve Dawson killed herself must have

178

been purchased from the little town of Highdale, an interesting little place near the mountains fifty or sixty miles from Fresno.

'As soon as I learned of this, I realised that the evidence might be of some value to you. Since we have, on occasion, been on opposite sides, I welcomed this opportunity to co-operate with you.'

Selby nodded.

Carr extended the long paper package which he was holding. 'With my compliments, gentlemen.'

Selby cut through the strips of brown adhesive, unrolled the paper and inspected the knife which was disclosed to view. A carving-knife with the price written on the blade in grease pencil. T-E-M $7.65, together with a sales slip made to Alfonse Baker Carr, dated the day before and signed by Tom Kittson.

'Rather a coincidence, wasn't it?' Selby said.

'What?' Carr asked.

'That you should happen to stumble on to the one store in the State that sold this knife.'

'In a way,' Carr said disarmingly, 'there certainly seems to be the long arm of coincidence entering into the picture. But, as so frequently happens in such cases, when you know the facts, the situation ceases to appear even unusual.'

'And what are the facts?' Selby asked.

'The facts,' Carr said, 'are that Eve Dawson's mother lived in Highdale. I went up

179

to see her. While I was there…'

'And what did you want to see Mrs Hollenberg about?'

'Frankly,' Carr said, 'I wanted to forestall a certain cheap sensationalism. I also wanted to protect certain unnamed clients from any unethical and very much undesired publicity.'

'So you went to see Mrs Hollenberg?'

'That's right.'

'And what does *she* have to do with unethical publicity?'

'Come, come,' Carr said, smiling. 'I'm not on the witness-stand, but since you ask, I'll tell you. My unnamed client is a yachtsman. He had been on a yachting trip with some friends. Two girls were on the yachting trip. My client didn't even know they were going to be there. Unfortunately, one of the yachtsmen had a camera, and some pictures were taken. My client was somewhat concerned about that. Those things are so easily capable of a false interpretation.'

'Aren't they!' Brandon said sarcastically.

'And so,' Carr went on urbanely, 'I thought that I would get in touch with Miss Dawson's mother and ask her if perhaps her daughter had sent her any photographs.'

'That's rather a long trip.'

'It's not a bad drive, gentlemen. It gets tedious at times. I took the cut-off across the desert to come back to Madison City.'

'You knew Eve Dawson in her lifetime?'

Selby said.

'That's right.'

'And you know her room-mate, Eleanor Harlan?'

Carr pursed his lips thoughtfully for a moment, thinking that over. Then he said: 'Yes, I know Miss Harlan.'

'You might, perhaps, have saved us quite a bit of work if you had told us that you knew Eleanor Harlan, knew where Eve Dawson lived, and knew something about the dead girl's background,' Selby said.

'Of course,' Carr pointed out with a smile, 'I have my own professional life, gentlemen, and my own obligations to my clients. My primary purpose in practising law is not to save the officers of the law time. It is to protect my clients.'

'I'll say it is!' Brandon said.

'Come, come, Sheriff,' Carr said reproachfully. 'I have gone out of my way to present you with what I personally would consider to be a piece of quite valuable evidence.'

'And just how did you discover that bit of evidence again?' Selby asked.

'As I have said,' Carr continued easily, 'I was in Highdale on other business. I had occasion to go into the hardware store to make a small purchase, and while I was there, I looked down into the display counter, saw a knife and noticed that it seemed to be very similar indeed to the photograph I had seen of the knife with which Eve Dawson had stabbed herself. I couldn't believe that it would have an identical cost mark and sales mark on the blade, but I couldn't resist the temptation to look and make sure.

'Imagine my surprise, gentlemen, when I found that the knife was identical.'

'Don't make me laugh,' Brandon said.

Alfonse Baker Carr frowned reproachfully. 'I ascertained that the man who ran this hardware store had had a shipment of some three dozen of these knives. As it happened, this was the last one he had left. I realised, of course, that you might want this as evidence and wouldn't want the hardware store to sell it before you could get hold of it. I realised also that if I pointed out to the man in the hardware store the reason he should hold this knife subject to your inspection, I might be giving him information which you would prefer he didn't have.

'So,' Carr went on, smiling benignly at them, the timbre of his voice as melodiously vibrant as the low notes of an organ, 'I acted in the capacity of a casual customer, purchased this knife, and so that there could be no question about where it came from, had the man make out a sales slip in my name.'

'Your mysterious client, whose interests you are protecting, evidently is not at all hostile to our office,' Selby ventured.

182

'Oh, certainly not,' Carr said affably. 'On the contrary, I feel certain that my client wants me to give you all co-operation.'

'Then you might begin by telling us where you were at one o'clock on the morning of the twenty-eighth.'

'Where *I* was?'

'Yes.'

'Good heavens, gentlemen, what would my own whereabouts have to do with the problem under discussion?'

'We'd like to know.'

Carr frowned. 'Let me see—the twenty-seventh was Monday—and one o'clock in the morning on Tuesday. Why, yes, gentlemen, I was at my country home right here in Madison City, in my study there, reading.'

'Rather a late hour for you to be reading?' Brandon asked.

'Oh, not at all, Sheriff. You see, I'm pretty much of a night owl. I study and read and prowl—Oh, wait a minute, I begin to see a light, a pattern to your questions.

'Let me say this, gentlemen. Suppose you should by some strange chance be able to prove that the beautiful but despondent and erring Miss Dawson had, shall we say, a visitor, at perhaps one o'clock in the morning. You still wouldn't have anything. A young woman so situated might well have had either a business or a social engagement. She could so easily have had a caller about whom she wished her host and hostess to know nothing.

'It would have been very simple for her to have simply tiptoed down the stairs and unlocked the front door. Then her visitor could have entered the house whenever he came, tiptoed up the stairs and talked with Miss Dawson, or even brought her a suitcase with things she wished in it.

'But, gentlemen, even if you could prove *that*, you still wouldn't have a case. Eve Dawson could well have killed herself as soon as this man left. Your problem, your legal problem, Mr Selby, if you don't mind my saying so, is to prove and prove beyond a reasonable doubt that this despondent, unhappy, unfortunate creature, with her history of a previous suicide attempt, her medical history of suicidal complexes, was murdered. That, I would say, was practically impossible.'

'All done?' Brandon asked.

'All done,' Carr said, smiling.

'Then perhaps you can also tell us where you were at the time the shot was fired at Jim Melvin's house.'

'Why, certainly,' Carr said. 'To the best of my knowledge, talking at the moment with James L. Melvin, our host, and one of the guests. I believe it was Milton Granby. There were other people in the room, but we three were in a group, as I remember it.

'Of course, gentlemen, I am handicapped

because *I* personally don't think the sound so many persons took to be a shot actually was anything more than the popping of a champagne cork, or perhaps the back-fire of a truck. However, I was chatting with these two people when there was a loud "plop", and then someone said it sounded like a shot. I trust that answers your question?'

'It could have been a pistol-shot?' Selby asked.

'I believe it could, Counsellor, but of course you understand that's merely a layman's opinion. I'm not an expert in such matters, and I didn't think it was at the time.'

'Since then there have been developments which make you think it was?'

'Let's put it this way,' Carr said. 'I believe that subsequent developments have indicated there was the sound of a gunshot at some time during the evening, but of course...'

Carr broke off and made a little gesture with his shoulders.

'Subsequently,' Selby inquired, 'Melvin asked you to go upstairs and assist a man who had been shot?'

Carr smiled. 'Subsequently, my dear Mr Selby, I went upstairs with Mr Melvin and Mr Granby. I found a man lying on the bed, who *said* that he had accidentally shot himself, but I did not actually *see* the wound. Melvin asked me to assist the man down to his car. And I did so.'

'Do you know this man? Do you know who he was?'

'Do you mean had I seen him before? Or did I know his name?'

'Either.'

'I had seen him before. I believe he'd been there at the party, but I don't know his name.'

'Why didn't you report that to the officers?'

'There was no need for me to do so.'

'Why didn't you tell me about it when you saw me coming out of Melvin's house?'

Carr merely smiled and shook his head.

'When you say you had seen this man before, you mean you had seen him there at the party?'

'Yes.'

'Had you seen him before that?'

Carr frowned. 'Now there, gentlemen,' he said, 'you are taking what I call an unfair advantage of your official position. I'm afraid that I can't answer that question without betraying the interests of some of my clients.'

Brandon said angrily: 'Isn't it a fact that there was a shot, that that was when Eve Dawson either shot herself or someone shot her, and Melvin came to you and told you he had to account for a pistol-shot in some way, and you got hold of this stooge of yours and...'

'Come, come, Sheriff!' Carr said. 'You're making rather extravagant accusations! You'd have to prove them, you know.'

'I'm asking you if it isn't a fact.'

186

Carr said: 'It's too absurd to even warrant a denial, Sheriff. And may I say parenthetically that I'm somewhat surprised at this attitude on your part, in view of the attempt I have made to co-operate with you. After all, I'd have been much better off, so far as my peace of mind is concerned, if I had remained away from the office and taken no steps whatever to see that you discovered where the fatal knife had been sold.

'In short, gentlemen, I come to you bearing an olive branch. You snatch it out of my hand and start belabouring me with it. So now, if you'll excuse me, I think I'll be on my way.'

'Just a minute,' Brandon said, 'we're not done with you yet.'

Carr turned, and his smile was frosty. 'Yes, you are, Sheriff,' he said quietly. 'In view of the aggressive, hostile and unfriendly attitude that your questioning has taken, I have no desire to remain and be insulted further. You have, of course, the right to see that I am subpœnaed and testify before the Grand Jury, but that is *all* you can do. If you have any more questions of me you'll ask them in front of a grand jury.

'Good afternoon, gentlemen.'

Sheriff Brandon sat for several seconds without moving, watching the door through which Carr had departed. 'That man makes my mane bristle, Doug. He's dangerously clever, and he's magnetic, but he has the same effect on me that seeing a rattlesnake has.'

187

Selby nodded. 'He sure knows what trumps are, and he always seems to hold a fistful.'

Brandon said: 'I'd like to tear off that suave mask of his—and, damn it, I'd like to smash him in the face. If I could only see him at a loss for words some time—if I could only see him become embarrassed!'

Selby said: 'He'll always be suave. He may be sardonic. He may be affable. He may get angry. But he'll always have poise. He'll always have complete assurance. He's skating on thin ice this time, however, and he knows it.'

'I get the feeling that he's patronising me, and then laughing up his sleeve all the time,' Brandon said.

'I think Carr knows that,' Selby observed. 'Carr is essentially an actor. He is, therefore, always conscious of his audience. He's always putting on an act for his listeners. You don't give a hang about an audience. The only act you put on is for yourself. You like people who are the same way.

'I can appreciate Carr because the man is such a consummate artist. But that doesn't keep me from appreciating the necessity of clipping his wings.'

'Clipping his wings! I'd wring his damned neck!'

'We may do that, too, Rex ... if we can get the breaks. Let's begin by calling in Bob Terry, your finger-print man, and testing *this* knife for finger-prints.'

Brandon looked at him with incredulous eyes. 'Test *that* knife for finger-prints?'

Selby nodded.

'Shucks,' Brandon said, 'of course you'll find Carr's finger-prints on that. Why, he handed the knife to us ... No, he didn't either, come to think of it. He just handed it to you in the paper package. But, even if you do find his prints on it, that won't mean anything, Doug, because he must have handled it when he was buying it there at Highdale. In any event, he could say he did.'

Selby said: 'I'm not interested in Carr's fingerprints.'

'Whose?' Brandon asked.

'I'd rather not say until I find out if I'm right,' Selby said.

'Well, we'll find out what's on there,' Brandon announced, pushing back his chair. 'I'll take it to Bob Terry.'

He reached for the knife.

Selby lunging forward, grabbed the sheriff's wrist. 'Don't touch it, Rex,' he pleaded.

Brandon looked at him as though Selby had suddenly developed some form of insanity. 'What the heck are you talking about?' he growled.

'I want the knife tested for latent finger-prints. I want it just the way it is,' Selby said.

'But *you* handled it, Doug.'

'I had to,' Selby said, 'to avoid arousing Carr's suspicions.'

Brandon stepped to the door of the side office, called out: 'Oh, Bob! Can you come in here for a minute with the finger-printing outfit?'

Bob Terry, the sheriff's deputy, who had by diligent application and study taught himself how to develop, examine and classify latents, entered the room.

Sheriff Brandon indicated the knife on the table. 'Go over it carefully, Bob, and let's see what's on there.'

Terry glanced curiously at the sheriff and the district attorney, but without a word started dusting the knife with powder.

'There are lots of finger-prints on here,' he said. 'The thing is simply full of them.'

'See if you can get two or three good ones,' Selby said.

'Okay, here's one, Mr Selby. Here's another—here's another. There are lots of them we can use if we have to.'

Selby said: 'All right. Now bring in an ink-pad and some paper, if you will, Bob.'

Terry left the office, returning in a moment with a slab covered with printer's ink and some paper.

Selby, tamping tobacco in his pipe, surveyed the sheriff with twinkling eyes. 'Now, Rex,' he said, 'if you'll let Bob take your finger-prints.'

'What the heck!' Brandon said irritably. 'What kind of a joke *is* this?'

'Just let him take your finger-prints,' Selby

190

said.

Brandon started to say something, changed his mind, and in tight-lipped silence let Terry take the fingerprints from his left and right hand.

'All right, Bob,' Selby said. 'Take a look at the latents that are on the knife. See if you find anything there that matches the sheriff's finger-prints.'

'*My* finger-prints!' Brandon exclaimed.

Selby nodded.

'Why, hang it, I didn't touch the knife. Don't you remember? You grabbed my hand and...'

'I know,' Selby said.

'How the heck can my prints be on the knife if I haven't touched it?'

Selby looked inquiringly at Bob Terry.

Bob Terry, examining the latents and checking with the sheriff's finger-prints, suddenly stiffened to attention. He looked back and forth between the knife and the paper.

'Gosh,' he said. 'I can't say for sure, but...'

'What is it, Bob?' Selby asked.

'This latent,' Terry said, indicating one of the latents on the knife, 'why, that's the imprint of the middle finger of Sheriff Brandon's right hand. It's as clear as day.'

'I thought it might be,' Selby said dryly. 'Now, Rex, you can get the whole picture.'

CHAPTER SIXTEEN

Doris Kane and her daughter sat down to dinner in the dining-room of the big house.

Outside, a windstorm was starting, and the hot desert wind, whipping at the branches of the trees, made weird noises as it sucked around the eaves of the old-fashioned house.

It was Thursday night and the spell of Monday night's tragic events still gripped the big house.

Jim Melvin had been called to attend a meeting of the City Council at Las Alidas, a semi-secret meeting which had been convened as a 'Committee of the Whole'. He had left in urgent haste, almost running to the garage. He might, he explained, not be back until the small hours. He promised he would telephone as soon as he knew definitely what was up. From all appearances, the City Council was ready to give serious consideration to the parking meter question.

Doris Kane had cooked most of the dinner, making the lemon meringue-pie that had always been Paula's favourite dessert, a roast leg of lamb with small bits of garlic and other seasonings carefully worked into slits that had been cut into the meat, the whole basted with a sauce made from garden-fresh mint leaves. The potatoes had been browned in with the roast.

The avocado and tomato salad had a dressing which Doris Kane had carefully compounded. This dinner Doris had hoped would have a soothing effect on Jim's jumpy nerves—and now he had rushed out.

Paula had made the cocktails and Paula, Mrs Kane realised, had made them strong. After her second cocktail she was having a hard time keeping her thoughts on the subject she was to take up with Paula.

Paula had had three drinks and was feeling them, but there was none of the usual carefree lack of tension. Instead, Paula was as nervous as a high-strung horse fighting a taut rein. Not until after they had finished with the lemon-pie and had started on their cigarettes did Mrs Kane realise that Paula was desperately trying to manipulate the conversation into a channel which would make what she wanted to say appear to be the casual outgrowth of the conversation. Mrs Kane tried to help her— anything would be better than this terrific tension. They talked about the housing shortage, about the wind, about how sounds were magnified and distorted during a windstorm, about how Paula had recently had some difficulty in distinguishing certain sounds.

And then Paula raised her eyes and said: 'Mother, if it weren't for your statement that you saw someone standing there in the door of the bathroom, and your intimation that this

193

person might have been an intruder, the authorities would write off Eve Dawson's death as a suicide and the whole thing would be finished. Now, under the circumstances, *I* think it is only fair that you give the matter a little more thought.'

'I have given it a lot of thought, Paula.'

'Perhaps too much.'

'Perhaps.'

'Mother, Jim feels absolutely positive that the person you saw standing in the door of the bathroom was Eve Dawson. She must have been trying to make up her mind to end it all. She was lonely and despondent and neurotic. She had been pestering you earlier in the evening because she was in need of human companionship. You were tired, thoroughly exhausted, and didn't want to talk. It's unfortunate you weren't awake enough to have talked with Eve Dawson that second time, because then she might have sat on your bed and talked the whole thing out with you and forgotten all about her suicidal impulses.'

'I don't think it was Eve Dawson whom I saw in the bathroom, Paula.'

'Who else could it have been? Who do you think it was?'

'I *think* it was the person who murdered Eve Dawson.'

'Mother!'

'You asked me, Paula.'

'But, Mother darling, can't you see that Eve

194

Dawson wasn't murdered?'

'What makes you think she wasn't?'

'It was suicide just as plain as can be.'

'Then who was it I saw standing there in the door of the bathroom?'

'It was Eve Dawson, Mother.'

'I don't think it was, Paula.'

'Well, of course, if you feel that way about it, I guess that's all there is to it.'

Doris Kane looked at her wrist-watch, said: 'Anyhow, Paula, my testimony can't make very much difference. I was drugged with sleep. I looked up and saw someone standing in the door. I couldn't waken myself sufficiently to get my eyes in focus. I must have gone back to sleep almost immediately.

'However, looking back on it, I have the distinct impression that there was something menacing in the person's attitude.'

'Of course, the fact that your senses were drugged with sleep may have made for a certain distortion in your memory.'

'Perhaps. Anyhow, Paula, I'm going to be on my way. You tell Jim good-bye again for me and I'll try and give you a little more notice when I come next time.'

Paula said abruptly: 'Mother, there's one thing I have to tell you.'

'What?'

Paula was silent for a moment, then said: 'About the reason you didn't hear from us. I can understand a lot of things now that I didn't know then. This Eve Dawson was despondent. She had been trying to kill herself. She must have shot herself there that night we had the party.'

'Or someone shot her.'

'Nonsense. She shot herself, and Jim and I simply had to take her and nurse her.'

'Why?'

'I can't go into all the reasons, but, anyway, that was the way it worked out. We came over here and moved in. We weren't supposed to let anyone know where we were.'

'Isn't Jim well known here in Las Alidas?'

'Oh yes, he's working on that parking meter device, but no one knew he was here. We kept absolutely under cover for the first week, then went out very occasionally after the doctor assured us the girl was out of danger. It was then Jim felt it was safe to go to the Madison City house and pick up the mail and some clothes, and do a few of the business things he had to do. Aside from one trip to the grocery store, I didn't so much as set foot out of the house for ten days.

'I wanted you to know, because that was the reason you didn't hear from me. I didn't get your letter, and the day before your birthday I gave Jim a wire to send as a night letter, and—well, I guess he either forgot it or—well, he thought that it wasn't safe to send it.'

'It's all right,' Doris said, smiling. 'I was unduly anxious, but when I didn't hear from

196

you, I had all sorts of visions of things that might have happened. Well, let's get the dishes done, Paula, and then I'll be on my way.'

'Mother, I hate to see you start at night.'

'I like to drive at night.'

'But not tonight, Mother. This wind is going to make it very difficult.'

Mrs Kane shook her head and smiled.

'Mother, you're leaving because you feel that Jim doesn't want you here, aren't you?'

'No, Paula, I came just to make sure you were all right. I was anxious to see you. I wanted to drop in and say hello. I've seen you now. I know that you're all right and there's no reason why I should stay on any longer.'

'But we want you.'

She smiled. 'I have other things to do, Paula, other irons in the fire, and I really should be getting back.'

'But why not wait at least until tomorrow morning? You can get an early start if you want to.'

'I like night driving. It's a lot easier.'

But neither woman made any move to leave the table. Abruptly, Doris Kane asked: 'Paula, does Jim like this work he's in now?'

'I think he does, Mother.'

'I suppose it's necessary to play a lot of politics in order to make these sales?'

'Apparently it is.'

Again there was an interval of silence, then Paula said: 'Mother, please believe me when I

197

tell you that I don't know all the details, but this Eve Dawson was wounded at that party we gave there in Madison City and the whole thing had to be hushed up. The neighbours had heard the sound of the shot.

'This lawyer, Mr Carr, took charge of things. He arranged it so there wouldn't be any scandal. Even the people who were at the party didn't know what had happened.'

'How did he do it, dear?'

'First he had to get Eve Dawson out of the house and to a place where she was safe. He got busy on the phone. This house here in Las Alidas was vacated on an hour's notice so we could move in. I don't know how it was arranged. All I know is that Carr got busy on the telephone. The wounded girl was taken over here. A doctor was called, and within two or three hours everything was under control.

'Then Carr arranged with some former client of his to be found on the bed in the spare bedroom and say that he had accidentally shot himself in the arm. He had a blood-stained towel wrapped around his arm and—well, that accounted for the shot.'

Mrs Kane remained silent. Her silence conveyed her disapproval.

'It was absolutely essential that no one knew Eve Dawson had been shot and that no one knew where she was,' Paula went on. 'We simply hibernated over here in this house. We didn't stir outside. The doctor came and visited

198

Eve Dawson, and after a while said she was out of danger. I'll admit I didn't like the whole thing, Mother, but it was a matter of business—a business that's vital to Jim's career.

'I rang up my maid and headed her off from cleaning the house in Madison City, but, for the time, we forgot about the mail. That's why we missed your letter. Jim went over and cleaned out the mail-box the night before you came. Then the next morning there was this cheque which came from Mr Carr, the cheque that was to compensate us for—well, for doing what we did.'

There was a moment of silence, then Paula asked: 'Do you blame Jim, Mother—very much?'

'I'm afraid I don't know all the circumstances,' Doris Kane said. 'I'm no longer responsible for you, Paula. You have only to be loyal to Jim—and yourself.'

Paula nodded emphatic approval, but her eyes were doubtful.

'The trouble with concealment,' Doris Kane went on, 'is that one can drift quite easily into the habit of deception. Deception has always been so utterly foreign to your nature that I dislike to think of a situation such as you have described, Paula, but...'

'But what was the harm? She had shot herself, and certainly nothing was going to be gained by having the newspapers get hold of

199

the sordid facts and do a lot of speculating...'

'Are you certain she shot herself?'

'Yes.'

'How do you know?'

'She told me so with her own lips.'

'You don't suppose that was simply part of what she had been instructed to say?'

'I think she was telling me the truth.'

'Did she say why she shot herself?'

'She was despondent.'

'Over what?'

'I don't know.'

'She shot herself with Jim's gun?'

'Yes, it was in the glove compartment of the motorcar.'

'Jim didn't shoot her?'

'Don't be silly, Mother, it was nothing like that at all. We took care of her. It was a business proposition. Carr sent us the cheque for our services—$750 a week. The letter that you saw from Carr in the mail-box was a cheque he sent us for $1,500 covering two weeks. Carr wouldn't have paid us if Jim had been mixed up in it in any way.'

'And Mr Carr furnished the house?'

'Yes.'

'Isn't this man, Carr, pretty deeply involved?'

'He's an attorney. He's representing a client.'

'And why should Mr Carr's client go to all that trouble and all that expense to keep it from being known that Eve Dawson had shot herself?'

'Don't you see, Mother, because it happened at one of Jim's parties. It was a lousy break for him. I was so angry with that girl when I heard of it—the utter stupidity of it! Going down to the garage and taking Jim's gun out of the glove compartment! Of course, I suppose she was two-thirds tight.'

'I still don't see why Mr Carr's client should part with so much money to...'

'Oh, he simply couldn't afford to have his name linked with what had happened. You know how newspapers are. They'd make something mysterious out of the shooting and want a list of the names of the persons who had been at the party.'

'Do you have any idea who this client is?'

'It might be more than one person, Mother. Several people were there, several very prominent people who wouldn't want to have their names connected with anything that could possibly have been worked up into a scandal.'

Doris Kane nodded.

'So you see,' Paula went on, speaking rapidly now and smiling anxiously at her mother, 'it was all very logical. But that's the reason we didn't answer your letter, and that's the reason Jim didn't send the telegram that I gave him to send you the day before your birthday. He thought it better not to. You see, we simply didn't dare go out of the house except on matters of extreme urgency. Shopping and things of that sort. If you could only understand Jim's business a little more, Mother. He has all sorts of things on his mind, all sorts of responsibilities and worries, and—well, he simply must protect the people—the big-shots whom we have to entertain.'

'Can't you sell a device like this parking meter simply on its merits?'

'Heavens, no! Not when you're dealing with politicians. Sometimes there's less entertainment than other times. You see, Jim is trying to get started. This device is way ahead of anything else on the market because there are no periods of dead time. The minute a person takes a car out of the parking place, the meter goes back to zero and the next person has to pay for whatever time he's there. But we need to get it started in one or two cities so we can have something to point to, some record of performance.'

'Well, I'm quite certain, Paula, that Jim is thoroughly capable of running his business and knowing what is best for you and for him. Only, any sort of deceit has been *so* utterly foreign to your nature. You have always been so frank and...'

She was interrupted by the sound of the telephone.

The alacrity with which Paula jumped from the table to run to the telephone showed that she welcomed the interruption.

She talked spiritedly for a few moments, then hung up, returned to the table and said to Doris Kane: 'It's Jim, Mother. He wants some papers right away. He's up at a secret meeting of the City Council. He told me to get a taxi and bring the papers up right away. But I'm going to have trouble getting a taxi, and I thought that perhaps...'

'Why, certainly,' Mrs Kane said, 'take my station wagon, Paula. Here are the keys.'

'I'll be back in a jiffy, Mother. Don't bother with the dishes. Just stack them, and then if you insist on leaving, you can be all ready to go when I get back. It won't be long.'

Mrs Kane smiled indulgently. 'Don't worry, dear. Just run along.'

Paula rushed up the stairs to her bedroom and within two minutes was down again, out of the back door, and then Doris Kane heard the sound of the motor starting on the station wagon, the sound of the car backing out of the driveway. Then there was only the big lonesome house and the sound of the wind in the trees.

Doris Kane cleared the table, then washed and dried the dishes. There was no sign of Paula, no call from her.

Mrs Kane sat down to wait, and as she waited, the noises made by the wind became louder, seemed somehow more sinister.

CHAPTER SEVENTEEN

Doris Kane realised that this hot, dry wind was filling her with a strange restlessness. Her nerves were taut and jumpy. The bookshelves on each side of the fireplace, which ordinarily would have seemed so inviting, now held no appeal for her.

She walked over to the window, pulled the curtains to one side and tried to look out, but the light behind her enabled her to get only an indistinct glimpse of the moonlit yard.

She walked back and switched off the lights in the living-room, then returned to the window. The moon, slightly past the full, was flooding the yard with long shadows, and touching the trees with silvery highlights.

Everywhere was motion. The violent wind, dry and hot, whipped the tree branches, turned the fronds of a tall palm tree into glistening silver.

The steady ominous sound got on Doris's nerves. She sympathised with the trees, her imagination conjuring up a conscious resistance, as though the trees were waving their branches not with the wind, but against it, trying to fight it back; but the irresistible rush of dry air made the gesture one of empty futility.

Standing there in the dark room, looking out

at the alternate stretches of moonlight and shadow on the yard, Doris Kane began to think about Eve Dawson's death.

The living-room was directly under the room where the murder had been committed. The killer had been very, very sure of himself. He or she must have known the house well.

He probably did not know that Doris Kane had come to visit her daughter, that she was sleeping in the bedroom which adjoined the front room where Eve Dawson had been killed. Aside from that, however, the murderer must have been very sure of every move that was made. The mere fact that he expected to find no one in the other bedroom indicated a knowledge of the house and its tenants.

Had it been a man? Had perhaps the person who had shot Eve Dawson returned to finish the job which had been bungled that night of the party in Madison City?

Abruptly, Doris Kane's breath was sucked in with a gasp of startled apprehension—one of the shadows in the yard was moving.

She stood in the window, motionless, frozen with the realisation of her own helplessness, waiting. The shadow moved again, and this time she saw the bulk of a dark figure moving surreptitiously along the yard.

A moment more and she saw the white gleam of a flashlight. Then the man was bending low over the ground and the beam of the flashlight was moving back and forth in a short zig-zag on the ground directly beneath. The crouched figure came slowly towards the house. Whoever it was was completely absorbed in the search he was making.

Nearer and nearer the house came the light, shielded as much as possible by the crouching figure.

Doris realised that the light was following a sort of predetermined pattern. Apparently the intruder had entered at the south-east corner of the property, at the side of the garage, and had followed along by the big hedge which bordered the adjoining lot. Then he angled directly towards the front door.

So engrossed was Doris Kane in watching the motion of the man with the light, that for the moment she failed to anticipate what must be his obvious ultimate destination if he continued his present course.

When that realisation did suddenly crash home to her consciousness and she comprehended the fact that a few more yards and he would be on the front porch, she stood rooted to the spot, too startled for the moment to think clearly.

Then she resolved on a course of conduct. She would not answer the bell, but she would tiptoe to the telephone and summon help. But what help could she summon? Not the police, surely. Jim would never forgive her for that. Nor could she phone either Jim or Paula. They were at a meeting somewhere—a secret meeting of the City Council.

Then the obvious course occurred to her. She would simply turn on the lights. That would warn the intruder that there was somebody home. And she would telephone the residence of the city clerk, explain who she was, and ask him where she could reach Jim on the phone.

The house was still somewhat unfamiliar. Enough moonlight came through the parted curtains over the big living-room window, from which Doris had been watching the prowler, to enable her to avoid furniture. The telephone, unfortunately, was in the front hall, and, once there, she'd snap on the lights as she picked up the phone, and...

She became rigid. Not only were there sounds on the front steps, but there was the scrape of metal against metal, as though the man might be trying to pick the lock.

For a half second, Doris Kane hesitated. Then she plunged boldly towards the telephone. No matter what Jim thought, she wasn't going to stand for *this*. She would scream, if necessary. She...

The latch lock clicked back. The front door swung quietly open. The figure was standing there, silhouetted against the moonlight.

In that moment Doris Kane thought something was going to burst within her. Her lungs all but refused to function. Her heart was pounding so fast the beats seemed to overlap.

Then the lights switched on.

Seeing the ludicrous dismay on the man's face, Doris was for the moment heartened, but she still wasn't certain whether she could trust her voice for just the right intimation of cold disapproval.

She mustered her courage, said: 'I *beg* your pardon!'

The man's right hand no longer held the flashlight. It went in swift motion to his head, removed the hat and that simple, instinctive gesture was all that Doris Kane needed to send reassurance flooding through her veins like some heady stimulant.

'Will you please explain the meaning of this?'

The man smiled apologetically; then he laughed, low, rich laughter, and said: 'Of course! You're Mrs Kane. You're Paula Melvin's mother.'

'That still does not explain your reason for entering this house.'

His laugh was hearty. 'I'm Hudson Parlin,' he said. 'Jim's boss.'

He said 'Jim's boss' as though feeling certain that the words would cause a melting of Doris Kane's icy reserve, but she was not ready as yet to surrender her advantage.

'That still doesn't account for your manner in entering this house.'

His laugh died away. He was frowning annoyance now. 'Come, come, I'd entirely forgotten about you. That is, about you being *here*. Jim's on a job, pinch-hitting for me, and he telephoned Paula to join him. He thought you'd left immediately after dinner. At least he told me those were your plans. Then, ten or fifteen minutes after Paula left the house, Jim remembered certain additional papers that we simply had to have. I didn't dare to let him break away from the meeting. They're trying to undermine us there. One of the rival companies is questioning the validity of our patents and a few other things, threatening to bring injunction suits and all the rest of it, so I told Jim to give me his key and I'd go pick up the papers. The house was dark, and I had no idea you were here; I guess I gave you a scare. I'm sorry.'

She said: 'I had intended to leave immediately after dinner, but when Jim telephoned for Paula to join him, I insisted Paula take my car. Naturally, Jim thought I wasn't here.'

It was all so simple, so absurd for her to be frightened, so matter-of-fact an explanation, that her attitude seemed old-fashioned and melodramatic. She was shaking all over with nervousness.

She found she was the one now who was apologising. 'After all,' she heard herself saying, 'in view of what has happened here ... Well, you can understand...'

'Perfectly!' he exclaimed heartily. 'That

209

suicide must have upset you. I certainly should have tried the bell before I came in. I just never thought of it. I was so certain the house was empty, and these papers that we need are so important, that I just came barging on in.'

'Well, don't let me detain you. Go right ahead and get them.'

'Thank you.'

He walked past her into the living-room, said: 'I'll have to switch on the lights. I suppose the house was dark because you were just getting ready to go upstairs.'

She didn't answer that question.

The light switch clicked on in the living-room. For a moment he stood puzzled, looking at the window where the curtains had been drawn back.

He paused, standing near the light switch.

'Why *were* the lights out?' he asked.

She said: 'The wind made me nervous. I felt like a cat on a back fence. I switched out the lights and went over to stand at the window, and then...'

Her throat suddenly contracted so that the cords choked off.

The numbing fear that had heretofore been in her mind came surging back. This was the man who had been so surreptitiously searching the grounds, who had been bent over shielding his flashlight, who...

'You were standing at this window?' he asked casually, almost *too* casually.

She made no answer. There was no answer she could make.

He said: 'Well, let's have some more light.'

She saw his hand reach towards the wall, heard the click of the light switch as the room was plunged into darkness, leaving only the light in the reception hallway which he had switched on when he had entered the room.

He said: 'My dear girl, you're all upset,' and moved towards her.

She knew she was screaming. She dashed towards the front door, conscious of the steps behind her.

She struggled with the knob—the door, of course, opened inwards—the steps were almost on her.

She screamed again, a wild, terror-distorted scream that was so shrill it cut her own ear-drums.

CHAPTER EIGHTEEN

Doris Kane's fear-numbed fingers struggled with the door-knob.

Hands of iron gripped her shoulders from behind, jerked her away from the door and back into the hallway.

As the hands jerked her back, however, she managed to twist the knob so that she unlatched the door. The wind did the rest. The wind whipped the door open with a bang.

A big car was parked at the kerb just outside the house. Doug Selby and Rex Brandon were coming up the walk towards the front door and were within a distance of some fifteen feet of Doris Kane as the wind banged the door open and disclosed the two figures in the lighted hallway.

Parlin said: 'Madam, please calm yourself. Good heavens, what's the matter?'

'Let me go! Let me go!' she screamed at him.

Selby and Brandon ran forward.

'You're hysterical; you'll hurt yourself,' Parlin said. 'Please be reasonable. Can't you tell me what's wrong?'

'Break it up,' Rex Brandon said, pushing forward belligerently. 'What's the idea?'

'The woman,' Parlin said, 'seems to have gone completely crazy. I was talking with her, when all of a sudden she screamed and made a rush for the door. I didn't know whether it was hysterics, or whether she had gone suddenly insane. I tried to remonstrate with her, but she got the door opened, and if I hadn't restrained her, I really believe, gentlemen, she would have rushed screaming out into the night. Perhaps she can tell us what it is. Apparently something has frightened her to the point of hysteria.'

Doris Kane felt grateful that Parlin's explanation had given her a chance to collect her senses. After all, this man was Jim Melvin's boss. He could now tell his story to the officers, and perhaps in telling his story he would trap himself. If he did, there was no need for her to make any accusation: If he didn't, she could tell her story to the officers in private.

Selby turned inquiringly to her. 'What is it, Mrs Kane?'

She laughed nervously, and was alarmed to notice the note of hysteria that crept into that laughter, despite her effort to make it appear well modulated and thoroughly sane. 'I'm afraid,' she said, 'that what Mr Parlin says is all too true. I'm *terribly* jumpy. I am particularly nervous tonight.'

'It's the wind,' Brandon said. 'These hot, dry winds will do it to sensitive people every time.'

She led the way back to the living-room, smiled at him gratefully. 'The wind, I suppose, has something to do with it, and the events of the past few days. I was alone here in the house and Mr Parlin called . . .'

'A most unfortunate occurrence,' Parlin hastened to explain. 'I thought, of course, the house was empty. Jim Melvin and his wife are out doing some work for me. I had to have some papers, and I didn't want to send Jim for them because Jim is up to his neck in a conference. So I borrowed his key and came out here to pick up the patent papers. He told me where to find them. I was using my flashlight to find my way to the door. The house was all dark and . . .'

'I'd turned out the lights and was looking

213

out at the moonlight,' Mrs Kane explained.

Parlin smiled indulgently. 'I had turned on one of the light switches,' he explained to the officers, 'and then when I started to snap on the other, I made a mistake and turned off the one I had already turned on. Mrs Kane screamed and started for the door.'

Brandon frowned. 'You unlocked the door and opened it without knocking?'

'I confess I did,' Parlin said. 'I had no idea anyone was home. Both Jim and I thought Mrs Kane had started back home.'

'I had intended to,' Doris Kane said, 'but because Jim was away and Paula here alone, I was in no hurry to get started.'

Brandon said: 'Well, we wanted to look the place over a little more and ... by the way, Parlin, where did you leave your car?'

Parlin hesitated for just a fraction of a second, then said: 'Around the next block. I came down the alley and cut through across the lawn.'

'Why?' Selby asked.

Parlin laughed. 'To tell you the truth, I am not familiar with the streets here. I got on the wrong street, then, when I realised my mistake, felt I could run through the alley and save time, after all. And if you gentlemen will pardon me, this brings to my mind the extreme urgency of my visit and the necessity for haste. I want to get those patent papers and get back to the conference as soon as I can. There's an attempt being made to sabotage everything I've accomplished by the claim that my patents are not sufficiently broad. I have copies of my patents and a letter from one of the best patent attorneys in the country.

'Perhaps,' Parlin said to Mrs Kane, 'you can show me where Jim's bedroom is. He told me he left the papers in the bureau drawer.'

'Right this way,' Doris Kane said, and started firmly up the stairs, praying that her knees would not buckle and let her fall ignominiously, sensing that for some reason Selby was appealing to her for her co-operation.

Brandon turned to Selby: 'What's the idea, Doug?'

Selby said in a low voice: 'Take it easy, Rex. There's something going on here. Mrs Kane isn't the type to get as jittery as she claims she did, unless there was some reason for it. Let's just stand here and wait.'

'I don't get it,' Brandon said, frankly puzzled.

'You're sure he was in Los Angeles the night of the murder?' Selby asked.

'Gosh, yes, Doug. I talked again with the lawyer in that car accident case. As it happens, he's a man I was able to get a line on. One we can trust. He says Parlin was standing within fifty feet of the crash and saw the whole thing, describes it minutely and is willing to testify. The accident was at precisely ten minutes past one.'

'Then,' Selby said, 'Parlin is looking for some evidence, something the murderer must have left, or dropped, or—Rex, that spectacle case!'

'What about it?'

'Granby dropped that *in your office* the night of the murder. But Granby has never said a word about it. Suppose he didn't miss it until Tuesday morning, and suppose he thinks he dropped it here! And suppose Parlin knows about it.'

Brandon whistled.

'Of course,' Selby went on, 'that, by itself, won't convict him of murder. As Carr pointed out, a man *could* have visited Eve Dawson, and then left, but ... hang it, Rex, that must be it. Where is that spectacle-case, Rex?'

'In the glove compartment of the county car.'

'Sneak out and get it,' Selby said.

Doris Kane led the way with calm confidence down the upstairs corridor, said: 'Here's their room, the one over here on the right.'

Parlin moved over and held the door open for her. 'Would you mind waiting?' he asked.

'Not at all.'

She switched on the lights. Parlin walked over to the dresser, opened the upper right-hand drawer, rummaged through a pile of papers, and then emerged with a copy of a

216

patent and a letter written on the embossed stationery of a law firm.

'These are the ones,' he said, smiling.

'I'm glad you found them.'

He stood near her, said: 'Jim Melvin is a very nice boy. I have plans for him, Mrs Kane. I think you ought to be congratulated on your son-in-law. I intend to give him every opportunity to advance. As you no doubt know, he has a substantial interest in this *Karpay* device. There is an additional bonus that is to be turned over to him under certain conditions. A very substantial stock interest.'

'I'm glad to hear it,' she said.

And now he was smiling quizzically at her. 'So will you please tell me what's so terrible about me? Should I see my dentist, or am I just repulsive to you?'

'Why, I...'

'Yes, go on.'

'I don't know what you mean.'

'Yes, you do. I've never had any delusions of grandeur, but neither did I think that mine was a face to frighten little children.'

He was so charming now, so quizzical in his self-appraisal that she found her nervousness leaving her. She was laughing with him in spite of herself.

'The truth is,' she said, 'I'm terribly upset tonight. I think the wind makes me nervous, and thinking back on the thing that happened in this house—well, I'm afraid I put a wrong interpretation on...'

'Wait a minute,' he interrupted, cocking an incredulous eyebrow. 'You don't possibly mean that you thought I...'

She nodded.

For a moment he was indignant, and then he threw back his head and laughed uproariously. 'Wait until I tell Jim!'

She went towards him, putting out her hand, her fingers resting pleadingly on his arm. 'No, no, please,' she said. '*Please* don't tell Jim!'

'Then you'll have to pay a forfeit.' He dropped his bantering tone and his voice took on a note of appeal. 'Mrs Kane, would you do something for me?'

She laughed nervously, touching her hair. 'That depends.'

'Will you look around here to try and find something for me?'

'But I'm not going to be here; I'm leaving almost immediately.'

'No!' he said incredulously. 'You just came. You can't leave Paula like that, and you can't leave me.'

Her determination showed in manner and voice. 'I'm going within the next hour, as soon as Paula gets back with my car.'

'Oh, look here, Mrs Kane, give a fellow a chance. Stay on for two more days and give me a dinner date tomorrow. I know a place where...'

'No, I'm leaving.'

He studied her, saw her determination, asked: 'Do I get your address?'

'Why?'

'I'm going east within the next thirty days. I want to stop off for that dinner date.'

'We haven't any.'

'Oh yes, we have. It's in escrow.'

'We'll talk about that later. What was it you wanted me to look for?'

She felt him tighten. 'Just a small object—but if you're not going to be here you can't help.'

'Why don't you ask Jim or Paula or...'

'I may have to, but I'd hoped you could do it.'

'But you didn't know I was here until after you walked in.'

He laughed. 'Yes, Miss Prosecuting Attorney, but I didn't expect to have to hunt for it until after I found it wasn't on the lawn—oh well, skip it.'

'But what is it? What's so important about it?'

Parlin said: 'It belongs to a person who was here Monday night. I think it must have been dropped when—well, I think he had an appointment with Eve Dawson. I'm trying to check on it and find out. If I can find this particular object, I think it would help.'

'What makes you think he left it here?'

'Because I know he's lost it somewhere, and I know he's very much upset about it, trying to find out where he lost it, thinking back and cudgelling his brain.'

'And suppose I should find it and give it to you, then what?'

He laughed. 'You can't. You won't be here.'

'You think this "object" has something to do with the murder of Eve Dawson?'

He slid his arm around her shoulder. 'It may prove to be a clue. But let's not call it a murder, at least as yet. It would be a lot better for Jim, for all of us, if we could let it appear Eve Dawson committed suicide. And, after all, it isn't going to bring her back to life to hatch a lot of scandal. However, if we can once get proof as to who did it—a confession, perhaps, then it would be a different story. We wouldn't mind a clean-cut murder trial. It's the probing and poking in the dark that's dangerous. Eve was playing around with some politicians, and they're all scared stiff.'

'Of what?'

'Of publicity.'

'And one of them killed her?'

'Don't be silly. A politician wouldn't kill anyone. A politician talks. He perpetuates himself in office by talk. He will denounce, he will accuse, he will raise his voice in righteous accusation, but he hasn't the guts to kill.'

'Then who did kill her?'

'Someone who had nothing to do with our crowd.'

'You're certain?'

'Yes.'

'Then you must know who did it.'

Doug Selby called out from downstairs: 'Finding what you want up there?'

'We've just located it,' Parlin said. 'Coming right down.'

He bestowed a reassuring pat on Doris Kane's shoulder. 'Now look, beautiful, you and I have a date. Some time within the next three weeks I'll be seeing you. And remember, our interests are exactly the same in this case. I'm going to try my best to put across the idea of suicide, but if it should turn out to have been a murder, then I'm going to try to put evidence in the hands of the officers that will point to the killer.'

She walked towards the stairs with him, his hand on her arm. 'The officers aren't going to fall for that suicide idea.'

His laugh was vibrant with assurance. 'Don't make any mistake about those boys. They'll pull in their horns. The foreman of the Grand Jury is going to put enough pressure on them to crush a steel safe. You mark my words, the Grand Jury won't touch an investigation of Eve Dawson's death with a ten-foot pole.'

'But can't the district attorney go ahead with proceedings of his own if he feels someone is guilty and ...'

Parlin placed his palm underneath her elbow as he assisted her down the stairs.

'Not after the Grand Jury tells him to mind

his own business and not try to get notoriety by torturing a suicide into a murder.'

'That seems dreadfully unfair.'

'Sure it's unfair, but that's the way politics are played ... Well, thanks a lot, Mrs Kane,' Parlin said, raising his voice as they encountered Sheriff Brandon and Doug Selby in the reception hallway. 'I couldn't have found it without your help—how are things coming, Sheriff, okay?'

'Okay,' Brandon said.

'If I can be of any assistance, let me know.'

Selby said: 'There was one thing we wanted to check up on, Mrs Kane. It will only take a few minutes. I'm wondering if you...' He glanced at Parlin.

'I'm on my way,' Parlin said. 'Got to rush these papers up to the conference.'

He turned, extended his hand to Mrs Kane. He was smiling at her. His eyes, somewhat wistful, seemed to exclude every other person in the room except Doris.

'Within three weeks,' he said.

He bowed to Brandon and Selby and opened the front door. A blast of wind fluttered the papers in his hand, blew into the house, billowing the curtains over the windows. Then he had pulled the door shut and they heard his running steps crossing the lawn on the side of the house.

'What frightened you so?' Selby asked Doris Kane.

She laughed: 'I'm absolutely the world's worst ninny, Mr Selby.'

'I'm not so satisfied that you are.'

'I know that I am now.'

'Tell me about it.'

She said: 'I was standing here with the lights off, looking out across the lawn, then I saw him in the moonlight—a dark shadow, and he was crossing the lawn with a flashlight. I didn't know, of course, who it was, and I stood here wondering what to do. Then, without any warning whatever, he had opened the front door.'

'I understand that,' Selby said, 'but there must have been something else.'

'That was enough. Of course, Jim thought I had gone, and he had already telephoned Paula to bring some papers, and then afterwards remembered that he had to have still additional papers. He'd given his key to Parlin and asked him to run up here and get them. It's all simple enough when you understand the facts.'

'Except for two or three things,' Brandon broke in. 'For one thing, why did Parlin leave his motor-car in the next block and cross the lawn? What was he looking for?'

She said: 'I want to be frank about this. I don't want to keep things from you, but—well, you must understand that my son-in-law is working for Mr Parlin and I—well, after all, I'm one of the family.... Sheriff, would it help if I should tell you that he had confided in me and

I know that ... well, everything is explained now.'

'What terrified you?' Selby asked.

She laughed outright at that and said: 'The man was making a pass at me, but in my muddled, nervous state I thought he was coming towards me, intending to choke me. I could see he had me listed in his mind as tonight's target, and I wasn't in the mood to be bombarded.'

Selby smiled, said: 'You had quite a conversation after you got upstairs.'

'Yes, he was explaining to me—well, you know, what had happened and—well, he tried to get our relationship on a more personal basis.'

'Forward pass?' Selby asked.

'He didn't make any yardage, but he was trying to make a pass.'

'And did he tell you anything else?'

She hesitated.

'You've played fair with us so far,' Selby reminded her.

'Please don't ask me that question, Mr Selby. I talked with him about something that—well, I'm quite certain he'd want to have it kept confidential. He was looking for something.'

'What?'

She said: 'Frankly, Mr Selby, I don't know. You understand I'm leaving.'

'When?'

'Immediately. Just as soon as Paula gets back with my car. I'm all packed.'

Selby slowly shook his head.

'What do you mean?'

'That's not so good.'

'But I have to get out. My presence here is irritating Jim and...'

'You'll have to be a witness sooner or later.'

'When?'

'I can't tell you exactly when it will be. It may be some time soon if we go before the Grand Jury.'

'I'll come back. You have my word on that, but I simply cannot stay here. It's not fair to Paula. It's not fair to me.'

'There's one thing we want before we go,' Brandon said. 'We want you to go to your room, lie on your bed, relax as much as possible, and then when one of us comes through the other door and stands in the door which connects with your bedroom from the bathroom, you can perhaps give us some additional information.'

'In what way?'

'You can tell whether it was a man or a woman who was standing there.'

She shook her head. 'I can try, but I doubt if it will do any good.'

'Well, we'll try, anyway,' Selby said, 'if you can give us a few minutes.'

'Certainly. I'm waiting for Paula to bring my car back, and I'll be only too glad to do what I can.'

She led the way up the stairs.

'Now then,' Selby said, 'can you fix the lights just about the way they were the night Eve Dawson was killed?'

'Yes, I think I can. This room was dark, and there was light in the bathroom ... no, wait a minute. I don't think it was the bathroom light that was on. I think a light was on in Eve Dawson's bedroom, and then the door between her bedroom and the bath was open, and I saw the figure standing in the bathroom, silhouetted against that somewhat diffused light.'

'All right,' Selby said, 'you try and fix the doors so that the illumination is about the same as it was when you looked up and saw the figure.'

She went over to the bed, changed the position of the bathroom door once or twice, then, leaving it half open, worked on the door of the room where Eve Dawson had been sleeping.

'Now I think I have it about right. I think that's just about the way the illumination was when I wakened there at night.'

Selby said: 'The door between the bath and Eve Dawson's room is about half open. The door to your bathroom is about half open.'

'That's right.'

'Now lie down and relax. I want to see if you can tell us anything about the figure that stood

226

there in the doorway.'

Doris Kane stretched herself out on the bed.

'Close your eyes,' Selby said, 'and then open them just part way.'

'I'm ready,' she said.

'All right. Now I'm going to come through from the bedroom and stand in the door of the bathroom.'

There was only one light on in Eve Dawson's bedroom, the reading-lamp over the bed. Selby, tiptoeing through to the bathroom, moved slowly across to the door of Doris Kane's bedroom.

'How's this?' he asked.

'No,' she said, 'I can see your profile. The figure was standing so that his face was towards me. That made it silhouetted against the light and...'

'Wearing a hat?' Selby asked.

'No, there was no hat.'

'Standing about like this?'

'That's right.'

'And then he turned back?'

'Yes, but quickly, so I couldn't see his face. He ... wait!' she said. 'I remember something now! Why, isn't it strange! It never occurred to me before, but I can remember it now as plain as can be.'

'What?' Selby asked.

'Boots,' she said. 'The man had on high-heeled cowboy boots, and when he was standing—just the way you're standing now,

227

Mr Selby, I remember light coming through from the heels of the cowboy boots.'

'Not a woman wearing high-heeled shoes?' Selby asked.

'No, no, Mr Selby. They were regular cowboy boots, with the heels pushed forward.'

From the drive-way came the sound of a melodious horn.

Doris Kane said: 'Oh, that's Paula. She's back with my car.'

Selby said quickly: 'Say nothing about this to anyone, Mrs Kane. We'll all go downstairs and meet your daughter when she comes in. We'll tell her we were making a routine check.'

They moved rapidly down the stairs and were in the reception hall when feet sounded on the porch outside. Paula Melvin called: 'Yoo hoo, Mother,' and fitted her latch-key to the door.

As the door opened, a gust of wind swept into the corridor. Paula Melvin entered and, immediately behind her, Milton Granby turned back to wrestle the door shut.

Paula said: 'Milton Granby came home with me and . . .'

She broke off as she saw the county officials.

Selby said: 'Good evening, Mrs Melvin. We were just checking up on some measurements.'

'Oh, hello. My husband isn't here. He's at a very important meeting.'

'Yes. Mrs Kane let us in.'

'Did you—do you have everything you

want?'

Selby nodded. 'I think so.'

Milton Granby said: 'Some wind outside. What's new, anything?'

'Nothing much,' Brandon said.

Paula Melvin was talking rapidly: 'Mr Granby didn't want me to come home alone, Mother. He said he'd drive home with me; and then when you left, you could drive him back and leave him up-town.'

'We're going back that way,' Brandon said. 'You can come with us, Granby.'

Granby hesitated.

'Well, come on in and have a drink or something,' Paula said. 'Let's not stand here.'

She led the way into the living-room, talking over her shoulder as she switched on lights. 'Jim's having quite a time up there. His competitors have claimed his patents are invalid and the city can be sued for infringement if it installs Jim's device. I guess you thought we had a procession coming after papers, Mother. Mr Parlin said you were very nice, helping him get those other papers Jim sent for.'

'He got the right ones all right?'

'Yes. He arrived just as we were leaving.'

Granby said importantly: 'Well, I don't think the competition's going to get anywhere using dirty tactics like that. Now, of course, I'm not an official member of the trustees, but my brother-in-law certainly drags some

229

influence around here, and I know *him* well enough to know how *he* feels.'

Paula flashed him a grateful glance.

'Well,' Sheriff Brandon said, 'we're on our way. Want to come with us, Granby?'

Granby hesitated, apparently trying to find some tactful way of refusing the invitation, then said: 'That's fine. Thanks. I'll ride along.'

Paula smiled graciously. 'Thanks ever so much, Milton!'

'Not at all. Don't mention it.'

The three men said good night and pushed their way out into the wind. Granby, walking across to the county car and said: 'Well, I've fixed things all up for Jim Melvin. He's really hit the inside track now.'

'That's fine,' Brandon said dryly. 'Where did you want to go?'

'Up to the city hall. They're having the secret meeting up there.'

'Who is?'

'Not a *secret* meeting,' Granby corrected himself hurriedly. 'It's a committee of the whole, just for the purpose of having a more informal discussion.'

'Hop in,' Brandon said.

The big county car swung around the corner, then doubled back towards the centre of town at the next block.

Granby started to say something, then caught himself just before the words were uttered, and lapsed into silence.

The sheriff drove the car without a word to the Las Alidas city hall.

'Looks as though you have quite a gathering here,' he said. 'Lots of cars parked in front.'

'They're having a confab,' Granby said, 'but everything's all right,' and then added self-importantly: 'I should be in a position to know.'

'You should be,' Brandon agreed.

'Well, good night. Thanks a lot.'

'Good night.'

Brandon turned on the red spotlight on the county car, started the needle of the speedometer quivering up into the higher speeds.

Brandon said musingly: 'Cowboy boots.'

Selby said: 'That probably means someone from Madison City, someone who was dressed for the celebration.'

'Hang it!' Brandon said. 'I keep thinking of old A. B. Carr.'

'And somehow *I* keep thinking of Carr,' Selby said. 'We can involve him in that knife deal, Rex. What happened is pretty well subject to proof. Eleanor Harlan had a knife in her apartment. And that must have been the knife that was used as a murder weapon. Carr wanted to keep us from finding that out. He found out that the price mark and cost code mark were still on the blade of the fatal knife. He knew that eventually we'd trace the knife from that. He wanted to beat us to it.

'He rushed to Highdale, bought the only knife Kittson had left, then telephoned us from Fresno, stating that he had it and would deliver it to us some time the next day, but Carr didn't stay in Fresno. He must have rushed to Los Angeles, and planted that knife in the suitcase in Eleanor Harlan's apartment.

'When we went to Eleanor Harlan's apartment, she produced the knife for us and you handled it. She refused to let us take it.

'Then, the next day, Carr brought us a knife which he said was the same knife he had purchased at Tom Kittson's hardware store, and he had the sales slip to prove it. But that knife was exactly the same knife we had previously inspected in Eleanor Harlan's apartment. The things can be proved mathematically by the fact that your own finger-prints were on the knife.'

Brandon said: 'I tipped Sylvia Martin off, and she's covering Eleanor Harlan's apartment, trying to get an interview. As soon as she gets it, she'll notify us.'

'The opposition newspaper will squawk that we're giving Sylvia all the breaks,' Selby said, smiling.

'Let them squawk! Sylvia and *The Clarion* are entitled to all the breaks ... Hey, what's this car ahead? It's throwing a spotlight in our eyes. Watch out, Doug! You can't tell just what it ... Wait a minute, they're signalling us.'

'It's Sylvia Martin!' Selby exclaimed as the

sheriff pulled to one side of the road, tugging at his gun.

'Hanged if it isn't,' Brandon said. 'I thought that someone was going to try to crowd us into the ditch.'

Brandon brought his car to a stop.

Sylvia Martin jumped out of her car, came across to stand by the sheriff's machine, her hair blowing out from under the hat she was desperately holding with her right hand while she fought her wind-whipped skirts with her left.

'Thank heavens I've found you!' she said. 'No one seemed to know just where you were. Then someone gave me the lead that you might have gone over to Las Alidas.'

'What is it?' Selby asked.

'Eleanor Harlan,' she said. 'She took an overdose of sleeping pills.'

'Who found her?' Selby asked.

'I did, Doug. Sheriff Brandon tipped me off that I could get a story there. I tried phoning and got no answer. I kept watch on the door of the apartment house. After a while I skirmished around and located the window of her apartment. There was a light on. Then I used a ruse to get through the outer door, went up to her apartment and knocked. She didn't open the door, but I could see lights were on through the transom. I had a hunch something might be wrong. I wanted most desperately to look inside that apartment, Doug. I went to the

233

building superintendent and got him to go with me and open the door.

'She was lying there on the bed. There was a bottle of sleeping-pills about half empty, some pills spilled over the floor.'

'No note?' Selby asked.

'Nothing. Just the sleeping-pills and the girl lying there half undressed on the bed, her face dark, and her breathing very shallow.'

'Good work, Sylvia,' Brandon said. 'What happened? Is she alive?'

Sylvia said: 'Yes, she's alive. I'm trembling all over. I took a chance. I wanted to get that girl's story and—well, anyway, here's the way it happened. I entered her apartment, and it was quite evident she'd taken an enormous dose of some sleeping medicine. Well, I remembered Dr Deming. He's about the only doctor I know in the city, but he's really a good one. Well, I rushed over to the telephone and, as luck would have it, I caught him at home. I asked him if he could come at once.

'The building superintendent took it for granted that I was some sort of a close friend or relative, and, as soon as I called the doctor and told him to come at once, the building superintendent stepped out of the picture.

'Dr Deming came and said there wasn't a minute to waste. I'd told him over the phone what it was all about, and he pumped out her stomach, administered some stimulants, and we worked over her for about an hour, I guess.

And then she began to come to.

'The point is, she's groggy from the medicine, but she has some sort of a talking jag. Dr Deming says they sometimes give this drug, sodium amytal, to make people talk, because it makes them too drowsy to be on their guard, but they can still talk.

'It's positively shameful the way I took advantage of that woman. I started asking her questions, and then I asked her why she had tried to commit suicide, and she said she hadn't. She seemed very much surprised to think that anyone would have thought she had. She said she must have been drugged.'

'Doesn't she know who drugged her?' Selby asked.

'Not unless it was in the candy. It seems Milton Granby called on her late this afternoon and wanted her to leave the country. He brought her a box of candy. It seems she knows something he doesn't want to have come out. Gosh, she's talking a blue streak right now, and I was so afraid you wouldn't get there in time.'

'She thinks Granby drugged her?'

'There was a box of candy. She ate some.'

'Where is she now?' Selby asked.

'In my apartment. Oh, Doug, I know I'm taking the darndest chances, but I just didn't know what to do. Dr Deming says she's out of danger. And that,' she went on, laughing nervously, 'brings us up to date.'

'She's talking?' Selby asked.

'Like a house afire. Dr Deming says powerful stimulants on top of a barbiturate make people do that.'

'And when she snaps out of it,' Selby said, 'she won't admit a thing and we won't be able to use a single bit of all this as evidence, but at least we'll get the low-down now. Let's see what we can find out.'

'You mean we can't use anything she'll tell us?' Brandon asked.

'Not a word of it. Old A.B.C. can prove she's under the influence of drugs.'

'Then let's get our haying done while it's haying weather,' Brandon said. 'Get your car turned around, Sylvia, and tag along. Our siren will clear the way. You're going places fast. Let's go.'

CHAPTER NINETEEN

Paula Melvin said: 'I still wish you'd change your mind about going tonight, Mother. The wind's a howling gale. It'll be blowing sand all over the road.'

'I'll be out of the wind after the first fifty miles. I want to get started, Paula.'

'You won't find any place to stay. Hotels and motor courts will be all crowded—'

'I like to drive at night.'

'At least, Mother, wait for Jim. He'll be home any time now. He'll want to...'

'No, I just want to get off and be by myself. I'm nervous and jumpy. I'm going to put my stuff in the car. The bags are all packed.'

She marched determinedly up the stairs.

Paula followed, saying: 'I think it's positively idiotic, but if you must, I suppose you must.'

They took Mrs Kane's bags downstairs.

Mrs Kane said: 'Don't worry about me, Paula. I'll feel like sleeping tomorrow. I'll go into a motor court somewhere and sleep the clock around.'

'I hope you do. You let me hear from you.'

'Of course.'

Paula smiled and said: 'I won't be so remiss in my own correspondence next time. You understand how it was, Mother. How about a glass of milk and a cheese sandwich before you go?'

Mrs Kane hesitated.

'Come on,' Paula urged. 'We'll just have a little snack. I'm hungry too.'

They went out to the kitchen. Paula fixed a couple of toasted cheese sandwiches. They ate the snack in silence. When they had finished, Mrs Kane started through the living-room, paused at the bon-bon dish, picked up a chocolate cream, said: 'Well, I guess my figure can stand this.'

She munched the chocolate cream, smiled at

Paula and said: 'Invite me again some time, will you, Paula?'

Paula laughed. 'I wish you wouldn't be so frightfully sensitive, Mother.'

'I'm not. I think this whole trip was under the auspices of an unlucky star.'

Paula took one of the chocolate creams. 'You're a goof.'

'No, I'm not. I've brought bad luck with me. I've placed Jim in an embarrassing position and ... Oh, what's the use, Paula? You've been a perfect angel, but I guess things just had to happen that way. Anyhow, I'm taking off. I think the long night drive will calm my nerves a bit.'

'Be careful of the wind, Mother. When you get out on the rim of the desert it may be blowing a terrific gale.'

'A little wind won't bother me.'

'Well, it usually goes down before midnight.'

They kissed each other. Paula stood wistfully in the hallway.

Mrs Kane adjusted her hat, smiled, and said: 'One more piece of candy. Paula, where did you get it?'

'I don't know. It must have been some Jim brought.'

'It's nice and fresh. Going to join me?'

'May as well.'

'That leaves only two pieces,' Doris Kane said, and added laughingly: 'Let's split the temptation, Paula.'

They each had one more piece, finishing the candy. Then they loaded the baggage into the station wagon. Doris Kane waved her gloved hand. Paula waved back, stood watching Mrs Kane back out of the drive-way, then waited until the tail light was a blur in the distance.

Paula returned to the house, started switching off lights. She looked at the clock, stretched, yawned, picked up a book, adjusted herself in an easy chair and started to read.

Slowly, almost imperceptibly, her eyelids fluttered shut. She raised them with an effort, concentrated for another few minutes on the pages of the book, then, having finished a chapter, placed her head against the back of the chair and closed her eyes "just to rest them for a moment".

Thereafter there was silence in the big house, save for the sound of the wind tugging at the corners, howling around the eaves, and the gentle, rhythmic breathing of Paula Melvin as she sank into a slumber which became progressively deeper.

CHAPTER TWENTY

Dr Deming said: 'Of course, gentlemen, I can take no real responsibility for this. It's been deuced irregular. I'm glad that your presence now gives it a certain official sanction.'

'Of a highly irregular sort,' Selby said, grinning.

'How is she?' Sylvia asked.

'About the same. You may go on in if you want.' Sylvia nodded, vanished through the door to the bedroom.

'Is she out of danger?' Brandon asked.

'Completely—subject, of course, to the remote possibility of some unforeseen secondary complication. She's entirely normal except that she has a talking jag. You may have read about a somewhat similar case in one of the national magazines a month or two ago. The drugged condition in that case was deliberately brought about to test the so-called "truth-serum". It is, of course, of no legal value as evidence, but it is an interesting psychological manifestation and may well have some distinct importance in criminology. The patient, through fortuitous circumstances, has absorbed a very large dose of one of the barbiturates. I would say probably sodium amytal. She has also received a very powerful stimulant. Her system is, therefore, torn between the lethargy induced by the drug and the restless wakefulness produced by the stimulant.

'As you probably noticed in the magazine article, where it was tried out, the patient had lost the ability to lie, simply because the sedative effect of the barbiturate made the mind follow the course of least resistance. On

240

the other hand, there is a distinct desire to be talkative.'

'Does her conversation make sense?' Selby asked.

'Oh, it's perfectly coherent, perfectly rational, but she's simply on a synthetic talking jag. Her inhibitions are dulled.'

'To what extent can we depend on what she says being the truth?'

'That is something that will have to be determined by future experiments,' Dr Deming said. 'Apparently it is all the truth. But you can't use it in a court of justice, because I would have to testify that her mind was still completely under the influence of the drug she had been given.'

'You don't think she's lying?'

'I'll stake my reputation that she's not lying in the ordinary sense of the word. But there may be room for certain hallucinations. Want to go in?'

Brandon and Selby nodded.

'Let me take a look,' Dr Deming said.

He peered through the bedroom door and then beckoned to the two men.

Eleanor Harlan, fully dressed, propped up on Sylvia Martin's bed with pillows behind her, her eyes shining, was talking a blue streak to Sylvia Martin.

'Oh, hello,' she said, looking up. 'What is it this time, Doctor? More medicine or ... oh, I know these two people, the sheriff and the district attorney! Well, you found the knife, didn't you?'

She threw back her head and laughed, and once more, as she laughed, the face suddenly ceased to be beautiful.

'How are you feeling now?' Selby asked.

'Fine! Fit as a fiddle. And why do you suppose people say that? What's fit about a fiddle? When you take one out of its case you have to putter around with it, tinkering and tuning. Why should people think it's fit? I'd hate to think people had to twist and turn to get *my* strings in tune after they lifted me out of a case.'

She giggled.

'Who gave you the drug?' Selby asked.

'Well, now, I don't know. I could only make a guess.'

'How about making a guess?'

'That might not be fair. You see, I don't *know*. That's just the point, Mr ... What was your name? Selby, wasn't it?'

'That's right.'

'And the other man, the cowpuncher-hat man? What's his name?'

'Sheriff Brandon.'

'That's right. But you're all cowpunchers here in Madison City. When Miss Martin was taking me here, I was surprised. I thought I'd moved to the Wild West. For a while I thought I was completely goofy. I just sat in the car and watched people walking around in cowboy boots and whiskers. Now I'm talking kind of fast, Mr Selby. I didn't mean walking in whiskers.' Again she threw back her head and laughed.

'And while you're making guesses,' Selby said, 'how do you *think* the knife got in your apartment?'

'Bless your soul, Mr Selby! Don't be so naive. It's something I wouldn't even want to *think* about. It might not be healthy.'

'Why wouldn't it be healthy?'

'I don't know. I would no more try to speculate on how the knife got into my apartment than I would try to speculate on how the knife got *out* of my apartment.'

'You mean the same knife both times?'

'No, not the same knife both times, Mr Selby,' she said with tantalising mockery in her voice.

'You mean there were two?'

'Of course there were two.'

'Let's talk about the first knife first.'

'That sounds like a wise-crack. The first knife first. The first first. First is first and last is last.'

'Did you take it to kill Eve Dawson?'

'Don't misunderstand me about that. I didn't kill Eve. I wouldn't have killed her for the world after I failed in that first attempt.'

'What first attempt?'

'The night I shot her. I suppose I shouldn't be telling you this, but, after all, I'm in a talkative mood tonight, and we may as well get the whole thing cleared up. I shot her the night of the party. Now why am I telling you all this?'

Selby realised that if he could keep her in the mood to exchange light banter with him, she would make incriminating statements, with no particular regard for their significance, but the minute he became serious and let his manner impress upon her the gravity of the situation, she would fight back the impulse to confide in him.

The effects of the drug were beginning to wear off. While she still wished to talk, and would at the faintest excuse rattle on about her personal affairs, she was recognising the folly of confiding in the district attorney even as she talked.

Selby, casting about in his mind for just the proper approach, heard the sound of angry voices in the other room of the apartment.

Dr Deming's voice was raised in a statement of protest. Then Selby heard Sylvia Martin saying: 'Well, you certainly can't search my apartment without a warrant.'

A. B. Carr's voice, richly resonant, vibrant with authority, said: 'We'll have a search warrant here within five minutes. We'll also have a writ of *habeas corpus*, and if that doesn't do the work, we'll have the F.B.I. on the job.'

Eleanor Harlan giggled. 'That's old A.B.C.,' she said to Selby. 'Smart, isn't he? He figured the whole thing out, but you couldn't catch

244

him at it. He never leaves a back trail. But you have to watch him. Don't ever let him offer you a drink if you go to his house. He has a portable bar. When he opens it, a hidden microphone starts relaying everything you say to wax records. Then old A.B.C.'s got you hog-tied.'

'He bought you some candy this afternoon?' Selby asked.

'Bless your soul, not old A.B.C.! *He* didn't bring me any candy. Milton Granby came to see me. He brought the candy.'

A voice, shouting to make itself heard, said: 'I'm Ellery Fairbanks, foreman of the Grand Jury, and I guess *I* have something to say about what goes on in this county! The Chief of Police of Madison City is on his way up here with a search warrant and I'm going to stay right here until he arrives.'

Brandon and Selby exchanged glances.

'Well,' Eleanor Harlan exclaimed airily, 'sounds like quite a little commotion, doesn't it? I guess we're giving a party.'

Brandon pushed his way towards the door to the living-room. Selby hesitated a moment, then followed.

As Brandon opened the door, Selby was careful to hold it so that as he followed Brandon into the other room it was impossible for the others to look through the door and see Eleanor Harlan on the bed.

Ellery Fairbanks was standing in the centre of the room, pounding the table, his face red with anger.

Dr Deming, perched on the arm of an over-stuffed chair, smoked a cigarette nonchalantly.

Carr, tall and dignified, had discarded his cowboy regalia and was dressed in a neat-fitting, double-breasted business suit. His calm authority and conscious power made Sylvia Martin's apprehensive eyes gravitate towards him, despite the table-pounding vehemence of Ellery Fairbanks.

'Well, well,' Carr said. 'Surprise, surprise! The sheriff and the district attorney! Now *what* would you gentlemen be doing here?'

Fairbanks paused in his table-pounding tirade to glare at the two county officials. 'So *that's* it!' he said.

Sylvia Martin slipped quietly through the door into the bedroom, taking advantage of the diversion created by the appearance of Selby and Rex Brandon.

'What's the search warrant for, Carr?' Selby asked.

'The search warrant,' Carr said, with cold anger, 'is for the person of my client, Eleanor Harlan, who, I understand, has been deliberately drugged by this newspaper woman in an attempt to get an interview from her. I don't mind telling you, Selby, I've secured a writ of *habeas corpus*, I've secured a search warrant, I'm having both of those documents served. I am also intending to make a complaint to the Federal Bureau of

246

Investigation concerning a kidnapping and abduction.'

'A fine lot of advertising you're giving *this* county!' Fairbanks shouted. 'A couple of trigger-happy politicians trying to even up a lot of political scores. You two have gone nuts on publicity. You have a common, ordinary garden variety of suicide, and you try to torture it into a murder simply so you can stir up a local political stink involving the people who have been on the other side of the political fence.'

'You talk a lot,' Brandon said.

'I talk a lot,' Fairbanks yelled at him, 'and you haven't heard anything yet! I have a majority of the Grand Jury behind me. I know how they feel about this thing. The minute you fellows learned that this suicide could be made to involve some politically prominent people in this county, you were off to the races. Well, I'll tell you right now you're not going to get away with it. The Grand Jury is behind me to a man! We're going to . . .'

Carr did not seem to raise his voice, yet his words cut through the tirade of Ellery Fairbanks, brushing that irate individual's words to one side with effortless ease.

'I'm warning you, Selby, I intend to take this up with the Bar Association.'

'Take what up?' Selby asked.

'You people have exceeded your authority. You have invaded the privacy of my client's apartment. You have, by artifice and trick, administered a drug for the purpose of getting her to talk. And then you have spirited her out of the county in which she lived and into this county. You are planning to take the statements of a drugged girl and spread them out on the pages of the public Press for the purpose of trying to prop up a purely synthetic murder case you have dreamed up in your own imagination.'

'You are accusing me of having administered a drug?' Selby asked.

'It was administered with your connivance, I'm satisfied of that.'

'And of kidnapping your client?'

'You've either kidnapped her or you're an accessory after the fact. You're taking advantage of the kidnapping.'

Dr Deming said: 'Gentlemen, my patient is . . .'

'Just a minute,' Selby interrupted. 'If you don't mind, Doctor, we'll make no statements of any sort. We'll give these two no information.'

Fairbanks said: 'Well, Chief of Police Otto Larkin is on his way up here with a search warrant and a writ of *habeas corpus*. You're in the city limits of Madison City, and just because you happen to represent the county authority, doesn't mean you can ride roughshod over . . .'

Heavy steps sounded outside the door. The

knob twisted, and Otto Larkin, Chief of Police of Madison City, pushed his big, paunchy frame through the door. His face twisted into a synthetic grin. His eyes, glittering out from above the folds of fat on his face, were alert to every move that was being made.

'Well, well, what's the trouble here?' he asked, striving to make his voice sound jovial.

'You have a warrant!' Fairbanks screamed at him. 'Go ahead and serve it.'

Larkin asked the sheriff: 'Are you detaining an Eleanor Harlan as a prisoner?'

'As a prisoner?'

'That's what I said.'

Brandon shook his head.

'I've got a writ of *habeas corpus* directed to you.'

Brandon extended his hand. 'Go ahead and serve it.'

'It's served,' Larkin said, pushing the folded paper into Brandon's hand.

'That writ of *habeas corpus* orders you to produce the body of Eleanor Harlan in the Superior Court of this county at two o'clock tomorrow afternoon,' A. B. Carr said. 'And it is ordered that she be released on bail in the sum of one thousand dollars, pending the hearing of the writ of *habeas corpus*. I have the cash bail in my possession. I want her released.'

'So I understood,' Brandon said.

'Now, I've got a warrant to search the apartment of Sylvia Martin,' Larkin said. 'I don't want to have any trouble here, and I'm calling on every man in this room to assist me in the enforcement of the law. Where's Sylvia Martin?'

'She was here a minute ago,' Fairbanks said. '—I guess she went through the door into the bedroom. And if there's been any drugging of Eleanor Harlan in order to make her a witness, in other words, if any drugs have been administered to her by anybody without her consent, there's going to be an investigation by the County Grand Jury that will blow the lid off this county.'

Larkin, waving the search warrant in his hand, said: 'Well, we'll mighty soon find out whether she's drugged or not.'

He approached the bedroom door, started to put his hand on the door-knob, then paused for a moment, raised his knuckles and pounded authoritatively on the door.

There was no answer.

Otto Larkin said: 'This is the Chief of Police of Madison City. I have a warrant to search this apartment for the purpose of finding the person of one Eleanor Harlan who is being illegally detained. Open the door or I'll break it down.'

There was no sound from behind the door.

Larkin twisted the knob and pushed the door open. Selby and Brandon, moving quietly, fell in behind Larkin as he entered the bedroom.

The room was empty.

CHAPTER TWENTY-ONE

As Brandon and Selby entered the sheriff's outer office, the night man who was on duty at the telephone looked up and said to the sheriff: 'I've been trying to get you everywhere. A call came in from the traffic department.'

'What is it?' Brandon asked.

'A woman driving a station wagon, apparently completely under the influence of drugs, zig-zagging over the road, asleep at the wheel, and before the officer could catch up with her to stop her, she'd side-swiped another car. Nothing serious, but just because the woman got the breaks. Otherwise, she'd have been facing a manslaughter charge. She's completely goofy.'

Brandon glanced at Selby. 'What else?'

'That's all. Just before she passed out entirely, she told the motor-cycle officer to get in touch with you. She said: "Tell Sheriff Brandon chocolate creams," and then added: "I'm Paula Melvin's mother." Then she became unconscious.'

Brandon said: 'Get on the phone. There's a Dr Deming in town. He's just finished treating one of these same cases. Tell him to rush to Las Alidas and call at that place where Jim Melvin

251

is staying. You may locate the doctor at Sylvia Martin's apartment. Have Mrs Kane taken to that house in Las Alidas.'

'Come on,' Selby shouted, making for the door. 'Seconds may mean a lot.'

They pell-melled down the steps of the court-house.

As Brandon slammed the car door, Selby said: 'Rex, we need some candy.'

'Why?'

'The murderer never would have left any drugged candy in Eleanor Harlan's apartment. Yet there was candy there, candy that was just as pure as any candy that left the candy factory.'

'I don't get it.'

Selby said: 'The undrugged candy is Granby's alibi, in case someone connects him with candy and a visit to Eleanor Harlan's apartment.'

'Why should we take candy along with us?'

'We may want to do a little sleight-of-hand stuff ourselves,' Selby said.

Brandon stopped the car in front of the Palace Confectionery Store, then followed Selby into the store.

'A pound of your best chocolates,' Selby said. 'I want the mixed variety. Hurry!'

They waited impatiently while the girl behind the counter, watching their haste with ill-concealed curiosity, grabbed a package, handed it to Selby, rang up the sale in the cash register.

The two officers hurried out of the candy store, heedless of the curious glances of people who had drifted in from the movie across the street for sundaes and sodas.

The two officials walked rapidly across the stretch of pavement, jerked open the door of the big car and jumped inside.

Brandon sensed motion in the rear of the car as the balance of the body shifted on the rear springs. Suddenly he whirled, his hand darting to his shoulder holster.

'Don't shoot!' Sylvia Martin's mirth-choked voice said from the floor by the back seat. 'It's a friend.'

'Sylvia! What the deuce are you doing there?' Selby asked.

'Hiding from the law,' she said. 'I'm crouched into a ball. Would it be too much to ask you to start the car and get out of the lighted district? I think I'm a fugitive from justice and my muscles ache.'

'What happened?' Selby asked as Brandon started the car in motion.

She said: 'I have an idea Otto Larkin wants very much to throw me in the cooler.'

'How did you dodge him, Sylvia?'

'Eleanor Harlan was fully dressed. There was a door from my bedroom into the corridor, and...'

'Not that,' Selby said, 'we know all about that, but Larkin put in a general alarm. Every officer in the city got on the job.'

Sylvia laughed. 'I knew if I cruised around the streets they'd pick me up. So I made a sprint for a motor court and grabbed the last vacancy they had. I'll bet I was inside the court within three minutes of the time I left my apartment.'

'Larkin will search the courts,' Selby said, as Brandon gunned the car into speed.

'Sure, he'll search 'em,' Sylvia Martin agreed. 'But he won't actually search the courts. He'll search the registers. I registered as "Anita Smith and sister from San Diego" and gave a phony licence number.'

'Larkin will check up on the time and...'

'Ten to one, he doesn't,' Sylvia said. 'You're thinking about what you'd do under similar circumstances. Gosh, I've got a *whale* of a story, but it's so hot I don't dare to publish it until it's given some sort of an official sanction. You've got to get that girl before the Grand Jury!'

'You know how the Grand Jury is stacked against us,' Selby said.

'*I* don't think Fairbanks has the thing sewed up half as much as he thinks he has,' Sylvia said. 'You folks have got some good friends on that jury, and once they hear Eleanor Harlan's story...'

'Will she tell her story after the drug wears off?' Selby asked.

'She's got to!' Sylvia said.

'She admitted to me that she shot Eve

254

Dawson,' Selby said. 'She certainly is not going to get up in front of a Grand Jury and . . . .'

'I think she is, Doug. I think she'll have to.'

'How come?'

She said: 'Here's the story—but first, where are we going?'

Selby said: 'Mrs Kane, Paula Melvin's mother, was in an accident.'

'Doug, you mean she was—that someone tried to—'

'Not in the way you mean,' Selby said, 'but it amounts to about the same thing. They evidently managed to give her a big dose of sleeping-pills in the same way that pills were given to the Harlan girl.'

'In candy?'

'That's right.'

'Then that's what—What *were* you doing buying candy in there?'

'Getting bait for a trap. Anyway, we're going to Las Alidas to see Paula Melvin.'

'Do you think she knows something about it?'

Selby said: 'I wouldn't be too much surprised if we found *her* sound asleep.'

'Oh, oh,' Sylvia Martin said.

'Go on,' Selby urged, 'tell us about Eleanor Harlan, Sylvia.'

Sylvia said: 'These politicians do quite a bit of entertaining. When they entertain, they need gals to spice up the party and keep the boys interested. Eleanor Harlan and Eve Dawson were good scouts, and they were invited along on quite a few of these parties.

'Eleanor didn't make any particular secret about it. She liked the life and liked the idea of getting out on yacht trips, doing night clubs, and stuff like that, but she always maintained financial independence. She got a job—I think it was a job she got through political pull and didn't take too much of her time, but nevertheless it was a job.'

'How about Eve Dawson?' Selby asked.

'Eve Dawson was inclined to drift along and take things a little more easy.'

'Then what happened?'

'Well, Eleanor Harlan became Hudson Parlin's personal property in the course of time. She became his accepted girl friend. She went along on these trips as a sort of semi-official play-girl hostess. She got to know a lot about his business.

'Parlin had some pretty hot stuff on Morris Sheldon, the Mayor of Las Alidas. Parlin intended to use that, not resorting to anything as crude as blackmail, but, nevertheless, he intended to see that Morris Sheldon got certain documents back under such circumstances that Sheldon realised very clearly he was obligated to Parlin.

'The papers, whatever they were, were given to Eleanor Harlan for safe keeping and somehow Eve Dawson found out about them. Eve was becoming bitter and disillusioned and

256

kept talking about how she would like to quit the life if she could make one big shake-down.

'She evidently thought the Sheldon deal was her opportunity. On the night Jim Melvin was giving the party, she stole the papers and went out to try and shake down Morris Sheldon. Eleanor Harlan found out what had happened and followed. They met in the garage out at Melvin's place and there was quite a fight. Eve Dawson had a gun. She pulled it and Eleanor Harlan, who certainly has nerve and spunk, waded right in and tried to grab the gun. They struggled for it and—well, it's the same old story. While they were struggling, the gun went off.

'Morris Sheldon wasn't there at the party, but Milton Granby was. And Granby apparently had had some telephone conversation with Eve Dawson about those papers. They were papers that Morris Sheldon wanted to get back the worst way—something about a kick-back in a paving deal.'

'What happened to the papers?' Selby asked.

'Babe Harlan regained them and made her getaway. Milton Granby found Eve Dawson on the floor of the garage. He evidently was somewhere near-by and came running as soon as he heard the shot.'

'No chance of their lying about that and that Granby was the one who shot her?'

'I don't think so, Doug. The Harlan girl was talking like a house afire, and I think she was telling me the truth. She seemed incapable of lying. She just kept going on and on.'

'Okay, what next?'

'Granby consulted Melvin and the two of them got Carr. They decided that each would give the other an alibi. Carr told them a story to tell about everyone having all been together when this shot was fired. Then he told them to tell about finding one of the guests at the party who had become pretty much intoxicated and had shot himself through the arm.

'He rehearsed them in their stories and made a pretty good job of it.'

'I'll say he did,' Brandon said fervently. 'Darned if Granby didn't fool me with the yarn about the guy on the bed with the towel wrapped around his arm.'

'Who killed Eve Dawson?' Selby asked.

'Eleanor Harlan doesn't know, but someone stole that murder knife out of her apartment. She says she doesn't have the faintest idea who it was. And for some reason, Carr was deathly afraid that knife was going to be traced into her possession. He wanted to be certain that she had a duplicate knife that she could pass off as the one that had been in her possession all along.'

'Do you really think Eleanor Harlan fired the shot that wounded Eve Dawson?'

'She says she did.'

'But she did tell you that the story that Milton Granby told us about Carr and Melvin

258

being with him at the time the shot was fired was a story that Carr fixed up?'

'That's right.'

'Then the three weren't together when the shot was fired.'

'No.'

'No one knows where Melvin was?'

'No one knows where Melvin was. No one knows where Carr was. No one knows where Granby was.'

Brandon said: 'When we get done in Las Alidas we're sure going to talk with that Harlan girl.'

CHAPTER TWENTY-TWO

Brandon stopped the car in front of Jim Melvin's house.

'Lights on,' Brandon said.

'That doesn't necessarily mean anything,' Selby pointed out.

They ran up the steps of the front porch and rang the bell. There was no answer, no sound of motion within the silent house.

They rang the bell twice more, pounded with their knuckles on the front door, kicked with their feet on the bottom of the door, setting up a reverberating racket which boomed through the interior of the house.

Their efforts were without avail. The house

remained utterly silent.

Standing on the sheriff's shoulders, Selby was able to remove a screen from the pantry window, raise the window and crawl through.

Paula was sound asleep, completely dead to the world, slumped over in the chair, the reading-light showering her with soft illumination which turned her hair into a fluffy halo. Her book lay on the floor where it had fallen from her lifeless fingers.

Selby gave her only a glance, then ran to open the front door, letting Brandon and Sylvia Martin in. The three of them tried to arouse Paula, but their efforts met with no success. She was as unresponsive as a wet sack, her muscles completely limp.

They were trying cold water applications, when they heard the sound of a siren, and a few seconds later the night deputy and Dr Deming entered the house.

'What have we here?' Deming asked.

'Another one,' Brandon said grimly. 'And still another coming. Get busy.'

Dr Deming took Paula's pulse, listened to her breathing, nodded his head.

'In time?' Selby asked.

'I think so,' Dr Deming said. 'Let's get her into a bedroom and get her clothes off.'

They carried Paula up the stairs to the bedroom. Dr Deming opened his instrument bag and started to work.

He nodded to Sylvia Martin and said: 'All

right, Sylvia, this is where you get busy. I want all of her clothes off. Then turn cold water in the wash-bowl in the bathroom and hot water in the bath-tub. Get out all the towels you can find, get me some lukewarm water in a pitcher and then I'll tell you what to do next.'

Dr Deming jerked his head towards the door, glanced at the sheriff and district attorney, and said: 'I'll call you as soon as we know where we stand.'

The siren of an ambulance faded from a scream to a mournful groan. Steps sounded on the porch and stretcher men brought in the unconscious figure of Doris Kane.

'Take her upstairs,' Brandon said. 'A doctor's on the job up there.'

He waited until Mrs Kane had been put to bed and the ambulance men had departed, then said to Selby: 'Let's take a look around, Doug.'

They found a bon-bon bowl on the table in the living-room. There was some small fruit-flavoured gum-drops in this bowl and some hard candy, but no chocolate creams.

'Suppose *this* candy was drugged?' Brandon asked.

'I doubt it,' Selby said, and opening the box of candy which he had purchased in Madison City, he proceeded to arrange two chocolate creams temptingly on the top of the bon-bon dish.

'Only two?' Brandon asked.

261

Selby said: 'I wish I knew the answer to that one, Rex. Two should be enough. However, I'll try one more.'

'Does it make any difference, if you get too many?'

'A lot of difference. The man who put out chocolate creams containing the drug would know how many he put out. In order to bait our trap he must know that Paula and her mother have been drugged. Therefore there must be at least two or three less chocolate creams remaining in the dish than he put there. If there are the same number or if there are more, we've defeated our own purpose.'

Brandon nodded, said: 'This is your play, Doug. Go to it.'

Selby hesitated a moment, then put down a fourth chocolate cream, stepped back, looked at the bon-bon dish, shook his head, picked up the fourth chocolate cream and returned it to the box, leaving only three.

'Figuring it that way,' Brandon said, 'it just about has to be Jim Melvin.'

A car came to a stop outside the house. There were steps on the porch. Then a latch-key clicked in the door and Jim Melvin's voice, laughing triumphantly, said: 'Well, it was quite some smear!'

The wind had gone down now, leaving a stillness of chilled dryness in the air, a lack of humidity which made the chill highly insidious.

Hudson Parlin's genial laugh boomed in

approval. 'Jim, my boy, you did a real job! You really did a job.'

'I think we owe quite a bit to Granby,' Melvin said.

'Granby!' Parlin snorted. 'He...'

Parlin broke off in the middle of a sentence.

'What's the matter?' Melvin asked.

'You seem to have visitors.'

Melvin pushed ahead into the room, said to Brandon: 'What are you doing here? Who let you in?'

'We want to talk with you,' Brandon said.

Melvin's face was angry. 'It seems to me that's all you've been doing—talking with me. How did you get in here? Where's Paula? What kind of a deal is this?'

'Sit down,' Selby said. 'Keep your shirt on.'

'I wondered what all these cars were doing out here ... Say, who's upstairs?'

'People are visiting your wife,' Selby said. 'Sit down a moment, I want to ask you something.'

'Well, go ahead and ask it and get it over with.'

Parlin said: 'Gentlemen, it does seem to me that...'

'Yes, go on,' Selby said.

'Nothing,' Parlin said.

Melvin took one of the chocolate creams from the bon-bon dish. 'Go ahead, let's have it.'

Parlin promptly reached out, scooped up the

remaining chocolate creams and a dozen or so of the small gum-drops and sat back in the chair Paula had been occupying, munching candy, listening.

'Your wife is upstairs, in the hands of a physician,' Selby said.

'Paula is! What happened?'

'She evidently received a large dose of one of the barbiturates.'

'What doctor?' Melvin asked.

'A doctor that I brought.'

Melvin slid off the edge of the table, took the stairs two at a time.

Parlin said: 'Good heavens, Selby, Paula Melvin had no reason to want to make away with herself. She—why, it's absurd!'

'I didn't say that she was trying to make away with herself,' Selby said.

'Then what do you mean? Surely you can't mean she was—that someone gave her the drug without her knowing it.'

'It's possible.'

'I don't see how.'

Melvin, his voice excited, called from the upstairs bedroom: 'Parlin, come up here a minute, will you? I want a witness.'

Parlin started for the stairs. He was near the foot of the staircase when steps sounded on the porch, and the bell rang.

'Want me to answer the door?' Parlin called up the stairs.

'It's probably Granby. Let him in.'

Selby glanced significantly at Brandon, then arose and put two more chocolate creams in the bon-bon dish.

Parlin opened the door and said: 'Hello, Granby,' and then added in a quick warning: 'We have visitors—official visitors.'

'Oh, hello,' Granby said. 'How are you, gentlemen? Everything all right?' He stood in the hallway.

Selby said: 'Mrs Melvin seems to have taken an overdose of sleeping-pills.'

Granby made clucking noises with his tongue against the roof of his mouth.

Parlin said: 'Isn't that rather a premature statement, Selby?'

'Perhaps,' Selby admitted laconically.

Jim Melvin called from upstairs. 'Parlin, would you mind coming up here?'

Parlin said: 'Not at all,' and then to the others: 'Excuse me, please.'

He walked heavily up the stairs.

Selby caught Rex Brandon's eye, slipped the brown spectacle-case from his pocket and placed it on a smoking-stand near the table on which the candy-bowl had been placed.

Granby entered the room, said: 'My gosh, that's too bad! I saw the county car go through town.'

'And surmised it was coming here?' Selby asked.

Granby moved over towards the bowl containing the candy. He said: 'Poor Jim certainly is having his share of bad luck. However, I've got things all fixed up for him on the contract with the city, and that'll help.'

'Anything new on that deal?' Selby asked.

'No, nothing, except that it's all sewed up for him.'

Selby glanced at Rex Brandon.

'I thought perhaps there was some new angle, that was why you wanted to see him.'

Granby cleared his throat. 'Well,' he said, 'I just thought I'd talk with him a little about some of the details.'

He extended a hand towards the candy-dish, then checked the motion, turned over towards the window, said: 'Well, I may as well stick around a while,' and seated himself in the chair by the smoking-stand.

Selby caught the sheriff's eye. 'I wonder how things are going upstairs,' he said.

'We might get in touch with the doctor,' Brandon said. 'I'm very much interested.'

Granby lit a cigarette, dropped the match into the ash-tray and, as he did so, his hand came to rest on the brown spectacle-case. He picked it up and started twisting it around in his fingers. 'A very bad business,' he said.

Brandon said suddenly and savagely: 'Go ahead, Granby, and put it in your pocket.'

Granby looked up at him in surprise.

'Put what in my pocket?'

'Your spectacle-case.'

'It's not mine.'

'Yes, it is,' the sheriff said. 'You recognised it. You picked it up. You started to put it in your pocket, then you suddenly realised that if your spectacle-case had been found here by someone and placed on that smoking-stand, you must have dropped it the night you murdered Eve Dawson.'

'Are you crazy?'

'You're the one that's crazy,' Brandon said. 'Why didn't you take those chocolate creams a minute ago?'

'Oh, those,' Granby said. 'I'm quite fond of chocolate. I happened to remember, however, that I have a leaky filling, and the last time I ate a chocolate cream I got quite a sharp pain, so I decided not to eat any more until I saw my dentist.'

'When was it that you experienced the pain?'

'This afternoon.'

'Where?'

'Here in town.'

'You're sure it wasn't in Los Angeles?'

'I wasn't in Los Angeles this afternoon.'

'You're a liar,' Brandon said. 'You went to Los Angeles. You went to see Eleanor Harlan, and you took her a box of candy.'

Granby's face twisted spastically.

'Do you deny it?'

'I don't have to tell *you* what I did with my time.'

'You bought candy for Eleanor Harlan. You drugged part of it. Then, after she had gone to sleep, you put the rest of the drugged candy in your pocket, planted a bottle of sleeping-pills as evidence that would make it seem she committed suicide, and then tiptoed out.'

'I tell you you're crazy.'

'Then you came here and encountered Selby and me. You still had that candy in your pocket because you hadn't had any opportunity to dispose of it. Or, perhaps, because you deliberately intended to kill Paula and her mother. You put the drugged candy in the bon-bon-dish.'

'Are you accusing me of murdering Eve Dawson?'

'You're damn right, I am,' Brandon said.

Selby nudged the sheriff with his elbow, and said: 'We're not putting it as bluntly as that, Granby. What the sheriff means is that we want an explanation. We want to know more about why you went to see Eleanor Harlan; why you took her candy and...'

'Well, I'm tired of being pushed around by you people,' Granby said. 'I guess I have a little influence in this community, myself. You may have forgotten it, but I'm related by marriage to some pretty influential people.'

Granby glowered at them.

Brandon reached over and took the spectacle-case. 'All right,' he said, 'we'll just take this as evidence before you manage to get rid of it somewhere.'

They heard voices, as two men came down

the stairs. Then Jim Melvin and Hudson Parlin entered the room, sensed the tension in the attitudes of the three men, and Melvin asked: 'What's the matter? What's coming off here?'

'They're trying to frame a murder rap on me,' Granby said.

Melvin laughed and said: 'Welcome to our lodge. You can be a charter member. They've tried to do the same thing to me.'

Selby brushed against Hudson Parlin's coat. He felt two round lumps in the right-hand side pocket.

'Wait a minute, Rex,' Selby said.

Parlin suddenly became conscious of Selby's touch on the side of his coat. 'Hey!' he shouted. 'What are you doing?'

Parlin jerked away. Selby's hand grabbed the edge of the coat, crushed the two chocolate creams into a sticky smear on the inside of the coat pocket.

'What's the idea of carrying candy in your pocket?' Selby asked.

'I like chocolates,' Parlin said. 'I saw two chocolates in the bon-bon dish. I scooped up some candy and intended to eat it all together, but the fruit gum-drops were so tart I didn't want to mix the flavour with the chocolate, so I dropped the chocolates temporarily into my side pocket. Then Melvin asked me to come upstairs, and I...'

He broke off, to regard the two chocolates which remained in the bon-bon dish with wide, startled eyes.

'So!' he said suddenly. 'A plant!'

Selby said: 'The drugged ones are the ones in your pocket. Parlin. You planted them here earlier, when we surprised you as you were about to choke Mrs Kane. And it was *your* spectacle-case. You thought you lost it when you murdered Eve Dawson.'

Parlin's eyes narrowed in shrewd speculation. Then suddenly he threw back his head and laughed. 'All right, Mr District Attorney,' he said, 'you think you're pretty smart. You're running a bluff. I'm calling it. Prove this candy is drugged.'

Selby nodded to Brandon. 'Put handcuffs on him, Rex.'

Brandon jerked out handcuffs, started towards Granby.

'No, no, not Granby,' Selby said. 'Hudson Parlin.'

'This is an outrage!' Jim Melvin said. 'Why you slap-happy dopes!'

Hudson Parlin extended his wrists. His mouth was twisted in a sneer. 'Go right ahead, boys,' he invited. 'You've laid an egg; now sit on it and see what hatches. It's going to surprise you.'

CHAPTER TWENTY-THREE

Selby and Sylvia Martin got into the back seat of the county car. Sheriff Brandon hustled his prisoner into the front seat, said: 'Don't try making any sudden moves,' and then walked around to climb in behind the steering-wheel.

'I want to communicate with my attorney,' Parlin said, 'and I want to be taken before the nearest and most accessible magistrate.'

'You've been told all about your legal rights, haven't you?' Brandon sneered. 'You've been given a line of patter that you've memorised against the time when this would happen.'

Parlin said: 'Don't get funny about it. Jim Melvin knows what to do. He'll telephone A. B. Carr, and old A.B.C. will be waiting for us when we get to the jail.'

'Then he'll have a long wait,' Brandon said. 'You're not going to the jail—not just yet.'

'Where am I going?'

Brandon said: 'You're going to be confronted with Eleanor Harlan. It happens she's in a talkative mood and has spilled everything she knows. She's told us the whole business, from the time she shot Eve Dawson on up to the time you took the carving-knife out of her apartment and went out to finish the job.'

'In the first place,' Parlin said, 'Babe Harlan

271

never told you anything of the sort. In the second place, Babe didn't shoot Eve, and in the third place, I didn't kill Eve. If it gives you any pleasure, go right ahead with your pipe dreams, but I demand that I be taken before the nearest and most accessible magistrate.'

'I heard you the first time,' Brandon said, 'but unfortunately we're out making an arrest now.'

'An arrest of whom?'

'Eleanor Harlan.'

'You boys certainly are leading with your chins,' Parlin said.

Brandon turned to Sylvia Martin and said: 'What's the name of the auto court, Sylvia?'

'The Columbian.'

'What cabin?'

'Number twelve.'

Brandon devoted no more time to conversation, but whipped the big car into speed, sending it tearing over the road, rocketing past slower moving vehicles, clearing the way from time to time with the intermittent flashes of his red light and the scream of his siren.

'Paula Melvin was conscious when you left?' Selby asked Sylvia Martin in a low voice.

'Yes.'

'Any idea how it happened?'

'She said there were...' Sylvia Martin leaned over and put her lips close to Selby's ear, so that there was no possibility of Parlin

272

hearing ... 'said that there were chocolate creams in the bon-bon dish. She didn't know where they came from. They tasted all right. She settled down in a chair to read and became terribly sleepy, simply couldn't keep her eyes open. And that's the last she remembers.'

'And the mother had some, too?'

'Apparently they shared them.'

'Well, the mother's getting emergency treatment and should be all right,' Selby said. 'It's fortunate she got such a big dose that it showed up before she left the county.'

'It gives me the creeps just to think of it,' Sylvia said.

Selby said: 'Well, let's hope Eleanor Harlan is still in a talkative mood.'

Sylvia said: 'There's something that puzzles me about her, Doug.'

'What?'

'When I left the auto court she had started to get very sleepy. She began to yawn and yawn, and then she nodded her head a few times, and then quit talking. I thought that was an entirely natural reaction after the stimulant began to wear off, but I was talking with Dr Deming about it while we were working on Paula, and he says it shouldn't work that way; that the barbiturate should work out of her system, but the stimulant should last longer.'

'We'll be there in a few minutes,' Selby said, 'and see for ourselves.'

They saw that Parlin was holding his head

273

rigidly at an angle, straining his ears to hear what they were talking about, so they became silent.

The car rushed on through the star-studded night, screaming its way over the pavement until they could see the lights of Madison City, and then an electric sign, now dark, bearing the words: 'Columbian Auto Court.' Down below that sign was a small illuminated sign bearing the words: 'No vacancy.'

The big tyres on the county car crunched on the gravel drive-way as Brandon swung the car around, to stop in front of cabin number twelve.

The cabin was dark and silent.

Brandon glanced back with an inquiring look at Sylvia Martin.

'It's all right,' Sylvia said reassuringly. 'She's gone to sleep. I'll go in and wake her.'

Selby opened the door for her. She flashed him a smile of thanks, jumped to the gravelled drive-way and ran quickly across to the porch of the cabin. She paused briefly, then tried the knob of the door. The door opened and the darkness swallowed her.

'I suppose this is another bluff,' Parlin said, 'like the chocolate creams that are now a sticky mess in my pocket. I'm going to expect the county to buy me a new suit.'

The county officials said nothing, watching the interior of the cabin.

Lights flashed on, showing oblongs of soft
274

illumination through the drawn window curtains. They could hear Sylvia Martin moving around, but could hear no sound of conversation.

Then Sylvia came to the door. The anguished look on her face as she glanced at Doug Selby and from him to Brandon, told its own story. 'Just a minute,' she said, 'I want to talk with the manager.'

Sylvia ran to the front of the auto court and rang the night bell of the building marked 'Office.'

After a few moments, lights came on and a woman's voice said irritably: 'Can't you see the sign "No vacancies"?'

Sylvia said: 'I want to talk with you a minute.'

They heard the door open and close, heard low-voiced conversations. Then Sylvia came back, beckoned to Selby.

Selby went over to join her.

She said: 'We're licked, Doug. She slipped one over on me.'

'What happened?'

'She must have been putting on an act. She certainly seemed dead to the world when I left. But the manager said I hadn't been gone more than two minutes before Eleanor Harlan came running into the office and demanded a phone. She said she had to have one fast.'

'I suppose,' Selby said wearily, 'she called Carr.'

'That's right. The woman made a note of the number because she charges five cents apiece for local calls. Eleanor called Carr and told him where she was. Within ten minutes Carr had driven down and picked her up and driven away.'

From the motor-car, Brandon was looking at them anxiously.

Selby caught his eye, shook his head faintly in an all but imperceptible negative.

They walked back to the machine.

Parlin threw back his head and laughed. 'Another bluff gone wrong!' he said. 'I knew damn well you didn't have Eleanor Harlan. And now I demand that you take me to the nearest and most accessible magistrate.'

CHAPTER TWENTY-FOUR

It was nearing midnight when the county car stopped in front of the palatial residence which Alfonse Baker Carr had purchased on Orange Grove Heights.

The front of the house was dark, but there was a light in the back where Carr had his study, and Doug Selby, after a low-voiced conversation with Rex Brandon, pressed a firm thumb against the bell button and held it there until he was satisfied that the sound of the chimes had penetrated through to Carr's study.

Selby waited for something over a minute before the porch light clicked on. A small steel slide slipped back in the heavy door so that the unseen eye of the man in the shadows could survey the porch.

Then the door was flung open. Carr's resonant voice said: 'Well, well, Major Selby!'

'Just plain Doug Selby, if you please.'

'I'm sorry. I'm trying to make you keep your military title. It becomes you. It's rather late for a call, isn't it?'

'Quite late. This isn't a social call.'

'Official?'

'In a way, yes.'

'Well, well, *do* come in! Where's your inseparable companion? The worthy, somewhat naive, but conscientious sheriff?'

Selby said: 'I thought we might talk to better advantage alone.'

'Rather considerate, Counsellor. I appreciate that sort of an approach. Come right in.'

Carr escorted his visitor back to the study, a room lined with books, dominated by a huge desk in the centre, surrounded by deep over-stuffed chairs, a room that was conducive to comfort, relaxation and concentrated study.

The desk was piled with books, placed one on top of the other, opened at places marking the important passages which Carr had been studying.

'Do sit down, Counsellor. Make yourself at home.'

'Thank you.'

Selby stretched himself out in one of the deep leather chairs, making himself thoroughly comfortable.

Carr watched the district attorney with shrewd, twinkling eyes. 'Cigar?' he asked. 'Cigarette?'

'Thank you,' Selby said. 'I have my pipe. I'll stay with it, if you don't mind.'

The district attorney took his pipe from his pocket, pushed fragrant tobacco down into the crusted bowl and lit up.

Carr said: 'Really, Counsellor, you're not on duty now. This must be in the nature of a call that's off the record. I have some very nice rum here. It's something over a hundred years old. It's mellow and syrupy. Mix it about half with Benedictine and you have a marvellous drink.'

'Why not?' Selby said.

Carr walked over to a liquor closet which had been built in the side of the wall, selected glasses, bottles, mixed the drinks, placed one before Selby, took one himself, smiled at the district attorney over the brim of the glass, said: 'Here's to crime.'

The two men touched their lips to the glasses, getting the delicate flavour and aroma of the drink.

'It's really marvellous,' Selby said.

'So glad you appreciate it, Counsellor.'

Carr settled comfortably in a chair across from Selby. 'And now,' he asked, 'what is the object of this visit?'

Selby said: 'I have been thinking about you quite a bit this evening, Carr. I remember when you first came to town.'

'Not too very long ago,' Carr said.

'It's been several years.'

'Yes, I guess it has!'

'You remember,' Selby said, 'you came here because you wanted to retire. You wanted to get away from the city. You wanted to get away from the class of people whom you had been representing.'

'That's right,' Carr said.

'You wanted to rest and relax.'

'Exactly.'

'But,' Selby went on, 'as you explained to us from time to time, your clients wouldn't let you relax or rest. They hounded you, followed you here, insisted that you represent them.'

'That's right.'

'It's a shame things had to happen that way.'

'Isn't it? Oh, well, that's the penalty for success. However, I hardly feel you came here at this hour of the night to discuss *my* troubles, my desire to retire.'

'Oh, but I did.'

'Indeed!'

Selby said: 'It would be nice if I could help you realise your ambition.'

'To retire?'

'Yes.'

'Carr smiled. 'I don't think I need any help, Selby.'

'The county will do everything in its power,' Selby said.

Carr threw back his head and laughed melodiously and heartily. 'I take it, Selby, I'm becoming a thorn in the flesh.'

'Exactly.'

Carr said: 'Of course, Counsellor, while I put on an act of righteous indignation earlier this evening in connection with the Eleanor Harlan matter, you will understand that I personally don't believe that you administered any drug to her or that you kidnapped her. However, after all, we're on opposite sides of the fence and, as far as my public utterances are concerned, I certainly intend to accuse you of taking unfair advantage of a witness, of violating the law and various and sundry other irregularities. I trust you appreciate that behind all this mud-slinging, I have the highest personal regard and respect for you?'

'Thank you.'

'However, you and the sheriff have placed yourselves in a rather unenviable position. And I'm frank to admit, Selby, that I intend to apply the pressure, just as the sheriff would, were the situation reversed.'

Selby said: 'Sylvia Martin took Eleanor Harlan to the Columbian Auto Court.'

'Did she, indeed!'

'Registered under assumed names and took the last cabin that was available.'

'Clever of her,' Carr said. 'You know, that girl really thinks with considerable rapidity in an emergency. If she had stayed on the streets in her car, she would have been apprehended in no time at all; but by this clever ruse, she threw Otto Larkin off the trail. Of course, I don't mind telling you in confidence, Selby, that Otto Larkin is no intellectual giant.'

'And,' Selby went on, disregarding Carr's comment about the officious chief of police at Madison City, 'when the effects of the drug began to wear off, Eleanor Harlan showed she was capable of some pretty fast thinking herself. She played 'possum and lulled Sylvia into a false sense of security. Sylvia, thinking she would sleep for several hours at least, tiptoed out of the cabin and went out to work on some other angles of the case Eleanor Harlan promptly telephoned you and you came and got her.'

'Very interesting!' Carr said. 'I take it that when it comes to substantiating your charge that *I* got her, you have some witness?'

'Frankly, I haven't.'

'Well, well,' Carr said, 'this is a conversation off the record. Don't expect me to admit anything, but keep right on talking, Selby.'

Selby said: 'Earlier in the evening, Eleanor Harlan had confessed in the presence of witnesses that she had been the one who shot

281

Eve Dawson on the night of the seventeenth—or rather, in the early morning hours of the eighteenth.'

'Tut, tut, Counsellor, you should know better. The girl was under the influence of drugs. Someone had administered or attempted to administer a truth-serum to her.'

'Someone had tried to kill her.'

Carr once more laughed heartily. 'Selby, you do have the most naive ideas. Think of how a statement like that would sound in front of a jury.'

'I think it would sound like the truth.'

'My dear Counsellor, you have been associating with the estimable, but somewhat bucolic, sheriff too long. Imagine you standing up in front of a jury and trying to explain to them how it happened that when I found Eleanor Harlan in your custody, there was a newspaperwoman taking down everything she was saying, there was a doctor, who had been selected by you and whom Eleanor Harlan had never seen in her life, treating her, administering drugs which she had not requested and did not want, and, as a result of the administration of those drugs the patient was becoming talkative, having hallucinations, making wild statements under the influence of delusion—and, incidentally, being prompted by you. And then you have the nerve to try to tell that jury that all this was a fortuitous chain of circumstances, that the girl either tried to commit suicide or someone tried to murder her. You try to explain that it was merely due to a series of coincidences that she happened not to be in a hospital, not to be in the custody of her own doctor, not to be among her own friends, not even to be in the county where she had her own residence, but to have been spirited out of that county, to have been in the hands of a strange doctor, talking her head off to a newspaper-woman as the result of drugs that had been administered purely for the purpose of making her talk! My dear Selby, don't let me think that a man of your intelligence would ever willingly place himself in such a position. It would be a massacre; it would be too one-sided even to be a contest.'

'Nevertheless,' Selby said doggedly, 'I believe what Eleanor Harlan told me. I believe that she shot Eve Dawson in Jim Melvin's garage in the early morning hours of the eighteenth of this month. I have caused a complaint to be filed, charging her with that crime and I now have a warrant for her arrest.'

Carr shook his head mournfully. 'A most unwise procedure, Counsellor. You'll have to dismiss the charge. You won't dare to stand up and press that charge even at a preliminary hearing.'

'Nevertheless,' Selby said, 'I intend to do so. I intend to try and pin that crime on her because I think she's guilty.'

'The crime of assault with a deadly weapon?'

'That's right. Assault with a deadly weapon with intent to commit murder.'

Carr again shook his head mournfully. 'I had hoped for better things from you, Counsellor.'

'Therefore,' Selby said, 'in the event that you are now harbouring Eleanor Harlan, you now know that she is a fugitive from justice; and so there will be no question about your knowing it, I'm showing you the warrant of arrest which I hold here in my hand.'

For a moment Carr drew back, frowning, his face dark with anger. Then he smiled, and his smile became once more laughter, though this time it sounded a trifle forced.

'Clever, Selby! Damned clever! I will now admit that you are in every way coming up to, if not exceeding, my expectations for you.

'It really is a clever play! You wouldn't dare to go ahead and prosecute Eleanor Harlan because you haven't the evidence, but you have gone ahead and secured a warrant for her arrest, which you show me. Therefore, if I harbour her now, after having personally seen that warrant of arrest, you are in a position to accuse me of being an accessory, of harbouring a criminal wanted by the police. Rather a clever move. Unfortunately, Selby, it won't avail you anything, because I don't know where Eleanor Harlan is at this moment.'

'If you do,' Selby said, 'I call on you to surrender her.'

'I understand the legal point,' Carr said, smiling. 'You have done it very cleverly, Counsellor. You don't need to dot the i's and cross the t's.'

'Thank you,' Selby said. 'I just wanted to be sure you understood it.'

Carr raised his glass, sipped the mixture of rum and Benedictine, said: 'In this case, Selby, you and the sheriff are going to come a terrific cropper. I don't mind telling you that as far as you are concerned, I'm sorry to see it. But, as far as Sheriff Brandon is concerned, he's been asking for it. I'm sorry that you two are tied up together. However, I do feel that in private practice you will make a great deal more of a success than in working for an unappreciative county. I don't suppose you'd be interested in considering an association with an older man?'

'How old?' Selby asked.

'About my age,' Carr said.

Selby smiled and shook his head. 'You're going to retire.'

'Well, there's no hurry about retiring,' Carr said. 'After all, I find it very delightful here.'

Selby said: 'Let's not mince words, Carr. You're a fascinating rascal; but since you came to this county you've brought an entirely new problem, one that we don't like to have in a rural community.

'You have "connections". You handle your practice in such a way that you have built up contacts and thrown a huge web across this county. In the course of time, people who get into trouble come to you for help, and once they've become enmeshed in your web, you use them in turn to help in your future cases. You have so much on them that they *have* to co-operate.'

'Well, what's wrong with that?' Carr asked. 'That's the way any good defence lawyer builds up a lucrative practice.'

'In the city, perhaps, but not here. Now take this case, for instance.'

'All right, what about this case?' Carr asked.

'Eleanor Harlan shot Eve Dawson. Milton Granby appealed to you for help. You devised a scheme by which each one of three people gave the others an alibi. You worked out a story that would account for a pistol-shot.

'You had sufficient power, because of your previous connections and contacts, to call up the people who owned that house in Las Alidas and tell them to vacate on half an hour's notice and stay out of the county until you advised them it was all right for them to return. You offered Jim Melvin money and immunity to take the wounded girl and to see to it that she was given sanctuary.

'All the way along the line you were protecting Hudson Parlin, who was your real client. You knew, subsequently, that when Eve Dawson recovered her health, she was still trying to use the information she'd gained, in order to get enough money to make a stake and start in some sort of business for herself. She didn't realise how dangerous it was to play that sort of a game with Hudson Parlin.

'Eleanor Harlan's brother had given her a carving-knife. She had never used it, because the girls didn't eat very often in their apartment, and when they did, it was a meal composed mostly of canned foods and knick-knacks they could pick up. When Hudson Parlin realised Eve Dawson was trying to blackmail Morris Sheldon on a matter that Parlin considered his own personal prerogative, Parlin went to see Eve Dawson. He had taken a carving-knife from Eleanor Harlan's apartment just in case he might need it. It never occurred to him there would be any possibility of tracing that carving-knife.

'After his interview with Eve Dawson, he found that she was adamant. He may have intended to use the knife to frighten her, but he was angry and he committed a murder.

'When it appeared that there was a price mark on the knife and that it might be traced, he became panic-stricken and called on you.'

'What's wrong with that?' Carr asked.

'Everything,' Selby said. 'You didn't simply advise him, but you became an active participant. You tried to manipulate things so it would appear that Eleanor Harlan still had her knife.'

'*Doesn't* she still have it?'

Selby smiled. 'An interesting thing, Carr.

287

Brandon did not touch that knife when you brought it to his office, but he *had* touched the knife that had been in Eleanor Harlan's apartment the night before. We found his latent finger-prints on the knife.'

'Clever!' Carr said, his eyes showing sudden admiration. 'Damn it, Selby, that *was* clever.'

'So you can see,' Selby said, 'where that leaves you.'

Carr shook his head and smiled. 'Evidence that a sheriff could fabricate by the simple process of touching his own fingers to a knife blade ... come, come, Selby! No jury would ever believe that.'

'A jury in this county would,' Selby said doggedly. 'They know the sheriff.'

'That would have been true,' Carr conceded, 'when I first came here. I don't mind telling you frankly, Counsellor, that I don't like to see such extreme confidence on the part of jurors in the district attorney and the sheriff. Since we're having a talk that's off the record, I don't mind saying that I am endeavouring to introduce an element of friction here and there. I'm making the political fights become bitter, personal fights. I don't think you could get any jury now that would accept the sheriff's word that way. I think they'd consider he was playing some fast politics.'

'You're being very frank.'

'I can afford to be,' Carr said, 'because only you and I are here. Incidentally, Counsellor, you've done some rather nice deductive reasoning in this case.'

'And,' Selby went on, 'when Parlin realised that Eleanor Harlan knew too much, he decided to put her out of the way. So he used the key of her apartment that he had been carrying for some months now and dropped in to see her. He found her sitting there, eating candy that had been brought to her earlier in the afternoon by Milton Granby.

'That gave him an idea. He went out and bought some similar candy, drugged it heavily with one of the barbiturates, came back and substituted the drugged candy for the other. After she had taken enough of the drug in the candy to constitute a fatal dose and had gone to sleep, he set the stage for a suicide. But he didn't dare to eliminate *all* of the candy because Granby would have known Eleanor could hardly have eaten a whole box. So Parlin put the rest of the drugged candy in his pocket and left the apartment, leaving good, clean candy behind.'

Carr stretched, and yawned, said: 'Well, all this is very interesting, Selby, but I'm afraid I can't give you any more time listening to your wild theories.'

'Do you admit that there's some truth in them?' Selby asked.

Suddenly Carr smiled, and said: 'You caught me rather neatly on that knife substitution business, but you can never prove

289

it, Selby. As far as the other elements are concerned, I'm representing my clients. I'll meet you in court when it comes to a discussion of those matters.'

'Thanks,' Selby said. 'I just wanted to be sure you knew about the warrant being out for Eleanor Harlan.'

'Quite all right,' Carr said. 'Quite all right. I'm glad you told me. And that, in itself, was rather clever. It would have been a nice trap if I'd known where she was, but I don't. Good night, Counsellor. Good night.'

Carr showed Selby out of the house, switched off the porch light.

Selby got in his car, drove a hundred yards and stopped. The county car was across the street. It was deserted.

The district attorney stood by the sheriff's car, waiting. One minute passed, then another. Then suddenly there was the sound of a police whistle from the back of Carr's house, a voice raised in a shout, a scuffle and then a shot.

Selby calmly walked back to the front door of Carr's house and pressed the button, sounding the chimes.

There was an interval of some four minutes before the door opened.

Rex Brandon grinned at Selby. 'Come on in, Doug. I think we've got it.'

Selby said: 'He opened the folding bar in his study, Rex. The microphone must be in that bar and ...'

'We've found it already,' Brandon said. 'There seems to be a complete transcription of your conversation.'

Selby grinned. 'I thought so. He felt certain of himself. He didn't know but what he might want to tax me with what I was saying, so he had a recording just to protect himself. I think we can use it against him.'

'He's here in the front room,' Brandon said in a low voice. 'He doesn't know we found the recording outfit.'

'He was trying to spirit Eleanor Harlan out of the house?'

'Yes.'

Selby said: 'Good. We've got him now.'

Selby entered the living-room.

A. B. Carr was sitting angrily erect.

Selby said: 'I warned you, Carr.'

Carr said: 'Well, you've got nothing on me. I was simply returning one of my clients to her domicile. She had been taken away and kidnapped and...'

'But, my dear man, don't you remember that I *told* you there was a warrant out for her arrest?'

Carr sneered. 'Don't pull that stuff on me, Selby,' he said. 'You know damn well you never told me anything of the sort.'

'I never showed you a signed warrant for her arrest?'

'Certainly not.'

'Didn't tell you we had sworn to a complaint

291

charging her with assault with a deadly weapon?'

'Definitely not.'

'And that in the event she was in the house and you didn't surrender her, you would be harbouring a person who was a fugitive from justice?'

'Certainly not. Don't try to make a case against me by any such absurd frame-up as that.'

Selby grinned and said: 'Let's play it back to him, Rex.'

Brandon said to his night deputy: 'Have you found the controls?'

The man nodded.

'Play it back,' Brandon said.

The man flipped a switch. From the adjoining room came the sound of voices coming back over a loudspeaker.

Carr lunged up from the chair, drew back his arm.

Brandon cocked a gleeful fist, held the punch as Carr suddenly subsided.

Brandon said: 'Boy, I'm sorry you quit on that one.'

'What do you want?' Carr asked Selby, his face white with emotion.

Selby said: 'I told you, Carr, we want to help you retire.'

CHAPTER TWENTY-FIVE

Sylvia Martin pulled *The Clarion* Press car to the kerb as Doug Selby started walking from his apartment towards the Palace Café.

'Hello, Doug,' she said. 'Are you going to have breakfast with me?'

Selby grinned. 'You must have been waiting for me to get up.'

'I was. I wanted to go up and drag you out of bed, but, after all, there are the proprieties, you know.'

'You could have used the phone.'

'I wanted to surprise you, Doug.'

'With what?'

'Get in.'

Selby got in the car with Sylvia Martin. She said: 'I don't suppose you've seen the papers?'

He shook his head.

She opened *The Clarion*, spread it across his lap, and said: 'How does that look?'

There were big headlines across the top of the paper.

'SELBY AND BRANDON TRAP MURDERER.'

'HUDSON PARLIN TO PLEAD GUILTY
AND THROW HIMSELF ON MERCY OF
THE COURT TO ESCAPE DEATH PENALTY.'

'SELBY TRIPS PARLIN ON ALIBI.'

'A. B. CARR, NOTED CRIMINAL LAWYER,
ARRESTED EARLIER IN EVENING
BUT RELEASED ON BAIL, ANNOUNCES
RETIREMENT ON ACCOUNT OF
ILL HEALTH.'

'Brandon and District Attorney, Selby, at an early hour this morning, cracked the notorious Eve Dawson case wide open.

'The death, which political opponents had been loudly shouting was a suicide, turned out to be a murder, after all. Hudson Parlin now admits he did the stabbing, but claims it was committed in the heat of passion after he had been goaded beyond all self-control by a blackmailer who was insisting he part with a small fortune in return for documents that linked the Mayor of Las Alidas with a paving graft.

'Parlin, who had offered a perfect alibi covering the time Eve Dawson was murdered, suddenly cracked during the small hours of the morning when District Attorney Selby punctured that alibi.

'Having pointed out to officers that he had witnessed a traffic accident in Los Angeles at about the time Eve Dawson met her death, Parlin became confused when District Attorney Selby started grilling him, not about the murder, but about the details of the motor-car accident.

294

'After an hour of rapid-fire questioning, Parlin admitted he had faked this alibi. Knowing that there were numerous minor traffic accidents hourly in the metropolis, Parlin had consulted traffic records, learned of an accident at the corner of Figueroa and Adams at 12.55 a.m. on the morning of the murder, and then boldly proclaimed himself a witness. The attorney for the party who sustained personal injuries in that accident quite naturally welcomed Parlin with open arms, and through his questioning Parlin learned all of the details he needed to know to make it seem he really had been a witness to the collision.

'Selby's adroit cross-examination as to the detailed circumstances surrounding the traffic accident finally tripped Parlin, and, according to those who were present in the jail at the time when Parlin started to go to pieces, he went to pieces all at once.'

(Continued page 2, column 1)

*　　　*　　　*

Selby glanced up from the newspaper. 'Didn't you spread this on rather thick, Sylvia?'

Her eyes were glowing. 'I don't suppose *you* have any idea how wonderful you really are, Doug Selby.'

Selby looked at her, then let the discarded newspaper slowly slide down his knees to the

295

floor of the car. 'I guess I'll have to work out some scheme of hiring you permanently as my Press agent.'

Sylvia Martin said demurely: 'Well, I *could* be had.'

Selby said: 'I . . .' and then broke off as Rex Brandon slid the county car alongside and called: 'Almost missed you, Doug. Got a minute?'

Selby waved Brandon on. 'Beat it! I have a breakfast date, and I'm discussing an important matter.'

But Brandon only grinned as he eased his machine alongside. 'Hop in, Doug. Old A.B.C. got bail for himself in an amount of ten thousand dollars, then bailed Eleanor Harlan out, flew to Tijuana and got married. Now neither one can testify against the other.'

Selby's face showed his consternation.

'Doesn't that put him out of reach, Doug?' Sylvia asked.

'I guess it does,' Selby said. He was frowning thoughtfully. 'In this state neither husband nor wife can be made to testify against the other. Carr has pulled another slick one, but he's harnessed himself with a wife who will make things interesting, and he doesn't dare divorce her until the statute of limitations has expired on the criminal conspiracy assault-with-a-deadly-weapon case. There's a question whether divorce destroys the immunity, and old A.B.C. won't dare chance it. He's stuck with a wife for three years. However, we've still got Parlin on that murder case.'

Sylvia Martin sighed. 'Come on, Wage Slaves,' she said, 'we've got to cover the honeymoon of Mr and Mrs Carr. It's news.'

We hope you have enjoyed this Large Print book. Other Chivers Press or G. K. Hall Large Print books are available at your library or directly from the publishers. For more information about current and forthcoming titles, please call or write, without obligation, to:

Chivers Press Limited
Windsor Bridge Road
Bath BA2 3AX
England
Tel. (01225) 335336

OR

G. K. Hall
P.O. Box 159
Thorndike, Maine 04986
USA
Tel. (800) 223–6121 (U.S. & Canada)
In Maine call collect: (207) 948–2962

All our Large Print titles are designed for easy reading, and all our books are made to last.